SMOKY MOUNTAIN DOCTOR

FOGGY MOUNTAIN INTRIGUE

BOOK FOUR

ASHLEY A QUINN

TCA PUBLISHING LLC

Smoky Mountain Doctor

Copyright © 2022 by Ashley A Quinn

ISBN is 978-1-959943-01-3
Library of Congress Control Number: 2022921237

Printed in the United State of America

ONE

"Have a nice day." Piper Riordan held out the prescription bag and bared her teeth in some semblance of a smile for the woman who just berated her for the cost of her medication. It wasn't like she had control over drug prices. And she'd done everything she could to get the woman the best price. Apparently, it wasn't enough.

The woman snatched the bag, the paper crinkling and pills rattling as she took it. With a harrumph, she spun on her heel and exited the pharmacy.

Heaving a sigh, Piper closed her eyes and rubbed her forehead. She had a headache, and it wasn't even lunchtime yet.

A child's soft whimper drew her attention. She opened her eyes and forced a more genuine smile onto her face for the next customer. "Hello. How may I help you?"

The rest of Piper's day flew by. At the height of cold and flu season, the hospital pharmacy was hopping. She filled more prescriptions for ear infections and strep throat than she could count. It also served to remind her why she didn't have children. They were little germ factories.

"Phew! I'm beat." Piper's coworker, Melissa, followed her into the break room. She sank onto a chair at the table and popped open the spout on her water. "Is it my imagination, or did the entire population of Emery County come in today?"

Piper giggled and went to her locker. "It sure felt like it." She took out her coat and put it on. "I'm glad we're done, though. I'm ready to go home and veg on the couch the rest of the night. A glass of wine and a good book sound amazing right now." Her side ached, a holdover from being shot at her friend's wedding just a couple of months ago. Sitting down and not moving until it was time for bed sounded like her idea of a perfect evening.

"Oh, that does sound good. I'm surprised, though. You're not going out? It's Friday."

"I haven't been out dancing since I got shot." At first, she hadn't been able to because of her injuries. Then, she just didn't want to. It didn't hold the same appeal as it once did. She wasn't sure why. Now, she was more comfortable with her own company than with letting her hair down, so to speak.

"Why not?"

Piper shrugged, putting on her coat. "I'd just rather stay home. I'm pretty tired." That was no lie. She still didn't have all her strength and stamina back, even though she'd been discharged from physical therapy. Reaching into her locker, she removed her purse and slung it across her shoulders.

The door swung open and the pharmacy manager, Dr. Nikki Wells, walked in. "Oh, Piper. I'm glad I caught you. I need you to stay."

"What?" Piper frowned, her shoulders sagging. "Why?"

"Brandi called in. I need you to cover her shift."

"I just worked eight hours." Fatigue pulled at her limbs. She really wanted to go home and rest.

"I know, but it can't be helped. Maybe you can leave early. It always slows down after about ten o'clock."

Anger flared, swift and hot, in Piper's gut at Nikki's condescending tone. Did she actually think she was doing Piper a favor by letting her leave early from her forced second shift? "Let me get this straight. You want me to work a double shift—that I may or may not get off early from—then come back tomorrow morning and work my regular shift?"

Nikki frowned. The look on her face said she didn't see the problem. "Well, yes. Sometimes, we have to work unfavorable hours. Is that a problem?"

"Yes. Yes, it is." She propped her fists on her hips. "Why can't you call someone from that shift who's off today and ask them to come in?"

"It's too late. I need someone now."

"Okay, so I'll stay until her replacement can arrive." She held up a hand. "But not past six o'clock. It's been a long day, and I need to get some rest." The ache in her side seemed to double in intensity as she acknowledged it.

"I understand it's been a long day, but—"

Piper waved a hand. "No. Look, I know the doctor cleared me to come back to work, but I still don't have all my strength back. Long days like today wear me out. I *need* the rest."

Nikki's fierce frown said she didn't like that answer, but Piper wasn't willing to compromise. Her health was more important than leaving second-shift without a full staff.

"Um, Nikki?" Melissa lifted a hand. "I can take the shift if you're that desperate."

"Thank you for the offer, but it's Piper's turn."

Piper's frown deepened. "How is it my turn? I've had most of the overtime lately."

"Right. But you were out for ten weeks."

Was she for real? "Yeah, because I *was shot.*"

"We all still had to pick up the slack."

Piper snorted. "Glad to know I'm such a valued employee." She looked at Melissa. "Thank you for offering to stay. I appreciate it."

Melissa cast a quick look at Nikki, then smiled at Piper. "I'm glad too. The overtime will go toward Reed's birthday." She rolled her eyes at the mention of her son. "He has a list of video games eight miles long."

Piper grinned. "Glad I could help."

"Now, wait a minute." Nikki stepped closer. "I didn't agree to this."

"What's the issue?" Melissa said before Piper could open her mouth. "You need a shift covered. It's covered. Does it really matter who gets the overtime?"

Nikki crossed her arms. "That's not the point."

"Come on, Nikki. Show some compassion. She had part of a lung removed three months ago. Let her go home."

Their boss's mouth pursed for a moment, then she dropped her arms with a huff. "Fine." Whirling around, she stomped out.

Piper shook her head. Nikki had always been a bit of a hard-ass. She made sure her employees towed the line. But she'd been particularly hard on Piper since she returned. The only reason Piper could surmise was that she'd upset Nikki's orderly workplace with her prolonged absence. Giving Piper the lion's share of the overtime and weekends was her way of telling everyone to expect consequences for unexpected time off.

Sighing, she closed her locker and offered Melissa a soft smile. "Thank you again for taking the overtime."

Melissa waved a hand. "Not a problem. This just paid for Reed's birthday and then some, so I should probably be thanking you."

"Well, good. We're both happy." She adjusted her purse strap and headed for the door. "I'll see you tomorrow."

"See ya."

Piper left the break room and wandered down the hall to Nikki's office, where schedules were posted. There hadn't been time yet today for her to look at her schedule for next week. Hopefully, she had Sunday off. She hadn't had a day off since she came back last week. Undoubtedly more punishment for being out for so long.

She paused outside her boss's closed door and looked at the schedule on the wall. Anger swelled again. She was scheduled every day this week.

Furious, she didn't bother knocking on Nikki's door, just twisted the knob and thrust it open.

Nikki glanced up, frowning when she saw Piper. "Yes?"

"Okay, I get that I missed a lot of work, but is it necessary for me to work seventeen days straight? There are other people on my shift."

"Right, but I was forced to deny them all any time off while you were gone. Now that you're back, I'm working in their requests. The hospital was kind enough to allow us to roll our days over to the new year, so no one lost their vacation days because of your absence. I'd still like to limit the number used after the new year, though. It's easier on the people in accounting."

Piper took a deep breath and counted to ten. It didn't lessen her anger, but it gave her a chance to gather her thoughts instead of blurting out the first thought that came to mind. "I understand that, but forcing me to work more than two weeks straight is ludicrous. Even one day off would be great."

Nikki shrugged and rested her hands atop her desk. "Maybe, but that doesn't change the fact I need to make up for the time you were away. You'll get back to your normal schedule eventually."

"Mmm." Piper rolled her lips in as she hummed, pressing them together to hold back the words wanting to break free.

She couldn't get fired. Her savings took a hit when she was out. Short-term disability only covered so much.

"If there's nothing further, you should go home and rest. That's what you wanted to do, right?" Nikki arched an eyebrow.

Piper narrowed her eyes, but again, kept her thoughts to herself. "Yep." Without a goodbye, she left the office, barely stopping herself from slamming the door.

She was so done with Nikki's crap. Life was too short to spend all her time walking on eggshells at work. It was time for a change.

A plan formed in her mind as she left the pharmacy and wandered into the hospital's main lobby. There wasn't really anything left for her in Amandale now that her mom was gone. She had no other family to speak of. That meant she could go anywhere she wanted. Even out-of-state.

The main entrance doors swished open to let her out of the hospital. She stepped through and stopped as her brain registered the sight before her. Thick snow obscured the landscape. "When the hell did this start?" She huffed and ducked her head, walking into it. At least she'd parked in the garage and wouldn't have to clean off her car before she left. Getting home would be fun, though. The streets would be a mess. Now she knew why Brandi called in. And she was doubly glad Melissa took her shift. She couldn't imagine driving home in this later after working a double.

Hurrying down the sidewalk, she made a mental note to buy the woman lunch tomorrow. And coffee. She probably deserved even more than that.

Snow trickled down her collar, making her shiver. She quickened her pace. Her mind turned to her earlier thoughts. If she moved away, she should pick some place warmer. Like Florida. Or Texas. Hawaii would be amazing. But the cost to move her things there would probably be more than she could afford. She could always sell everything and buy new when she got there.

A small snort escaped her, and she rolled her eyes. Yeah, right. By the time she did that, she'd probably wind up paying just as much as to move it all there. She remembered the prices when she vacationed there a few years ago. Hawaii was expensive.

So, Florida, then.

She entered the parking garage and did a little shake, ridding herself of the snowflakes she'd accumulated. Walking forward, she pushed the button to call the elevator, then stepped back to wait.

Another shiver wracked her. Florida sounded better by the minute. But did she really want to go somewhere where she knew no one? She made friends easily, but it wasn't the same as being around people she'd known for years.

An image of her best friend, Mackenzie, popped into her head. She missed Mack. Her friend now lived in North Carolina with her new husband, Jake.

The elevator dinged, and the doors opened. Piper stepped on and pushed the button for the third floor. She rested against the wall, still lost in thought. It would be great to be close to Mack again. But could she live in the same place she nearly died?

She was getting ahead of herself, though. She needed to look up job openings and check the cost of living before she did anything.

With a jerk, the elevator stopped. The doors opened and Piper stepped out. Cold air whipped through the parking structure, bringing flurries with it. She shivered again, huddling deeper into her coat as she hurried to her car. Pushing the button on her remote to unlock the doors, the car beeped. She opened the driver's door and got in, tossing her bag onto the passenger seat.

"Damn, it's cold." She started the engine, cranking up the heat. Putting the car in gear, she backed out of her space, then drove down the aisle and left the garage, heading straight into the storm. Growling, she glared at the snow. "Wherever I go, there will not be as much of this crap." White-knuckled, she turned onto the road.

Two

"I can't thank you enough for flying up here to help me move." Piper looked around the side of a stack of boxes she carried at Mackenzie.

"Are you kidding? I could have flown here without the airplane when you told me you found a job near me and were moving down. It's going to be so great to have you close by again." She smiled as she wrapped a glass and put it in the box on the counter.

"Well, regardless, I appreciate it."

The front door opened and Jake stepped through, his gait slightly uneven.

Piper looked at him, then back at Mack. "And for bringing the muscle." She hooked a thumb toward Mackenzie's husband.

Mack grinned. "He was happy to come." She rolled her eyes. "Though I think it had more to do with keeping an eye on me and making sure I didn't lift something I shouldn't than anything else. I'm just glad he was able to get away. He went back to work a couple weeks ago, and we were afraid he'd catch a case."

"Well, he could have rest-assured I wouldn't let you lift anything too heavy." A slight frown marred her face. "Are you doing okay, by the way? Do you want to sit down?"

Mackenzie pointed a finger at her. "Don't you start too. I'm pregnant, not disabled. If anyone needs to take a break, it's him." Her finger ticked toward Jake as he walked closer.

"Huh? What are we talking about?" Jake lifted an eyebrow as he stopped next to Piper.

"Breaks," Piper said. "Do you need one?" She'd noticed his limp was getting worse as the day wore on.

Jake shook his head. "I'll be okay. Nothing some painkillers and a hot bath later won't fix."

"Are you sure?" Mackenzie put the glass in the box, her brows furrowed.

"Yes, I'm fine." He glanced around. "What's next?"

"Let me take these boxes out, then we can load up more furniture." Piper moved toward the door, smiling as she saw him move next to Mackenzie and give her a quick kiss. They were cute together, and Piper was elated her best friend had found happiness. She deserved it after that jerk, Brett Jorgensen.

Making quick work of putting her load in the moving van, she went back inside. While Mackenzie continued packing boxes, she and Jake moved things out.

"You know, I've got a lot more crap than I thought I did." Piper blew her bangs out of her face as she walked backward out the door, carrying one end of a chair. "And here I thought I was doing well at minimalism."

Jake grinned. "It hides."

"That's for sure." Piper hated clutter, so she kept her belongings to the necessities and some interesting art pieces. She still had more than she realized, though. Especially shoes. And books. She liked to read, so she had a lot of them. Fewer than if she didn't also use an e-reader, but there were still plenty. She liked the feel of a book in her hands at night as she wound down for the evening.

They loaded the chair into the van, then went back for more. By early afternoon, they had the apartment packed and loaded into the moving truck.

"Is that it?" Jake grabbed the handle to pull the rolling door closed.

Piper nodded. "Lock it up."

Jake tugged, and the door slid down. He stepped off the truck, pulling the door with him, then secured it. "Let's hit the road. The further we get today, the more time we have to unload you tomorrow."

Piper wasn't about to argue. She didn't want to be unloading in the dark. Turning, she locked her apartment, then headed for her car. Jake had offered to drive the rental truck. Piper gladly yielded to the policeman. He had more experience behind the wheel than she could ever hope for.

Waving, she got in her car while he and Mackenzie got into the truck. Excitement zinged through Piper's veins as they turned out of her apartment complex. She was still apprehensive about whether she'd made the right decision to leave Amandale. It was all she'd ever known, after all. But now that she was actually leaving, she could see the possibilities with much greater clarity. Her future looked bright, and she was excited to see where this move led.

THREE

"Dr. Tate!"

Stifling a yawn as he left the operating theater, Cullen Tate turned at the sound of his name. He hoped there wasn't another emergency. He desperately needed a nap before he drove to Foggy Mountain for his afternoon clinic.

A smiling, peppy young woman waved; her blonde ponytail bobbing as she jogged toward him in her flowy white blouse, gray pencil skirt, and mustard yellow heels. "I'm glad I caught you."

He frowned. "Okay? And you are?"

"Oh." She let out a little giggle. "Sorry. Jodie Berkshire. I'm with public relations." She held out a hand.

Cullen took it. "What can I do for you, Ms. Berkshire?"

She released his hand to remove a piece of paper from the clipboard she carried. "I'm following up with the doctors we haven't heard from in regards to our fundraiser email." She held out the pink sheet.

He frowned, his gaze flicking to the paper, then back to her face. "What fundraiser?"

Her eyebrows dipped. "Didn't you get the email a couple of weeks ago? Or the reminder I sent last week?"

Cullen shrugged and took the paper. "To be honest, if it's not about a patient or direct from my assistant, I rarely read my emails." He glanced at the page in his hand. Hearts rimmed the border. His stomach sank before he even read a word, then fell to his toes as he skimmed the text. "A bachelor auction? Are you serious?" Why would the hospital administration sanction something like this?

Her frown deepened. "Yes. It's a Valentine's auction."

He snorted and rolled his eyes, then thrust the paper at her. "I'm not interested." He didn't need help finding a date for Valentine's Day. He didn't want one.

She glanced at the paper, then back to his face. "It's for a great cause, Dr. Tate. Won't you at least consider it?"

"I'm not interested in plumping the hospital's coffers by auctioning myself. I'll gladly give a speech to prospective donors, though." His mind turned to his schedule, plotting where he could work in a fundraising dinner.

"It's not for the hospital." She frowned. "Did you even read it?" She pointed at the paper he still held.

Cullen's frown deepened. He turned the sheet and glanced at it again.

"It's for the women's crisis center Sheriff Davidson's wife and sister-in-law started."

Well, hell. Cullen held back a groan, seeing that now as he actually read the flier. "Right." He sighed and scratched his temple, dropping his hand back to his side. "Um, I'll have to check my schedule."

Ms. Berkshire smiled. "You're free. I talked to your assistant just a few minutes ago. He's the one who pointed me to your location."

Cullen bit back an epithet. No doubt Levi thought it was grand fun to sick the bubbly PR lady on him for such an endeavor. He should fire him and find someone more professional.

Mentally, he rolled his eyes. He'd never fire Levi, and the man knew it. Cullen's life had never run so smoothly. Levi Chambers was a master organizer. Not to mention a top-notch forensic investigator. Cullen would put up with his twisted sense of humor and his need to torture his boss for the level of ease with which his life now ran.

Sighing, he nodded. "Okay, then. I guess you can put me down."

Her smile grew. "Wonderful. I just need a candid photo of you and a short paragraph about yourself as well as what your date will entail."

Oh, Levi would definitely pay for this.

Cullen nodded. "How soon do you need it?"

"Friday by noon. We're sending the information to the printer that afternoon to get the pamphlets printed."

"Okay. Out of curiosity, why are you involved in this? The women's center isn't affiliated with the hospital."

Her smile dimmed a fraction. "No, but it's a cause close to my heart. I'm from up that way. Growing up, they didn't have resources like this. My sister had a baby at seventeen. Maybe if she'd had a place to go to, like this new center, she wouldn't have been forced to give up her baby. I know she regrets it."

"I'm sorry."

"Thank you." She waved a hand. "That's not the only reason I'm involved, though. I talked to Dr. North. She agreed to let us use the auditorium. And the hospital's endowment office said they would match all the donations." Her smile brightened and turned sly. "There's a reason I went into public relations."

A smile tugged at the corners of Cullen's mouth. "I can see that. You're very persuasive."

She chuckled. "So much so that I even got your assistant to agree to participate."

Cullen laughed. "Oh, thank you. I was wondering how I would pay him back for this."

"Well, wonder no more. Instead, you need to come up with an epic date. He mentioned something about outdoing you." Her smile turned knowing, and she moved forward to walk around him. "Have a good day, doctor."

Cullen rolled his eyes again. "Thanks."

She waggled her fingers and continued down the hall.

He let out a soft groan as she disappeared. Bowing his head, he pinched the bridge of his nose and sighed. This was going to suck. There was a reason he didn't date. Why he had few friends. He just didn't do well with other people in a social setting. Few people could match his intellect, so he was either bored or people looked at him like he was some sort of freak. Sheriff Davidson was an exception. As was his wife. Gemma was highly curious and not afraid to ask questions. They had lively discussions every time they were together. He doubted he would be so lucky as to garner a "date" with someone like her. No, he was far more likely to end up with some rich woman who only saw a handsome doctor. He was well-aware of how he looked and of his successes. Cullen never lacked for willing women. He just simply had no interest in what they offered.

Lost in thought, he failed to use the mirror at the end of the hall to see around the corner before he stepped into the intersection. He caught a quick glimpse of blonde hair and gray scrubs half a second before he collided with a woman coming from his right. She let out a squeal as she bounced off his arm and chest. He shot out a hand to catch her, snagging her arm before she fell to the floor.

"I'm sorry. I wasn't watching where I was going." His gaze

went to her face, and he frowned in surprise as it connected with a pair of jade green eyes. "Ms. Riordan?"

She grimaced as she got her feet under her. "Hey, Doc."

He continued to frown as he stared at her. "What are you doing here?" She'd returned to New York to continue healing from her injuries once he deemed her well enough to travel. His curious frown morphed to one of concern as a thought struck him. "Is your friend all right?" Something happening to her best friend, who lived in the area, was the only reason he could think she'd be at the hospital.

"She's fine. I work here." Piper lifted the lanyard and its attached ID, waving it slightly.

"You do?" He glanced at her badge, noting the hospital logo beneath her picture.

"Yes. You can let me go now." She pointed to her forearm, where he still clutched it.

"Oh, right. Sorry." He let go. "I didn't know you were back in town. So, you've moved here, then?"

She nodded. "I just got here about a week ago."

His frown turned curious again. "What changed? You were adamant about getting back to your life in New York."

A corner of her mouth tilted. "Once I returned, I realized there wasn't much of a life there." She shrugged again. "Coming down here seemed like the right call, so here I am."

"Oh. Well, welcome."

"Thank you."

She smiled, and Cullen's breath caught. Normally, his patients' appearance didn't affect him, but there'd always been something about Piper. With long blonde hair, light green eyes, and at nearly six feet tall, she was quite beautiful. But he'd treated other beautiful women in the course of his career, and none of them had ever affected him the way she did. She intrigued him, but he couldn't put his finger on why.

Clearing his throat, he thrust his hands into the pockets of his scrub pants. "Well, it was good to see you. I should be going." He took a step to his left.

"I'll walk with you. I'm headed that way too." She fell into step beside him.

Cullen bit back a groan. She upset his equilibrium and befuddled his brain, even as she intrigued him to no end. He didn't like it. When she was his patient, it was easy to shove away anything she made him feel. He didn't cross professional lines. But now that she was no longer his patient? There was nothing to stop those feelings.

"So, how have you been?" She glanced at him.

He shrugged, keeping his hands stuffed in his pants pockets. "Fine. You? Fully healed, I hope."

"Mostly. I still don't have the stamina I used to, but it's improving."

"Getting winded?"

"Sometimes. My strength took a hit, so I've been working to build that back up. Physical therapy only takes you so far. They got me functioning. I'm still trying to get to a hundred percent."

"You might always have a bit of a limitation just because your lung capacity is diminished."

Piper scrunched her nose. "No." She made a cutting motion with one hand. "I will get back to what I once was. My lungs will just have to breathe deeper. Don't most people only use a fraction of their actual capacity?"

"Around seventy percent, yes."

"I've still got eighty percent left. I will get back to normal."

Cullen smiled, admiring her determination. "I hope you do. Let me know if there's any way I can help."

"Unless you can exercise for me, I think it's all on me." She scrunched her nose again.

He chuckled. "What's the matter? Don't like exercise?"

"No. I was perfectly happy being my squishy self."

Cullen choked on a laugh at her candor and covered it up with a cough. "You were hardly overweight."

She laughed and touched his arm. "That's very kind of you to say, but we both know it's obvious I like food."

He rolled his lips in and did his best not to look like a lech and rake his eyes over her body. She'd lost some of her curves, but those she currently had were still generous. "You look lovely. You always did."

Pink tinged her cheeks, and a soft smile graced her face. "Thank you."

Heat crept up Cullen's neck. Why did he say that last part? He didn't want her to get the wrong idea and think that he'd ogled her when she was his patient. Deciding to ignore it and hope she didn't notice, he nodded. "You're welcome."

Silence stretched as they continued down the hall. Now that the pleasantries were out of the way, Cullen felt his normal social awkwardness rear its head. He had no idea what to say. His mind whirred as he fought to come up with a reason to speed up and walk away from her.

"You look tired."

"Pardon?" He glanced at her with a frown as her words pulled him from his thoughts.

"Tired. You look tired. Is everything okay?"

"Oh. Yes. Everything is fine. It's just been a long shift."

"How long have you been here?"

"Um—" A yawn cracked his jaw. "Excuse me."

She giggled. "That long, huh?"

He nodded, a smile toying with his lips. "It's Monday, right?"

Her eyes widened. "You don't know what day it is?"

Cullen gave a slight frown. "I'm pretty sure it's Monday. My assistant emailed me my schedule this morning. I glanced at it before I went into surgery. I think it said Monday at the top." He hoped that was right. If it wasn't, he wasn't sure where he was supposed to be right now.

"It's Monday, yes."

Thank God. "Good."

"Why is that good? Most people hate Mondays."

"Because it means I'm no longer on-call."

It was Piper's turn to frown. "But didn't you just get out of surgery?"

He nodded. "Because I'm working a half-shift today. I have clinic hours in Foggy Mountain this afternoon. Tomorrow and Wednesday I play catch up at the coroner's office, then I'm back here Thursday morning, clinic Thursday afternoon, then here all day Friday." And he had next weekend off. It would be a minor miracle if it stayed that way.

She shook her head. "I don't know how you do it. Or why, for that matter."

He shrugged. "I like to stay busy."

"Obviously. But don't you have any hobbies?"

"I go to the gym. Read."

She rolled her eyes. "You go to the gym so you can sustain the pace you keep. And I'm betting you only read medical journals."

Cullen's eyes widened a fraction before he schooled his features. How did she know that? Was he that transparent?

"When was the last time you did anything fun?"

His frown deepened.

"Don't tell me you don't know what fun is."

"Of course I know what fun is." He just couldn't remember having any lately. At least, not any that didn't involve work.

She stopped. "Oh, we need to fix this."

He paused beside her. "What?"

"You said you're working through Friday, but what about

this weekend? Are you free Saturday?" She stared at him, determination lighting her jade eyes.

"I have plans."

Piper propped her hands on her hips and narrowed her eyes. "To do what? If it's to read medical journals and go to the gym, those don't count."

His mouth flattened. How she had him pegged already from their short acquaintance, he didn't know. But he wasn't about to enlighten her of that fact. "Why are you so concerned that I have fun?"

"Because I've recently learned life is much too short." A hint of heartache crossed her face, then disappeared as she straightened and pinned him with an intense stare. "So. Do you have plans outside of reading and the gym on Saturday?"

He'd planned to play catch-up on his coroner duties, but he didn't think she'd let that count either. Unwilling to lie to her—for reasons he'd rather not explore—he shook his head.

Her face transformed as a bright smile took over her features. Cullen's breath caught again.

"Wonderful. You do now." She burrowed a hand into her scrubs pocket and came out with a pen. "What's your phone number?"

The digits flew from his tongue before he could stop them. Rattled at the ease with which she could draw information from him, he crossed his arms, shifting as he tried to regain some control. She blew through it again when she grabbed his hand.

"What are you doing?"

She paused, pen poised over his palm. One perfectly sculpted eyebrow rose. "Giving you my number."

"Oh." *Brilliant conversation, Cul.* His inner voice rolled its eyes.

Smiling, she scrawled her phone number over his palm, then let go and stepped back. "I'll call you. But make sure you keep Saturday free." Backing away, her smile grew. She waggled her fingers, then spun on her heel and strode away.

He stared after her until she turned down the next hallway and disappeared. What the hell just happened?

A nurse hurried around him, jolting him back to the present. He glanced down to see the black ink on his hand and realized he still stood there with his hand open and raised. Curling his fingers into a fist, he dropped his arms and blew out a breath, then hurried down the hall toward the elevator.

What was wrong with him? Why did one woman have him so flustered? Even in social situations, he didn't typically get flustered. Just bored, then awkward because he didn't know what to say. But no, she actually had him feeling confused and slightly agitated.

Grumbling to himself, he stopped in front of the elevator that would take him to his office and punched the button to call it. It arrived with a ding and he stepped on. He just needed a nap. He'd go to his office, close all the blinds, and lie down on his nice comfy couch. A quick power nap would restore his brain function and help him make sense of his encounter with the intriguing Piper Riordan.

Cullen pushed the button for his floor. He nodded to himself as the doors slid closed, confident his plan would work. It had to, because if it didn't, he wasn't sure how to fix things.

Four

P ep in her step after her conversation with the scrumptious Dr. Tate, Piper entered the staff only area of the pharmacy. She took her phone from her scrubs pocket and unlocked it, then opened her contacts and added Dr. Tate's number before returning the device to her pocket. She knew she could have entered it when she was with him, but something told her the more personal, old-school way of writing down his number would throw him off and make her more likely to get it. She'd been afraid he'd balk if she took out her phone.

A smile tugged at her lips as she clocked in. His face had said it all when she scrawled her number on his hand. She had him so flummoxed she probably could have gotten more than a phone number out of him. Piper still wasn't sure why she proposed what she did. But once the idea popped into her head, her mouth ran with it.

Oh, well. She wasn't upset about it. She rather liked Dr. Tate. He was nice. And handsome as sin. Though that wasn't why she wanted to get to know him better. It would be nice to have a friend at the hospital, even if she rarely saw him.

"Have a good lunch?"

Piper glanced over, her smile widening as she nodded at her coworker, Rosalina Morales. "I did."

"Good, because I think the boss has you down for inventory this afternoon." The dark-haired woman gave her a wicked smile.

Piper groaned and sagged, her good mood evaporating. "I don't know where everything is. It'll take me forever."

Rosalina giggled. "I think that's the point—for you to learn where stuff is."

Blowing her bangs out of her face, she nodded. "I guess so. I better go find her. Thanks for the heads up."

The woman giggled. "No problem. I trust you'll remember this if she tells you to pick a helper?"

Piper grinned. "Not you?"

Rosalina winked. "You're a quick study." Laughing, she walked away.

Shaking her head, Piper waded deeper into the pharmacy in search of her boss, Dr. Tillie Trufant. The older woman ran a tight ship, but unlike her former boss, had some compassion and understanding. She was also nice and didn't make unreasonable demands. So far, anyway.

"Hey, Tillie." She spotted the woman in the stacks.

Petite, with a little extra padding around her middle and hips, the older woman's dark hair was streaked with gray. A genuine smile lit her pretty blue eyes when she turned and saw Piper. "Hi, ready to get back to work?"

Piper nodded. "Rosalina mentioned inventory."

Tillie chuckled at Piper's despondent look. "It won't be that bad. And it'll help you familiarize yourself with the stacks. I know you've been here a week and everything is alphabetized, but this will help you understand the quantities we need to keep in stock. We do this once a quarter, but since you're new and starting so soon after we did the last one, I figured—

rather than let you flounder for two months—it wouldn't hurt to do it again." She motioned for Piper to follow her.

They walked through the stacks to the offices at the rear of the pharmacy. Tillie unlocked her door and went inside, picking up a tablet from the desk. She quickly showed Piper how to log into inventory control using her newly established username and password. After outlining what she wanted Piper to do, Tillie left her alone to accomplish her task.

Piper wandered back to the stacks and started at *A*, feeling a little daunted. There were thousands of medications listed. She had to check what was on the shelf against each one. Thankfully, she didn't have to count each pill. Only the number of bottles and then note the open one, if there was one. Tillie explained it was just a double-check of their computerized system. She liked to have actual eyes on what they had in stock, just in case something glitched.

Humming to herself, Piper worked her way down the shelves. The task went quicker than she expected and by late-afternoon she was in the *E*s. Tapping the tablet screen, she clicked in the box beside the next drug on her list, ephedrine. She glanced at the shelf, counting bottles, and noted the number left, and added it to the box on the screen. As she rearranged the bottles, she knocked over one toward the back. It rolled behind the medication next to it, just out of reach.

Piper put the tablet on the floor, then moved the bottles to get to it. She frowned as she picked it up. It was lighter than she expected. Removing the lid, she saw the foil seal was gone. Ephedrine had two bottles open.

Frowning, she checked the expiration date. This one was much older, but still good. Maybe it was the last of the previous shipment and got missed when they restocked, she mused. With a shrug, she recapped the bottle, then put it in front of the other open one and moved on after making a note on her tablet.

She made it to the end of the *E*s by the time her shift ended. Her side ached from all the reaching and bending and stooping, and she was ready to go home and get in a hot bath. Her new apartment boasted a soaker tub. It was the main reason she went with the slightly higher-priced place. She'd gladly pay an extra fifty dollars a month for that bathtub, especially when this job paid better than her old one.

"So, how far did you get?" Tillie asked when Piper took the tablet back.

"Through the *E*s."

"Not bad." Tillie took the tablet and smiled. "Learn anything?"

Piper nodded. "You guys fill a lot more prescriptions than the hospital I came from."

Tillie laughed. "I bet. We'll keep you busy."

"Oh, for sure." Piper smiled and walked to the door. "I'll see you in the morning." She waggled her fingers and crossed the threshold, but a thought hit her and she paused. "Oh, before I forget. I found a second open bottle of ephedrine. It was at the back of the shelf. I think it's been there awhile. The expiration date is a lot older than the others."

Tillie frowned. "How much was left in it?"

Piper lifted a shoulder. "A quarter of a bottle, maybe? I didn't count the tablets. The only reason I noticed at all is because I knocked it over. When I picked it up, it felt too light to be full."

"It wasn't marked with the date it was opened?"

"Come to think of it, no. And I didn't mark it open, either." She frowned. That's something she should have noticed. And done. She clenched her teeth, waiting for Tillie to lay into her about marking bottles. "Sorry."

"You're fine." Tillie waved a hand. "I'll take care of it. But if you come across anymore unmarked, make sure you mark them. And let me know. One is a mistake. More than that is a problem, and I need to send out a reminder. You've been marking others you open when you're filling prescriptions, right?"

"Of course." Piper's head bobbed. "I think I was just focused on the inventory and not paying attention to other things. It won't happen again."

Tillie smiled. "Good. Now go home and get some rest."

Some of Piper's anxiety lessened at Tillie's tone. It would take some time for her to recondition herself to a more understanding boss. If she'd done that at her old job, she'd be looking at a formal reprimand. "Thanks. Have a good night."

"You too."

With another waggle of her fingers, Piper headed down the hall to the locker room, even more ready for that bath.

FIVE

Cullen grabbed the last folder in his stack of death reports, eager to sign off on it so he could go home. It hadn't been a particularly long or taxing day, but he was still exhausted from yesterday. After leaving the hospital, he'd done his clinic hours, then been called back to Asheville for an emergency. A car accident left the trauma staff overwhelmed and in need of another surgeon. He'd been happy to help, but it made for a long evening. He planned to go home as soon as he finished here, eat some dinner, and crash.

Flipping open the folder, he paused as he read the name, and his heart sank. "Oh, man." Evan Dryden had been one of his patients about a year ago. He'd come into the E.R. with a bad bout of bronchitis and fractured ribs that punctured a lung and caused a massive internal hemorrhage. Cullen repaired the ribs, but also discovered the man had leukemia. He'd been making good progress, or so Cullen thought.

"Damn." He'd have to order some flowers and send a card to the man's widow and young children. He grimaced as he pictured those little kids' faces. The oldest was only six. The younger two might not even remember their father when they were older. He knew the youngest wouldn't; she was only eighteen-months-old.

Sitting back in his chair, he brought the file up and read the doctor's reports. It looked like things took a turn a few months ago and his leukemia returned. He was in the prep phase of a bone marrow transplant when he developed an infection that turned into sepsis.

Cullen frowned as he read the infection treatment course. He didn't understand why it didn't work. They'd caught it early, and it wasn't an antibiotic-resistant bacterial strain. When it became apparent they would need to postpone the transplant, his doctor gave him G-CSF—a blood cell builder—which set off an inflammatory response. The steroids they prescribed should have fixed that. Even with their immunosuppressive effect, he was producing enough white blood cells to fight the infection. He wondered if Evan had a secondary infection no one knew about.

In any case, it still sucked. This was the part of medicine Cullen didn't like—losing people who shouldn't have died, but for some inexplicable reason did anyway.

His expression tight, Cullen picked up the death certificate form and filled it out, marking natural causes as the cause of death, then scrawled his name at the bottom. Setting the form on top of the reports, he closed the folder and added it to his "done" stack. He was finished for the day, but now he had a sour taste in his mouth. This was not how he wanted to end things.

Turning off his computer, he pushed away from his desk and stood. He donned his coat and picked up his briefcase, then headed for the door.

"All done, Doc?" Cullen's assistant, Levi, glanced up from his desk.

"Yes. I left the signed reports on the desk."

Levi nodded. "I'll get them sent out." He frowned and tipped his head. "You okay?"

Cullen rubbed his forehead. "Yeah. One of the deaths was a former patient. It was just unexpected."

"Oh, I'm sorry."

"Thanks." He dropped his hand. "Anyway, I'm getting some dinner and heading home. Don't stay too late, yeah?"

Levi's smile held a hint of mischievousness. "Oh, I don't plan to. I have a date to plan."

Cullen frowned. "Date?"

"Valentine's auction? We have to turn our information in by Friday. You forgot, didn't you?"

Dammit. "Yes."

"Well, you still have a couple of days to plan. You better get busy, though. All the good restaurant reservations will be snatched up soon. If they aren't already." His grin was smug.

Cullen narrowed his eyes at the glint in Levi's dark eyes. "Is that what you're planning for your epic date? Dinner at a fancy restaurant?" He could top that easily.

Levi shrugged. "Guess you'll have to wait until you see the auction pamphlet."

Shaking a finger at him, a grin broke over Cullen's face. "And now I know it's not dinner. Or not *just* dinner."

With a deep chuckle, Levi turned back to his computer. "You can guess all you want. I'm not telling."

Cullen rolled his eyes, still laughing, but now his competitive streak was awake. Levi was going down. Tonight, he'd sit down and do some research. Come up with a date that would wow, but make it clear this was for charity, and that he wasn't looking for anything permanent. Or even temporary.

He left the office and crossed the parking lot to his car, snow crunching under his feet as he walked. It had been drifting down all day, but not very hard. A skim-coat of white covered the ground and obscured the grass. It was enough to make the roads slick, though. He hoped he didn't get called in again.

Unlocking his car, he tossed his briefcase inside and got in. Cold seeped through his pants from the leather seat. One day, he would remember to use the remote start function on the vehicle before he left his office.

He started the engine and let it warm for a few moments as he ran the wipers to clear the snow. Once he could see, he pulled out of the parking lot. Snaking his way through town, he was thankful he kept his main office in Foggy Mountain. He had one at the Asheville hospital, but he used the one at his clinic in Foggy Mountain as his primary space. It's where Levi worked and where Cullen did the bulk of his paperwork. He'd never been someone who liked big cities. It's why he'd chosen Asheville to practice in after he finished his residency and fellowship. He'd had his pick of hospitals, but knew he wouldn't be happy in one of the major cities. While he liked to stay busy, the crush of people there would have added an unhealthy amount of stress to his life. He'd barely made it through his fellowship in Baltimore because he felt so claustro-phobic in the city. Asheville was peaceful compared to there.

But he still preferred to be further away from the hustle and bustle, which is why he lived in Foggy Mountain and spent as much time working there as he could now that he had a clinic in town and was the county coroner.

Winding his way through what constituted rush-hour traffic in Foggy Mountain, he looked for a place with a short drive-thru line, ready to get food and point his car toward home. As he neared the stoplight at the shopping center, he slowed to a crawl. This intersection was awful in bad weather. Cars slid through the light with alarming regularity. He was honestly amazed there weren't more serious accidents here in the winter.

The thought no sooner crossed his mind than a black SUV

coming from his right slid through the intersection moments after the light turned red. Cullen held his breath as he noticed the smaller blue SUV in front of him that entered the intersection as the light turned green.

Metal crunched as the black SUV smacked into the smaller car. The blue SUV did a three-sixty before it came to rest thirty feet away in the opposite lane. The black car flipped onto its side and slid, coming to a halt when it hit the lamppost on the corner.

"Dammit." Cullen shut off his car and got out. He opened the driver's side passenger door and retrieved the medical kit he always carried, then headed for the closer of the two cars— the blue SUV. Feet sliding on the slush-covered roadway, he slowed down, so he didn't end up needing medical attention as well. His footwear, while comfortable and appropriate for his profession, was not designed for icy, snow-covered roadways. Neither were his dark gray slacks. Wind cut through them like a precision scalpel, chilling his skin beneath. He was grateful now that he'd splurged on his overcoat. The lined cashmere trench warded off the freezing wind.

As he got close to the blue car, he could hear a child screaming. His heart stuttered, but he forced his emotions away. They would do him no good here.

Reaching the car, he peered inside. A woman sat behind the wheel, staring forward in a daze. Behind her, a boy of about two screamed from his car seat.

"Ma'am?" Cullen knocked on the window.

She turned to look at him, her eyes glassy. Blood smeared across her forehead, darkening her blonde hair. He tried the door handle, but it was locked.

"Can you unlock the door?" He pointed to the lock.

She looked at it, then frowned, making no move to do as he asked.

Cullen bit back a curse. He needed to get to her. "Ma'am,

press the button to unlock your car, please. It's right there." He leaned closer and pointed to the controls on the door.

She lifted a hand and touched the buttons, but not hard enough to unlock the doors.

"That's it. Now press down. You only need to use one finger."

She stared at her hand, lifting it to look at the bloodstain on it.

"Ma'am, don't worry about the blood. I need you to unlock the car so I can get in to help you. To help your son."

At the mention of the boy, some of her confusion cleared. She glanced back.

Cullen knocked on the window again. She turned to look at him, more clear-eyed. He pointed to the lock button.

"The door? Unlock it."

This time, she touched the button and pressed. The locks clicked, and Cullen yanked on the handle. The door opened with a creak.

"Hi. My name is Cullen. I'm a doctor. Do you remember what happened?" He set the med kit on the floorboard by her feet, then crouched.

A frown wrinkled the space between her eyebrows. "Sort of. A car hit us." She glanced out the windshield at the other SUV, then back to him. "Did I run the light?"

He shook his head. "No. The other car slid through the intersection." He glanced at the other SUV. The driver had climbed out and stood leaning against his vehicle, hand pressed to his head as he looked around.

Cullen turned his attention back to the woman. "What's your name?"

"Um, Olivia."

"Okay. Can you tell me what all hurts, Olivia?"

"My baby. Is he okay?" She turned to look at him.

Cullen put a hand on her cheek and gently turned her to

face him. "Try not to move your head. He's fine. The screaming is a good sign. Can you answer my question?" He kept his tone gentle, but firm.

Her hand shook as she brought it up to touch the back of his, where he held her head before she let it fall back to her lap. "Um, what was it you asked?"

"Does anything hurt?"

"My head." She raised her hand again, going for the wound on her forehead.

Cullen took her hand in his and pulled it down, resting it in her lap again, then moved his hand back to hold her head. "Okay. Anything else?"

She started to shake her head, and he tightened his grip. "Just use words."

"Okay. Um, no. Nothing else hurts."

"Good."

"Dr. Tate?"

He glanced up at the sound of his name coming from outside the vehicle. His brows rose in surprise. "Piper?"

She stood near the hood of the vehicle. Wind whipped her long blonde hair around her face. She snagged the strand that covered her eyes and tucked it behind her ear.

"What are you doing here?"

"I was on my way home." She came around to his side. "What can I do to help?"

"That depends. How much medical training do you have?"

"Basic first aid, CPR, that sort of thing."

"Okay. Can you check the boy for visible injuries? See if you can calm him down?"

"Sure." She moved to the passenger door and pulled it open. "Hi, sweetie."

Cullen tuned her out to focus on the mom.

"Who's that? What's she doing with my son? Is he okay?" The woman's voice rose with each question.

"He's fine. That's my friend Piper. She's going to look after him, so you don't worry. I need you to focus on me right now, okay? You're hurt, and I need to assess how much."

Her head bobbed once in his grip. "Okay."

"All right. I'm going to probe your neck. You tell me if any of it hurts."

"Okay," she whispered. Squeezing her eyes shut, a tear leaked out to trail down her cheek.

Cullen slid his hands back and up to the base of her skull. Holding her steady with one hand, he probed the vertebrae with his other. "Any of this hurt?" He went bone by bone down her neck; each time, she answered in the negative. "Perfect. I'm still going to hold your head just to be safe. When the paramedics get here, they'll put a C-collar on you. Again, it's all precautionary. Nothing else hurts?"

"My wrist." She raised her right hand.

Cullen bit back a frown, concerned, but not surprised at the new development. Sometimes it took a few minutes—or more—for injuries to make themselves known, which is why he always asked multiple times about any new pain. "Okay. Just keep it resting in your lap."

She lowered her arm.

"Anything else?"

"No." Another tear slid free. "My son's okay?" Her gaze turned to the side as she tried to look at her shrieking child.

"He's fine." Cullen glanced around the headrest. Piper had climbed into the backseat with the boy to calm him. It wasn't working. "Take him out of his seat," he told her.

She glanced at him with a frown. "You're sure?"

He nodded. If the boy had any spinal injuries, he'd have already made them worse with his thrashing. With his back bowed, pushing against the restraints and his head whipping from side to side, he couldn't get much more agitated. "He'll probably calm down if you hold him."

"Okay." She reached for the buckles holding him in place.

"What's your son's name, Olivia?" Cullen asked.

"Cody."

Cullen glanced at Piper to see if she had heard. Her quick nod told him she had.

"Hey, Cody. It's okay. You're just fine," Piper crooned as she lifted the boy from his seat. "That was scary, wasn't it? But you're okay. And your mama's going to be all right. Dr. Tate will take good care of her." He pushed against her, wanting to get to his mother in the front seat. Piper slid out of the car, holding him. She looked at Cullen, then tipped her head toward the rear of the car.

He nodded, understanding her intentions.

"Where's she taking him?" Olivia's voice rose, and she shifted.

"Shh… It's okay. She's just walking around with him a bit, trying to calm him down. He's fine."

Sirens sounded in the distance. He let out a breath of relief. Olivia and her son needed to get out of the cold and to the hospital.

In moments, the ambulance pulled into the intersection. Cullen recognized the pair that climbed out. His patients would be in good hands with Maurice and Liz.

"What have we got?" Maurice rounded the car and paused when he saw Cullen. "Dr. Tate?"

"Hi, Maurice. The accident happened in front of me. The black SUV slid through the intersection and hit this car, spinning it around. I think the boy is fine." He tipped his head toward Piper. "But the mom likely has a concussion. And she says her right wrist hurts."

"Okay." Maurice set his bags down and glanced at his partner, Liz. "You want to check on the kid while I help with mom, here?"

She nodded and detoured toward Piper.

Maurice reached into his bag and came out with a C-collar. "Let's get this on her, then we can do a better assessment."

Cullen shifted with a grimace to give Maurice room to get his arms in the car. His calves screamed at him after being crouched so long.

The collar touched Cullen's hands, and he lifted one out, then the other, holding the curved plastic in place while Maurice strapped it around her neck. Once it was secure, he let go, then grabbed his kit and stood to get out of Maurice's way so he could check her vitals.

Blood rushed back into his legs, making them ache. He winced and glanced across the street. "I'm going to check on the driver of the other vehicle. You good?" he asked Maurice.

"Yep."

Carefully, Cullen crossed the slick roadway. The driver, who was little more than a kid, stood with several other people and a police officer.

"Hello. Sir, I'm Dr. Tate. I witnessed the accident. May I check you for injuries?"

The man waved a hand. "I'm fine. Just shaken."

"At least let me check your vitals. Shock can hide things."

"Let him check you out," the police officer said, nodding to Cullen. "This wasn't a fender bender."

The young man's shoulders slumped. "Yeah, okay."

"Let's go to the ambulance." Cullen held an arm out, urging the man forward. Together, they crossed the street to Maurice and Liz's ambulance. He stepped up to the rear door and opened it. Liz and Piper looked up from the child crying in Piper's arms. He'd calmed slightly, but fat tears still coursed down his cheeks and small hiccups interspersed his breaths.

"Sorry to interrupt. Liz, can I borrow some equipment to check out the other driver? Or is there another bus on the way?"

She shook her head and stood, moving to a bin on the wall. "We're slammed at the moment. The only way dispatch is going to send us another truck is if we have to transport multiple patients." She took out a blood pressure cuff and handed it to him. "You have your own stethoscope?" She pointed to the med kit in his hand.

Cullen nodded. "Okay. I'll let you know." He took the cuff and closed the door, turning back to the man.

"There was a kid in the car I hit?" The man's eyes were wide. Cullen watched the color leach out of his face, and he swayed on his feet. "Whoa, there." Cullen shot a hand out and grabbed the man's arm, tucking him close. "How about we find a place to sit down?"

"Yeah." The man leaned into him. "I'm a little dizzy."

Cullen glanced around for a suitable place. His gaze stopped on the police car. It wasn't ideal, but it would be warmer and dry. "Let's go sit in the police car for now." Holding the man's elbow, he led him to the cop car. With a sharp whistle, he drew the officer's attention and motioned to the car. The man jogged over, sliding on the slippery road.

"Can he sit in the backseat while I check him out?"

"Of course." The officer unlocked the car and opened the door.

Cullen helped the man sit. "What's your name?"

"Braden."

"Did you hit your head, Braden?" Cullen pulled the ends of the blood pressure cuff apart with a loud rasp.

"No."

"Any pain in your neck or back?" He wrapped the cuff around the kid's arm.

"No. I feel fine."

Cullen nodded once, then dug into his kit and retrieved his stethoscope. He put it in his ears, then laid the bell on the inside of Braden's arm. Pumping up the cuff, he let the air out slowly as he listened and watched the dial. Once he had both readings, he loosened the valve on the bulb and it hissed, then he tore off the cuff. "Your blood pressure is fine. Do you remember what happened?"

"I came down the hill and tried to stop, but I just slid. My dad's going to kill me. That's his car." He leaned forward, putting his head in his hands.

"I'm sure he'll understand and be happy you're all right."

The young man ignored him and continued to stare at the ground. Cullen took the opportunity to check his pulse. It was a bit quick, but under the circumstances, not unexpected.

"Okay, look up at me." He took a penlight from his pocket and turned it on. "Follow my finger."

Braden followed Cullen's movements.

"Good. Now pick a point past my shoulder and watch it." He flicked the light into and then away from Braden's eye to check his pupils. They were normal. He clicked off the light and put it back in his pocket. "Okay. Your vitals and eyes look fine. Do you have any pain anywhere?"

"My shoulder and right side are a little sore, but I landed against the console when the car tipped."

Cullen lifted his left hand, hovering near Braden's arm. "May I?"

The young man straightened. "Sure."

With efficient, practiced movements, Cullen checked his shoulder, arm, and ribs. Nothing seemed amiss and there were no outward signs of serious injury. He stepped back. "Okay. I think you escaped without any major damage done."

"What about them?" Braden pointed to the ambulance.

Cullen glanced back. Maurice and a firefighter were loading Olivia onto a backboard. "I think they'll be okay. A lot of what they're doing is precautionary because she bumped her head. Her son seems just fine, though."

"You're sure? I wasn't speeding. I don't know how this happened." Tears swam in his eyes.

"I'm sure."

Braden nodded, sniffing back his tears.

Cullen looked at the police officer hovering nearby. "I'm done with my assessment. He's okay." He turned to the young man. "We always recommend you go to the hospital and get checked out. Their equipment is more sophisticated than what I have here. Do you want to do that?"

Braden shook his head. "No. I think I'm all right. I just want to go home."

"Okay. If you start feeling more pain in your ribs or get short of breath, you need to go to the E.R. and get checked out."

"All right, I will. Thanks."

With a quick pat on the young man's shoulder, Cullen turned to the officer. "If you need me, I'll be with the ambulance crew."

The man nodded, and Cullen jogged off, slip-sliding through the slush.

Six

Under the harsh lights in the back of the ambulance, Piper sat on the bench seat, rocking Cody. The boy had finally calmed, but still hiccupped every so often. She smoothed his hair back, stroking the silky locks as he sucked on his thumb while snuggled up to her and watched Maurice and Liz work on his mother. The young woman was awake, though she seemed a little dazed.

The soft click of the door handle was Piper's only warning before the side door opened and Cullen stepped into the doorway. Her heart flip-flopped in her chest at the sight of him. She'd always found him attractive. But now, with his windswept dark blonde hair and his hazel eyes shining with intelligence and control—not to mention how massive he looked in that caramel trench coat—it was all she could do not to drool like the child in her arms. He was a man in his element and in charge. It was sexy as hell.

"How are things going in here?" He stepped up, leaning in to look at the paramedics.

"Just fine," Liz replied. "We'll be ready to head to the hospital soon.

"We just have one problem," Maurice added.

Piper frowned. They did? She glanced at Cullen to see a similar expression on his face.

"What's that?" he asked.

Maurice pointed at her and the boy. "What to do with Cody. He's fine, but obviously Olivia can't care for him right now. She said her husband is on his way, but he works in Asheville. With the weather—" He raised his eyebrow and twirled a finger in the air.

"I can come with you." The words were out of Piper's mouth before she knew it. "That is, if you don't mind." She glanced down at the boy. "I mean, he's comfortable where he is and with me, so..." Her voice trailed off, and she shrugged.

"That would be great, actually," Liz said. She looked at her patient. "Olivia? Is that okay with you?"

Eyes closed against the bright lights, Olivia tried to nod, but the collar around her neck and blocks beside her head stopped her. She sighed. "That's fine."

"Oh, wait. What about my car?" Piper bit the corner of her lip and frowned.

"I can park it at the shopping center and follow you to the hospital," Cullen said.

A crease formed between her eyes as she looked at him. "Are you sure?"

He nodded. "I don't mind." He held out a hand. "Give me your keys."

"They're still in it. So is my purse."

Cullen curled his fingers and withdrew his hand. "Okay. What kind of car do you drive? I'll move it now and bring your bag with me to the hospital."

"It's the purple Wrangler. You can't miss it."

A corner of his mouth rose. "Why am I not surprised?"

She grinned and said nothing.

"I'll see you at the hospital." He peered at Maurice. "Foggy Mountain General, right?"

Maurice nodded.

Cullen tapped the side of the ambulance with his palm once, then stepped down, closing the door.

"I take it you know our Dr. Tate?" Liz looked up and smiled.

"He was my surgeon."

Liz's eyes widened, then her forehead wrinkled as she frowned. "That's all he is to you?"

Piper lifted a shoulder. "We work together now. Sort of. I'm a pharmacy technician at the hospital in Asheville."

The other woman hummed and shifted, crossing her legs and resting her clipboard on her knee. A sly smile lit her face. "Oh, really?"

It was Piper's turn to shift under the woman's scrutiny. Cody groaned softly and snuggled deeper. She smoothed his hair again and looked down at his face. His eyelids fluttered. Poor kid had worn himself out.

She glanced up. "We're just friends. Sort of." Honestly, she didn't know how to categorize things with Cullen. He'd been her doctor, now he wasn't. Acquaintances? She knew she'd like more. He intrigued her. It was why she'd badgered him into doing something with her on Saturday. That and the fact the man seriously needed to lighten up. No one should work as much as he did.

Liz's giggle brought her out of her thoughts. "If you say so." The woman clicked her pen and jotted something on her clipboard.

Piper frowned. What did she mean by that? They'd had a conversation about her car. How could the medic read anything into that? What could she have possibly seen in such a short, innocent conversation?

Too tired to care, she lifted her shoulder once more and

turned her attention to the child in her arms. She'd think about Cullen Tate and all his sexiness later.

The ride to the hospital was a short one. Piper was glad they didn't have to go all the way back to Asheville. Getting back to Foggy Mountain had been treacherous enough the first time. She could only imagine how bad the roads would be once it got dark. While winters were warmer here than New York, Piper was finding the driving more hazardous simply because of the terrain. She was also glad she liked outlandish things. She wouldn't have her four-by-four vehicle otherwise.

"Okay." Liz stood, setting the clipboard on the stretcher by Olivia's feet. "Time for a better bed." The rear doors opened, and Maurice reached in to grab the end of the gurney.

Piper stayed where she was to give them room to maneuver, then went out the side door, still holding Cody. The boy sighed in his sleep, but didn't wake. She hurried inside out of the chill, following the staff into the treatment area.

Maurice gave the E.R. team a rundown of what happened. Even though he appeared fine on the scene, the doctor on duty directed the nurse to put Cody in the room next door to Olivia's. Piper couldn't fault the doctor for wanting to give the boy a good once over. Children didn't always react the same to trauma as adults.

Following the nurse, Piper went into the room and laid Cody on the bed. He rolled and whimpered. She put a hand on his back and gently patted him until he settled down.

"You're good at that."

Piper jumped at the deep voice coming from the doorway. She glanced up at Cullen, then back at the boy with a soft smile. "It's not hard to provide comfort when it's needed. He was just scared."

"Still." Cullen moved deeper into the room, filling it with his presence. "Not everyone has the magic touch. Not even some parents."

"Which is just sad." She kept her eyes on Cody so Cullen couldn't see the turmoil in her eyes. Her father had been that way. Any comfort she'd ever received had come from her mother.

"It is." He moved closer, standing behind her to look down on Cody.

The hair on the back of her neck stood up as awareness flooded her body. She clenched her teeth. Why was she having this reaction to him now? She'd been around him for weeks when she was injured. Other than recognizing just how damn handsome he was, she never got an inkling of this feeling. Now it was all she could do not to spin around and press her body to that massive frame of his.

"Dr. Tate?"

They both turned at the intrusion of another voice. Piper peered around Cullen to see a nurse in the doorway.

The woman frowned, eyeing first the child, then Piper. "Did someone call you? For him?" She gestured to Cody.

"No. Piper and I witnessed the accident. She accompanied the child to the hospital since the mother was incapacitated. I followed to give her a ride back to her car."

The nurse's frown deepened. "You weren't together? But you know each other?"

They nodded.

"Well, talk about coincidence." The woman's eyes widened, and she shook her head. "And fortuitous." She smiled. "Now one of you doesn't have to take a cab."

"It is lucky, yes." Cullen returned her smile.

Piper felt something stretch across her face, but she wasn't sure she'd call it a smile. She was still reeling from Cullen's closeness. He hadn't moved.

"So, how's our littlest patient?" The nurse glanced at Cullen.

"He seems fine, though I haven't examined him. Liz did."

He looked at Piper, a question in his eyes. "Did she say anything to you about him?"

Piper shook her head. "No. Though she said it was hard to tell with the way he was carrying on. Once he calmed, every time she came close, he started crying again and tried to wrap himself around me like a vine, so she backed off."

"Well, we'll take a good look at him here." The nurse smiled. "Is his father on the way?"

"Yes. Olivia called him from the ambulance shortly before we left the scene. He was already on his way home, so he should be here soon."

"Good. I'm just going to check his vitals, then. Make sure everything looks all right. I'll let the doctor know to wait until dad gets here before he comes in." She lifted the coiled wires from the hook attached to the monitor. After attaching a sticky pulse oximeter to Cody's finger, she wrapped a blood pressure cuff around his arm and pushed the button on the machine.

Piper said a prayer it wouldn't wake him. He deserved to rest.

Thankfully, he slept through the quick arm squeeze.

"He looks good, agreed?" She looked at Cullen.

He nodded.

"Perfect. And he's sleeping peacefully," she said as she removed the cuff. She left the pulse oximeter on, though. "Are you staying in here, Dr. Tate?"

"Yes."

"Okay. Holler if anything changes."

"I will, thank you."

She nodded once and left. Piper moved to the lone chair next to the bed and sat.

"So, you work here too?"

"Sort of. I have admitting privileges here, but don't work on staff. I'm more of a consultant. They call me where there's a trauma case they need stabilized or are unsure where to send them." He moved to sit down next to her.

She offered him a tired smile.

He didn't return it; instead, studying her face with a concerned frown. "You okay?"

"Yeah. Just tired. My boss had me doing inventory today. All the up and down and reaching wore me out."

His frown deepened. "You shouldn't overdo it. I know all us medical people have declared you healed and fit for work, but it takes time for the body to relearn and adjust to its new limitations."

She glared at him. "I already told you, I'm not limited in any way. I just need to regain my strength."

He held up his hands. "Right, sorry. But it still takes time for your body to adjust. And to rebuild that strength."

"I know." She was painfully aware of that. She hated that she couldn't carry on as she used to.

"If you'd like, I can talk to your boss. Let her know—"

Piper waved her hands. "No. I'm fine. Thank you, though." She did not want special treatment or favors. Particularly from Cullen Tate. It would just make the other staff members wonder what she'd done to garner such favor from the illustrious doctor. She didn't need them to speculate about her relationship with him. One, because they didn't have one. And two, it could damage his reputation. She knew before today that he was a skilled physician, but seeing him in action in a fast-paced emergency situation showed her how good he really was. The world needed him to be free of scandal so he could continue saving lives without interference from people with nothing better to do than create trouble.

"You're sure?"

She nodded. "I just need to soak in a hot bath and get some sleep. I'll be fine in the morning." After some painkillers and some stretches. She was only thirty, but nowadays, she felt twice that when she got out of bed in the mornings. "And the way I look at it, it's toughening me up for next week when I move to twelves."

"Twelves? You're not already on a twelve-hour shift?"

She shook her head. "The first two weeks are orientation and training. They're eight-hour shifts five days a week."

"Are you going to be able to manage that?"

Piper glared again. "I'll be fine." Her voice sank to a low growl.

His lips twitched, and he held up his hands.

A smile toyed with her mouth at the amused light in his eyes, and she shifted so he couldn't see her face. There was no need to encourage him.

"So, how is your job going? Are you enjoying it?"

Her head bobbed once, and she turned back. "I am. Tillie's a great boss. Much better than my last one."

"Good. So, how come you live here instead of Asheville? Is it because of your friend?"

"Yeah. We had to put our friendship on hold for so long. I wanted to be close, so we didn't have to plan outings. We could just call and say, 'I'm coming over.' Then show up with wine and chocolate for a movie night." An impish grin spread over her face.

A low chuckle emanated from Cullen's chest. "Have you done that yet?"

Her smile widened. "First weekend I was here. She came over with hot chocolate and cookies and helped me unpack, then stayed to watch a movie with me. It was nice." She tipped her head. "I know you said you don't get out much, but what do you and your friends do?"

Cullen shifted, crossing his arms. His brows pinched, and he shrugged. "I don't have many friends. At least not ones I hang out with regularly. Sometimes, I go to the Davidsons. Gemma likes to host barbecues."

A sharp pang of sadness pierced Piper's heart. Everyone needed someone. "What about your family?"

"My parents live in Arizona. So do my brother and sister."

"You have siblings?"

He nodded. "I'm the oldest." His brows dipped again. "I don't see them much."

Before she could question that statement, a man skidded to a halt in the doorway.

"Cody? Oh my goodness!" He hurried inside.

Piper turned, putting herself between him and the sleeping child. "Sir?"

"Sorry. I'm Isaac Grant. Cody's my son."

Shoulders relaxing, Piper stepped to the side. "He's doing fine. Just worn out. He made quite the fuss on-scene of the accident."

"Your wife is next door," Cullen said.

Isaac nodded. "The nurse said they were right beside each other. I just saw him first." He touched his son's hand, a tender look on his face. "He's really okay?"

Cullen moved closer. "Yes. The doctor on duty hasn't been in yet, but a nurse and I looked him over and so did a paramedic on-scene. His vitals are fine and he's responding normally to all questions and stimuli."

The man cast a quick frown at him. "Are you a doctor?"

"Yes. I was on my way home and witnessed the accident."

Isaac processed that information, then glanced at Piper. "And you?"

"Another witness. I helped comfort Cody at the accident scene and rode with him here since your wife couldn't hold him."

"Thank you. Is she okay?"

"She likely has a concussion, and maybe a broken arm or wrist." Cullen laid a hand on Isaac's shoulder. "You should go speak to her. We'll stay here as long as you need us."

Isaac touched his son's fingers once more and nodded. "I appreciate that. Thank you for all you've done."

Piper offered him a soft smile. "You're welcome. He's a sweet boy."

A half-smile tipped Isaac's mouth. "He is." He glanced at the door. "I'll be right back."

"Take your time," Cullen said.

With a nod, Isaac left. A moment later, they could hear his tearful reunion with his wife.

Piper cast a glance through her lashes at Cullen. He was so good with people. It made her wonder why he was so alone.

His stomach rumbled, breaking the silence. Red creeped over his cheeks, making Piper laugh.

"Sorry," he mumbled. "It's been a while since lunch."

"I know how you feel."

"Do you want to go get a snack?" He hooked a thumb toward the door. "I can wait with Cody."

She shook her head, another idea occurring to her. "No. We can just go get dinner once his dad comes back."

A slight widening of his hazel eyes was the only indication he gave that he noticed the meaning behind her statement. In a blink, it was gone. "Yeah. I'm just going to run through a drive-thru somewhere. At this point, anything will do."

Piper's mouth flattened as he chose to ignore her meaning. That wouldn't do. The man needed a friend.

Her brows dipped as her mind whispered that wasn't the only reason she wanted to go to dinner with him.

She ignored it. No matter what that voice said, being his friend was the only reason she wanted to have dinner with him. It had nothing to do with the way his massive, muscular body and dusting of beard stubble stirred her insides, or the way his eyes sparkled when he was amused. Or in the way his kindness toward his patients touched something within her.

She bit back a growl as want sent hot tendrils through her

body. He needed a friend. Not someone who found him gorgeous and intriguing and wanted to jump his bones.

"You know—" she cleared her throat. "Mackenzie turned me on to a place not far from where my car's parked. Jester's? She said it has great barbecue. I haven't been yet."

His head bobbed. "You should go. It's good."

"How about you come with me?"

Those green-gray eyes went wide again for a fraction of a second before he schooled his features. "I'm okay with a drive-thru."

She rolled her eyes. "No one is okay with a drive-thru when there's awesome barbecue around."

He chuckled, and one eyebrow quirked. "I suppose that's true."

Her expression brightened. "Does that mean you'll have dinner with me?"

Cullen studied her for a long moment. Piper clamped her lips together, keeping her expression blank.

Finally, he nodded. "Okay. I haven't had Jester's in a while. That sounds good."

Her inner woman fist pumped and did a dance, then fanned her face as she drank in the hunk standing before her. Outwardly, Piper just smiled and told her hedonistic inner self to shut up. "Great."

SEVEN

Cullen steered the car around the corner at a crawl as they left the hospital. Snow still fell at a gentle but steady pace. What was on the roads was freezing up, the slush turning hard now that the sun had set.

He cast a side-eyed glance at the woman occupying his passenger seat. What was he thinking, agreeing to eat with her? She'd already cajoled him into something this weekend. Why was he agreeing to dinner too? She had some sort of power over him, it seemed.

His gaze strayed lower as he cast another quick glance at her from the corner of his eye. He jerked his eyes back to the road and silently cursed. What was the matter with him? She was a patient. Former patient, but still a patient. He'd seen her insides and put them back together. That alone usually kept him from wanting to form any sort of attachment to someone he'd worked on. He could never stop thinking about what he'd done and seen.

But Piper was different. Yes, those images were there—sometimes—when he thought about her or looked at her. But not like they used to be when she was still under his care.

It had to be her sudden reappearance in his life. He'd never expected to see her again once he discharged her from his practice. Seeing her yesterday had thrown him. That had to be it.

"You're quiet."

Cullen jumped, hiding it by shifting positions. "I'm just tired. It's been a long day."

"That it has." She sighed and leaned against the window.

"Are you sure you want to go to Jester's? Maybe I should run us through a drive-thru and just take you to your car."

She waved a finger. "No. I want a good end to this long day."

Something in his chest warmed at the implication she'd find having dinner with him a "good" end to her day. He caved. "Okay. Jester's it is."

Navigating the rest of the way to the restaurant in silence, he turned into the parking lot and found a space close to the door. They got out and hurried inside, out of the cold.

"The temperature is really dropping." Piper looked up at him as the door shut behind them. She took off her gloves and put them in her pockets, then brushed a lock of her blonde hair from her face. "Driving to work tomorrow is going to suck."

Cullen nodded. "Give yourself a lot of extra time."

Her nose scrunched. "Great."

"Hi, welcome to Jester's."

They turned as a young woman greeted them from the hostess stand.

"Just two?" The girl reached for the stack of menus.

"Yes," Cullen said.

"Perfect. This way." She took two menus off the stack and motioned for them to follow. Leading them into the restaurant, she positioned them at a booth overlooking the parking lot and street beyond.

Cullen waited for Piper to sit, then slid into the other side. He shrugged out of his coat and let it fall behind him.

"What can I get you to drink?" The girl laid a menu in front of each of them.

"Water is fine for me," Piper said as she removed her coat.

"Same." Cullen looked at the hostess.

"Okay. Your server will be over with those shortly."

"Thank you." He offered her a smile, and she left. Picking up his menu, he opened it, even though he knew what he wanted. He just didn't want the awkward silence that always descended on a first date.

The menu hid his frown at that thought. This was not a date. It was dinner with a friend. Hell, not even a friend. An acquaintance.

His eyes closed for a moment. What was he doing here?

"What are you getting?"

Piper's lilting voice broke through his thoughts, and his eyes opened. He lowered the menu to look at her. Her gaze flickered to him, then back to the folder in her hands. Through her teeth, her tongue poked out to touch her lower lip as she concentrated.

Cullen bit back a groan. He wanted to taste that pouty lip too. He hid behind his menu again, teeth clenched. Man, he needed to get a grip. Swallowing once, he answered her. "Probably the brisket sandwich."

"Oh, that sounds good. What sides does it come with?"

He peeked over the top of his menu to see her head move up and down as she glanced through the menu items.

"It's on the second page. Halfway down."

Her eyes lifted to his again, and their gazes held for a long beat. Cullen blinked and looked down. "I usually get fries and okra." His grip on the menu tightened as he fought the attraction blazing through his veins.

"I've never had okra."

He lowered the menu, curiosity replacing a bit of the need he felt. "Seriously?"

She nodded. "What's it taste like?"

"Um, a bit like zucchini, I guess? They batter it and fry it here. It's great."

She hummed. "I like zucchini." Her eyes roved over her menu once more, then she closed it and laid it down, folding her hands over it. "Okay. I know what I want." She glanced around. "Now where's our server?"

Cullen closed his menu, laying it on the table as his lips twitched at the expression on her face. "Hungry?"

"Famished."

He was too.

Luckily, they didn't have to wait long. A teenage boy wandered over a few moments later with their water and took their orders. Cullen hoped it wouldn't take too long for their food to come out. He had a feeling one or both of them might start snacking on sugar packets if it did.

"So, Dr. Tate. Tell me more about yourself. You mentioned family in Arizona?"

He stiffened at her conversation starter, then forced himself to relax. This wasn't a date. There was no expectation of witty banter or wondering where the other person stood on displays of affection. She was just making conversation. As a *friend*. Maybe if that was the way he thought about her, he could curb this insane attraction.

"I think you can call me Cullen. I'm not your doctor anymore."

"Oh, first names. Okay." A corner of her mouth lifted.

He grinned, relaxing into the booth. "After today, I think we're there."

"Me too. So tell me about your family."

He shrugged. "Not much to tell. My parents and siblings

all live in Flagstaff, where I'm from. I don't get home as often as I'd like, but I see them a few times a year."

"What do they all do for a living?"

"My parents are both retired from teaching. My mom taught music and my dad was a math teacher and the wrestling coach."

"And your brother and sister?"

"My brother followed in my dad's footsteps and teaches math and coaches wrestling. My sister is a nurse."

"Oh, so medicine runs in the blood a bit?"

"I guess, maybe."

"Why did she choose nursing and not go for the medical degree too?"

"Too much school, I think." He shrugged. "I liked school, so I didn't mind the number of years it took to get where I am."

She shook her head. "More power to you. I'm in your sister's camp. I did well in school, but I could only take so much. I actually started out intending to be a nurse. I did well in my classes, but I dreaded going to school every day, so I quit and spent some time as a CNA at the hospital back home to see if I'd actually like being a nurse. It was just overwhelming and not at all what I thought it would be like." She wrinkled her nose. "Finally, I talked to my old academic advisor, and she turned me on to pharmacology. It was a good fit. I like my job. Seeing the number of drugs humans have developed is amazing. I learn new ones all the time."

He nodded. "The FDA approves, on average, about fifty new drugs a year."

Her eyes rounded slightly. "How do you know that? I mean, I know you're a doctor, but that seems like a rather obscure piece of information."

Cullen felt his cheeks heat. This was about the time every social interaction he had went off the rails. He'd mention some random fact no one else knew and people would look at him like he'd grown another head. "I read a lot."

"Obviously. But you remember things like that?"

Cullen touched the condensation on his glass, tracing the line a drop left behind. "I remember everything."

She blinked. "Everything?"

He met her gaze and nodded. "It's why I liked school. I remembered nearly everything I was taught the first time." He sucked in a breath. He might as well just cue her into his super brain. If she hung around, she'd figure it out eventually, anyway. "I'm a genius. I graduated high school at sixteen. I had my bachelor's degree in about two-and-a-half years. I slowed down after that. There's no fast-track for med school and residency. A lot of it's hands-on, clinical work."

Piper stared at him, her eyes wide green pools. Cullen shifted his gaze to the window, feeling heat creep up his neck.

"Sexy and smart as hell? Why are you still single?"

His eyes snapped to hers in surprise.

She covered her mouth and giggled. "Did I say that out loud?"

He tipped his head to the side and nodded.

Another giggle escaped, and she dropped her hands, her face turning pink. "Well, it's true. And it's a valid question." She lifted a brow, asking for an answer.

"You try being the smartest person in the room and no one ever knows what you're talking about." A muscle in his jaw ticked.

Ducking her chin, she stared at him for a beat. "I highly doubt you go around spewing medical articles verbatim on dates."

"No, but they inevitably ask about my work. When I mention a procedure I did or a case I had that was interesting, their eyes glaze over and they change the subject."

"That's because all those women only saw the outer trappings." She flicked a finger up and down, her gaze following it as she looked at him. "They just wanted to get in your pants and couldn't care less about what you've got behind those gorgeous eyes."

His face heated again. Man, she was blunt. He'd thought it amusing and a good thing when he was treating her for her gunshot wound. It gave her the strength she needed to recover. But now? It was coming out to bite him. He picked up his glass and took a drink before he replied. "Really? Some of them were other doctors."

"They're probably the worst ones. They want to get away from work and have some fun. You look like you could be a lot of fun." Her gaze traveled over his face and lower, then back up, and she smiled, a sexy glint in her eyes.

Cullen frowned as he thought about that. He knew he was no slouch in the looks department. Women flirted with him all the time. But he'd never thought of himself as a sex object before. Probably because he'd never been that interested in playing the field. After a short horny phase he went through as a teenager, he quit chasing girls and focused on his studies. Now, he wanted a woman who stimulated his mind, not just his body. There had been terribly few of those in his life.

"I'm getting a clearer picture of why you don't go out and do things with people." Piper leaned an elbow on the table, propping her chin in her hand. "And in a way, it makes sense. I wouldn't want to spend the entire time with nothing to talk about. But that's a two-way street. You can't talk about brainiac things the entire time, and the other person can't expect you not to say some smart stuff."

A smile toyed with his lips. "You make it sound so easy."

She shrugged and sat back. "It is."

"Not for me." His brow furrowed.

"Really? Because you're doing pretty well with me so far."

Cullen froze. Blinked. Blinked again. Well, hell. He took another drink. "You're easy to talk to."

"I'm just making conversation."

It was more than that. She was a natural conversationalist and was adept at teasing out information. Even from someone as reluctant to let people in as he was. But he wasn't going to argue with her. He liked the conversation.

"Tell me more about your family." She took a sip of her drink.

"Like?"

"Are either of your siblings married? Do you have any nieces or nephews?"

"They're both married. My brother has two kids—a boy and a girl. My sister just got married a little over a year ago. I think they're planning to start a family soon."

"You said they were both younger?"

He nodded. "Gavin's thirty-six, and Kari is thirty-one."

"How old are you?"

"Forty."

She let out a soft huff and shook her head. "I would not want my kids spread that far apart."

"Why not? Mom always said it was nice because the older ones could do things for themselves and help out while she took care of the baby."

"Yeah, but think about how long you'd have kids in the house. Little, tiny kids you'd need a sitter for." She shook her head.

Cullen lifted a shoulder. "I don't know. I didn't mind having such a younger sibling. In a way, I think it helped keep me young longer when my mind wanted to push off all the childhood trappings and pursue adult things, like college and a career."

Piper tipped her head. "I can see that in your case."

"Do you have siblings?"

She shook her head. "Only child. My dad wasn't around much. He was some boy my mom met in college. He was a reluctant father, at best, and they never got married. I haven't spoken to him in years. Mom dated some as I got older, but never met anyone special." Her expression turned sad. "She died early last year. Car accident."

Cullen's heart clenched. While he didn't spend much time with his family, he couldn't imagine life without them. "I'm sorry. Do you have any other family?"

"My grandma. And some cousins and an aunt and uncle —my mom's brother. We're not that close, though. All his kids are a lot younger than me. And my mom's family was kind of dumb when she got pregnant. They argued she was ruining her life by keeping me and pressed for her to either get an abortion or give me up for adoption. She did neither, though. And she flourished. I'm not saying we didn't struggle. The early years were rough. But once she earned her paralegal degree, things smoothed out. I had a great childhood." She picked up her water and took another sip, her gaze traveling to the window and the world beyond.

He was beginning to get an understanding of why she uprooted her life and moved down here. Her friend Mackenzie was her only family. He reached across the table and covered her hand with his. "I'm sorry about your mom."

She turned startled jade green eyes on him. Her head bobbed once, and she pressed her lips together. "Thanks," she whispered. After a quick glance out the window, she cleared her throat and looked at him again. "So, what else do you do besides work, read, and go to the gym?"

Cullen let go of her hand and sat back, some of the heaviness that surrounded them lifting with the change in subject. "That's about it. Music. I like music."

"Oh?" Her expression perked up, and she leaned forward, the sparkle back in her eyes. "Me too. What kind?"

"Jazzy, bluesy stuff in the car. I tend to favor rock when I work out. Otherwise, it's classical and instrumental. I grew up on that, and it's about all I played during my piano lessons."

A furrow formed between her eyes as she gave him an incredulous look. "How did you have time for piano lessons when you were busy graduating school two years early?"

"My mom was a music teacher, remember? She fit them in around school. Besides, I didn't have many friends. I wasn't a typical teenager who went to parties or sporting events. I stayed home and read or worked ahead." He'd spent many Friday and Saturday nights holed up in his room with his textbooks. Only a few times did he wish things were different. Mostly during his horny phase. He'd studied a little less, then, and tried to be more social. After a couple of quick flings with girls his age in the back of his car, he'd gone back to his books when it became clear none of them wanted to be the nerd's girlfriend.

Her incredulous look didn't disappear. "And the girls in your school let you do that?"

A wide grin broke over Cullen's face, and he chuckled. "I didn't always look the way I do now. This"—he lifted an arm and flexed slightly—"didn't develop until I got older. In my twenties. I needed an outlet—a way to shut off my brain. I was having trouble sleeping. I'd go home after a long shift and find myself going over case notes or classwork while I laid in bed. It wasn't really me processing what happened that day, but more of me trying to think of things I could have done differently and if it would have made a difference. One of my colleagues suggested going to the gym as a way to refocus my brain."

"And it worked?"

He nodded. "The first time I tried it, I didn't really know what I was doing, so I just went to the university gym and got on a treadmill and ran. It forced me to focus on myself instead of what was going on in my head. That night, I slept the best I had in years."

She hummed, a slight frown still present on her face. "Okay, I get that you weren't always this buff." She held up a hand, fingers splayed, and waved it in a small circle as she gestured to him. "But, I mean, didn't they look at your face? There wasn't one girl who asked you to come to a pep rally or to the movies?"

"They did, and I went to a couple of things, but we ended up hanging out with her friends, or it was like you said and she just wanted to get in my pants. That was only fun for a little bit. Then I wanted an actual girlfriend. When that didn't happen, I quit accepting invites and just stayed home."

Piper laughed. "I'm not sure I can imagine teenage you. He sounds so different from who you are now."

Cullen smiled. "Maybe a little. I haven't changed that much. I've gained some confidence, but that's about it. I'm still quiet and awkward."

Her smile grew, and one eyebrow winged upward. "Really? You've been chatty tonight."

"Like I said, you're easy to talk to."

She hummed again, still smiling.

"Enough about me. Tell me about teenage Piper."

She groaned and rolled her eyes. "Do I have to?"

He laughed. "It's only fair."

"Fine." She sighed. "Teenage Piper was—well, she was wild."

"Color me shocked." He grinned, not at all surprised.

A soft giggle escaped her lips. "Right?"

Their server appeared with their food. Cullen was amazed to discover he'd forgotten about his hunger as they talked. She'd thoroughly enraptured him.

They dug into their meals, silence falling as they satiated

their hunger. Once they both had several bites in, Cullen restarted their conversation.

"So, tell me more about this wild-child." He dipped a fry in ketchup and popped it in his mouth.

"I was hoping the food distracted you and you forgot."

He chuckled. "Nope."

She let out a sigh and speared a piece of okra with her fork. "She was a good girl, but liked to have fun. This is really good, by the way."

"I'm glad you like it. Elaborate on the fun thing." He took a bite of his sandwich and waited.

"Not much to tell. I was popular and went to all the parties. Probably gave my mom more gray hair than I should have by staying out past curfew and forgetting to call. But I didn't drink and didn't sleep around. I had the same boyfriend for three years in high school."

"How does any of that make you wild? A lot of high schoolers go to parties."

"Yeah, but they don't wear the mascot costume and dance on the roof of their boyfriend's house. Or convince the entire girls' volleyball team to die their hair fiery red for our state championship game."

"Oh."

She giggled. "Yeah." She lifted her sandwich. "And we won, too, so all the official pictures of us after the match are of all these happy, smiling teenagers with flaming red hair. At least it was one of our school colors." Grinning, she took a bite.

A burst of laughter escaped him. "Oh, I bet the school—and all the parents—loved that."

"Our principal was livid. He never said anything, but you could see it on his face. But most of the parents didn't care. There were a few who were all, 'What will people think?' But dyeing our hair was a morale booster, so they quickly overcame their objections. We were the underdogs. No one expected us to win. Dyeing our hair was meant to fire us up, so we didn't just roll over and hand the other team the trophy. It worked. We went out there and played like warriors. It was great." She speared another piece of okra. "Then, after we won, I went out and danced all night."

Cullen laughed again. He loved her *joie de vivre*. "You're fiery even without the red hair."

She grinned, eyes twinkling, and ate more okra. "I'm calmer than I used to be. Age and life"—she pointed at her chest and the scars he knew all too well were hiding—"have slowed me down. Taught me to think more before I leap." A glint entered her eyes. "You, though. You need to learn to leap some before you think."

"I leap."

She lifted an eyebrow.

"I do."

"Okay. Name one time—recently—that you've leaped without thinking."

"How recently?"

A quick, melodic laugh burst free of her lips. "Past five years."

Cullen dipped some fries in ketchup and ate them while he thought. Only one thing came to mind, but he wasn't sure he wanted to admit that to her. Though she'd probably find out soon enough. "I agreed to participate in the Valentine's bachelor auction that benefits the Foggy Mountain Women's Crisis Center."

Her eyes rounded. The fry she'd just picked up paused mid-air as she froze. Ketchup dripped off the end to plop onto her plate. "What?" She put the fry down. "You agreed to be auctioned off for charity?"

He nodded and sighed. "Yeah. The sheriff and his wife, Gemma, are friends. She and her sister-in-law started a crisis center for pregnant teens and women last year." He shrugged. "I was free, so I said yes." Though he'd wanted to say no. But as he told Piper, he had few true friends. He counted the Davidsons among them and would gladly help out. Even if it made him wildly uncomfortable.

A devilish smile overtook her face. "Can anyone come to this auction?"

Heat touched his face. "I suppose. I don't know that much about it except it'll be in the auditorium at the hospital."

"In Asheville?"

He nodded.

"Hmm, I might have to look into this. See if I can find myself a date for Valentine's Day. I suppose you'll be too rich for my blood, though. Some swanky heiress whose family donates to organizations like that will take one look at you and no doubt drive up the price."

Cullen's mouth pulled down. That's what he was afraid of. "I need to come up with a date that's very public. And maybe requires us to be far apart. Any ideas?"

She giggled. "Oh, um, let's see..." She bit her lip and looked up. "Laser tag? No, wait! Paintball!"

A low rumble emanated from his chest. "Would you play paintball?"

"Hell, yes, I would. I'd win too."

He laughed again. "As much fun as it would be to see some debutante try to avoid being splattered with neon paint, I should probably come up with something a little tamer."

Piper huffed, then picked up another fry, trailing it through her ketchup. "Hiking?"

"In winter?"

"Skiing, then."

A thoughtful crease formed between his eyes. That had possibilities. It would maintain some distance between him and his date, and there were always a million people at the ski resorts this time of year. "That might work." Plus, it would weed out the ones who only used their workout bodies for looks.

One perfectly shaped eyebrow rose again. "Desert boy knows how to ski?"

"I've been here for over ten years now. I've picked up some local sports." He actually quite liked to ski, but rarely went. There just never seemed like there was enough time. "Do you ski?"

"Snowboard."

"Of course you do."

She flashed a grin again.

"I'll have to add skiing to my list of possible dates."

"What else is on the list?"

"Dinner at some fancy place in downtown Asheville."

She stared at him, her forehead scrunching toward her hairline as the silence stretched. "That's it?"

"Maybe a museum or something."

The scrunch moved lower to her nose. "Oh, no." She shook her head.

"No museum?"

"No. Save that for later dates, when she knows you better and is more willing to listen to the science talk that will come out of your mouth."

"Science talk?" A smile toyed with his lips. He covered it by eating more of his sandwich.

"Yep. Spring your smarts on her slowly. You're kind of intense. Easing her into the idea of you being a genius will lessen the blow."

His smile died. "Being smart isn't a bad thing, Piper."

She winced. "That came out wrong. I didn't mean for it to sound like that. You said people get scared off by your brain. Maybe they feel like they can't keep up with someone with your intelligence. If you don't unleash it full force right away, they'll have time to learn more about you and see you're a nice, fun guy who just happens to also be a genius, instead of a genius who can talk circles around them in his sleep. I would never want you to pretend to be something you're not. Just be more selective about what you reveal and when you reveal it."

Cullen glanced away. He'd never thought about his intelligence from another person's perspective before. Always from his own and the way interactions with other people made him feel. He recognized that he made people uncomfortable sometimes, but he never really thought about why that was. He always assumed they thought he was weird, not that they were intimidated by him.

He bit back a scoff and gave a slight shake of his head. Why had he never considered that before?

"You okay?"

Piper's hand covered his, startling him from his thoughts. He looked at her.

"I'm sorry. I didn't mean to upset you."

He squeezed her fingers, then released her hand. "You didn't. Just gave me something to think about, is all."

"Oh."

"Anyway, all this dating advice is irrelevant. I don't intend for there to be a second date with whoever bids on me at the auction." He ate another fry.

"You don't want a sugar mama?"

Once again, she surprised a laugh from him. "No."

"Good. I don't think you'd be very good at being a kept man."

Grinning, he shook his head. No. No, he would not. He'd be so bored.

They finished their meals, their conversation turning to more mundane topics. When their waiter came with the check, Cullen grabbed it before Piper could look at it.

"How much was mine?" She lifted her purse from the seat beside her.

He waved a hand. "I've got it."

"What? No. Let me see it." She held out a hand.

"No." He lifted his hip and removed his wallet.

"Cullen." Her eyebrows slashed down over her eyes with a warning.

He smiled at her and removed his credit card and dropped it into the tray with the ticket. The server came back around, and Cullen held it up.

"I'll be right back with your receipt." The kid smiled and walked away.

Piper huffed. "Fine. But the next one is on me."

He just smirked, making the thunderclouds in her eyes darken. She was cute all riled up. Like a lioness. She probably had the claws to match.

The waiter came back with the check, and Cullen scrawled his name on the receipt, adding a nice tip for the young man. He slid from the booth, then held out a hand to Piper to help her from her seat.

"Thanks." She took his hand and slid out.

Cullen clenched his teeth against the onslaught of electricity that raced up his arm from her innocent touch. Their non-date was turning into the best date he'd ever had, and his body knew it.

She let go of his hand once she was standing, then put on her coat. He led her to the door, holding it open so she could pass through. Outside, she hunched her shoulders against the chill. Icy snowflakes pelted them in the face. The gentle snow had turned to a mix of snow and sleet, and the wind had kicked up.

"It's getting worse." She glanced at the sky.

"Yeah. Come on. I'll get you to your car so we can both get home." He ushered her toward his car and unlocked the door, opening it for her. She slid in with a quick thanks, and he shut the door. Trying not to fall on the icy sidewalk, he rounded the hood and got in beside her.

She rubbed her hands together. "I should have put my gloves on before we left the restaurant." She took them from her pockets as he started the engine and put it into gear.

"I should have thought to start the car so it could warm up. In my defense, I usually forget, so that's nothing new."

She gave a low laugh. "I'm guilty of that too."

Cullen navigated through the connected parking lots to where he left her car and parked next to it. "I'll help you clean it off."

"Oh, great. Thanks." She smiled and pulled on the door handle, getting out.

He grabbed his snowbrush from behind the seat and joined her. While she started the car and got her brush out, he attacked the passenger side windows. Snow had melted, then frozen to her windshield, but working together, it only took them a couple of minutes to clear the snow from the car. She tossed her brush into the backseat, then paused beside the driver's door, her hand on the handle.

"Thanks for helping."

"No problem. Be careful going home. In fact, let me know you make it there safely." The parking lot was a sheet of ice. No doubt the roads weren't much better.

"I will. You do the same?"

He nodded, then took a step back. "I guess I'll see you around at the hospital."

"Yep."

Cullen took another step back. "Drive safe." He turned to walk away, then paused, looking back. "Piper?"

She glanced up.

"I had a nice time tonight."

A soft, pretty smile lit her eyes. "Me too." Her smile widened. "Have a good night, Cullen."

"You too." He held her gaze a moment longer, then abruptly turned and headed for his car. She had him flummoxed again.

This time, though, it wasn't an altogether unwelcome feeling.

EIGHT

Piper's heart thumped as she walked down the hall to Tillie's office. She was done with inventory, and something seemed... weird. It worried her what her boss would think. Whether this was a legitimate concern, or Piper was seeing something that wasn't there.

Pausing outside Tillie's door, she hugged the tablet to her chest and raised a fist, hesitating only a moment before knocking.

"Come in."

Grasping the handle, she pushed it down and entered.

"Hi, Piper." Tillie smiled from behind her desk. "All done?"

"Yes." Piper chewed on one corner of her mouth as she hesitated in the doorway. Sucking in a breath, she closed the door and hurried forward to perch on the edge of the visitor's chair.

Tillie frowned. "You look like you have something on your mind."

"Yeah. Though I'm not sure it's anything." She set the

tablet on the desk. "So, when I did testosterone, it struck me that the supply of the single-dose ampules seemed low."

"Low?" The furrow between Tillie's eyes deepened. "How so?"

"Like there were boxes missing. The first day I started, Rosalina and I checked in a shipment of it. I swear there was another case."

"What? You're sure?" Tillie reached for the tablet and turned it on.

Piper nodded. "Pretty sure, yes. She had me reading labels and counting boxes while she input the data. There are twelve boxes in a case, right?"

Tillie nodded, not looking up from the screen.

"Well, there were ten boxes on the shelf. But I'm certain I counted two cases of it when we checked it in. Does extra stuff get stored somewhere I don't know about yet?"

"No. It all goes on the shelves." She glanced up. "This says only one case was delivered."

Piper's mouth turned down. That couldn't be right. "I don't know what to tell you. There were two. I remember because we were talking as we worked and she mentioned her son and how his voice keeps cracking. We opened that box and she started giggling, saying he'd think her the best mom ever if she brought him some home and sped up the puberty process, so he didn't sound like a squeaky mouse anymore."

"You don't think she took it, do you?"

"No. It was clearly a joke. And we verified there were two, twelve-count boxes, then moved on to the next item."

With one finger, Tillie scrolled through the inventory list. "Is that the only discrepancy you found?"

"Yes. But technically, it's not a discrepancy. The inventory is right according to that." She pointed at the tablet. "I only know it's wrong because I processed the shipment."

"None of the other items that came in with it are missing?"

Piper shook her head.

Tillie sighed and pinched the bridge of her nose. "Okay. I'll look into it."

Giving her boss a tight smile, Piper rose and headed for the door.

"Piper."

She paused, glancing back.

"Don't say anything to Rosalina about this, okay? Or to anyone. On the off chance something hinky's going on, I don't want to tip anyone off."

A soft frown overtook Piper's face, but she nodded. "Okay."

"Thank you. If I don't see you before your shift ends, have a good evening." Tillie's voice was strained, her face hard.

With a nod, Piper left. This did not bode well for her hope of having a boring job. If she'd wanted stress, she'd have stayed in New York.

There was nothing she could do about it, though. She'd given the information to the correct person. Now it was up to Tillie to figure it out.

Heading up front, Piper schooled her expression, hoping she didn't give away that something was wrong, and went to help Beth at the counter. She had an hour until her shift ended.

"Hi." She pasted a smile on her face as she approached.

Beth glanced at her with an answering smile. "Hey. Done in the stacks?"

Piper nodded. "I came to help." She tipped her head toward the line.

"Great. Log in." Beth pointed to the computer next to hers.

Scanning her badge and typing in her password, Piper beckoned the next person in line forward.

The next hour passed quickly and the line diminished to a manageable level. Piper signed off and turned to Beth.

"I'm out of here. I won't see you Monday, will I?"

"Nope. We're opposite each other. Unless one of us picks up an extra shift, we won't work together."

"Well, it was nice working with you while I learned the ropes."

Beth smiled. "You too. Welcome to the team."

"Thanks." Returning the woman's smile, she turned and walked away, heading for the employee lounge to get her things.

The locker door creaked as she opened it. Withdrawing her coat, she bundled up against the chill outside, then grabbed her purse and shut the door with a clank. She exited the pharmacy and entered the main hospital.

People bustled around her, all of them in a hurry to get somewhere. Piper kept to the side, out of their way. She passed through the lobby doors into the cold. At least it wasn't snowing. The weather tomorrow was supposed to be good too. Not that it mattered. Her plans for Cullen were indoors.

A soft smile tipped her mouth up. She hoped he didn't mind getting messy.

The stress of her day faded as thoughts of his hazel eyes and handsome smile entered her mind. It was too bad she wouldn't see him tonight. She could go for a dose of Cullen Tate. And not just because he was easy on the eyes. She enjoyed talking to him. The other women he'd dated were idiots. Yes, the man was brilliant, but he wasn't stodgy or weird. Just shy.

Oh well. It was her gain, and she was glad no one else had taken the time to get him to open up.

She rolled her eyes as she reached her car. Who was she

kidding? Just because he found it easier to talk to her than women in his past didn't mean anything would happen between them. The man was a brilliant doctor and drove a Mercedes SUV. She filled pill bottles and rode around in a two-door purple Jeep Wrangler. He was all class and sophistication. She was taking him to play paintball.

Her heart thumped. What was she thinking?

Getting in her car, she started the engine, her mood souring. Maybe she should come up with something different. Something safe. He liked museums. There were several in the area, and she'd never been to any of them.

But wasn't the point to show him there was more to life than learning?

She backed out of her space, pointing the car toward the exit. She'd just play it by ear. They'd go to the paintball place, and if he freaked, she'd come up with a new plan. Simple as that.

Turning out of the parking garage, she rolled her eyes again. Why did she have a feeling that nothing with Cullen would ever be simple?

NINE

The doorbell echoed through Cullen's house, pulling him out of the medical journal he'd been trying to read while he waited on Piper. He set his e-reader on the end table and got up.

His heart thumped as he neared the door. He could see her silhouette through the frosted glass panels on either side. Grasping the knob, he opened the door and nearly swallowed his tongue. In her work scrubs, she was beautiful. But with her hair hanging in loose blonde curls and wearing snug, faded jeans below a fitted wool peacoat? There were no words.

"Hi." Her bright smile hit him like a fiery lance to the heart.

Stunning. That was the word. She was stunning.

Cullen forced his vocal cords to work. "Hi." He stepped back. "Um, come in."

She crossed the threshold, her eyes straying from him to look around. "Nice place."

"Thanks."

"How long have you lived here?"

"Five years, maybe?" He'd picked the house for the land.

He was just outside of the city on five acres. Before that, he'd been in town. His neighbors there were nice, but they were nosy. He just wanted to be left alone after a long day, not make small talk.

Her eyebrows rose. "You've really lived here five years?"

Cullen glanced around, knowing what she saw. Artless walls painted the same neutral off-white they were when he bought the house. Stacks of books piled on and around his bookshelves. Worn leather furniture he'd had since he graduated college. At least there was no dust. He had a housekeeper who came once a week and cleaned. She'd been here yesterday.

"I'm not much of a decorator."

"I can see that." Her eyes roved over the room again.

"It's not like I'm home much, though." He shrugged.

She shook her head. "Still, you should have a place that's a refuge and can soothe your soul after a tough day. You work hard, Cullen. From what I see, your house is just an extension of your office." She gestured to the stacks of books, then looked at him. "Relaxation is a good thing."

"This is how I relax." He waved an arm at his books.

Piper sighed. "You have much to learn, young padawan."

He frowned, confused. "What?"

Her eyes widened. "Please tell me you've seen Star Wars."

Cullen shook his head. "I don't even own a television."

She blinked. "I didn't even know that was possible in this day and age." She shook her head. "But never mind. We'll tackle your lack of movie knowledge another day. You need to change." She pointed at him, flicking her finger up and down.

Cullen looked at himself. "What's wrong with what I'm wearing? You said casual. This is casual."

"I meant jeans and a t-shirt or a hoodie. Not khaki slacks and a polo." She narrowed her eyes. "You do own a pair of jeans, don't you?"

His brows drew down. "Yes." One. Maybe two if he looked deep into the depths of his closet.

"Go put them on. And a shirt you don't mind getting dirty." She looked him over once more. "And tennis shoes."

Grumbling under his breath about how it would have been nice if she'd mentioned this when she texted him about what time she was coming, he left the room to go upstairs and change. He wasn't sure this outing was a good idea. Well, a worse idea. He hadn't thought it a good one to begin with. Being in her presence unsettled him. Now she wanted to change him? Women like that were the reason he'd avoided relationships his entire adult life.

He paused at the top of the stairs as his anger grew. Dammit. She'd harped on him about being himself. Now she demanded he change. So why was he changing?

Jaw flexing, he turned around and ran back downstairs.

Creases marred her forehead as she took in his appearance. A wariness crept into her eyes as she noticed the storm clouds in his.

"I don't want to change."

Her frown deepened. "You'll be more comfortable—"

He cut her off. "You told me the other day that it wasn't me who needed to change. Why do you want me to change?"

"It's just clothes, Cullen." She blinked once, then her face cleared as her confusion morphed into a look of understanding. "Oh, wait. I think I understand." She walked forward until they were only inches apart.

Cullen swallowed at her nearness. At this range, he could see the flecks of gold in her jade eyes and smell her light floral perfume.

"I don't want you to change. Not the way you're thinking. I love your brain. But you're doing yourself a disservice by always burying yourself in your work. Did you ever stop to think that actually relaxing and letting loose and having a *life* might make you a better doctor?"

The frown on his face turned less fierce and more contemplative. "What do you mean?"

"Do you ever get stuck? You're treating someone and something's not going right, but you can't figure out why? Or things take a turn you weren't anticipating?"

"Of course. What's that have to do with not working?"

"Because sometimes the answer to the problem is a simple one, but our brains can't figure it out because we're too focused. Letting go and relaxing allows the brain to filter information while we're unaware of it."

Staring at her, he gave that idea some thought. He'd read studies that purported similar claims. But he always found an answer, eventually.

"Plus, constant work and stress aren't healthy. Doesn't the good doctor know that?" One side of her mouth lifted.

He couldn't help it and smiled back. His anger ebbed.

She framed his face in her hands. "I don't want to change you, Cullen. I just want to put a little fun in your life."

Her touch was like a brand. He covered her hands with his and took a step back, giving himself some breathing room. It was enough to allow him to process her words. Fun. He could do fun. "Okay. I'll be right back."

This time, when he went upstairs, it wasn't anger that stirred his blood. It was anticipation. And not a small amount of lust. Heat still infused his cheeks from where she'd laid her hands. He wanted to feel them elsewhere.

TEN

Noise on the stairs made Piper turn around. Her eyes grew round as she watched Cullen come down the last few steps and walk toward her. Those jeans were sinful. He looked good in a pair of khakis, but jeans? They showed off his lean hips and muscular thighs—as well as more interesting tidbits. She licked her lips.

He lifted the sweatshirt in his hands and put an arm in it. His t-shirt rode up, exposing a sliver of skin. Piper's core clenched.

Oh, this was bad. She should have let him wear the khakis and polo.

Spinning away before he could see in her eyes the desire to strip him naked, she headed for the door. "Ready?"

"Yeah. Are we taking your car or mine?"

"Mine." Even if he knew where they were going, she'd still want to drive. It would keep her hands occupied, so she wasn't tempted to touch those powerful thighs. She opened the door and stepped outside. On her way down the porch steps of his stunning farmhouse, she heard the door close, then his footsteps on the stairs. She didn't stop and wait for fear she'd turn back around and plant a hot kiss on that sculpted mouth of his and let her hands drift over all his muscles to see if they were as hard as they looked.

Yep. This was a bad idea.

Climbing into the driver's seat, she buckled up and started the engine as he got in.

"Where are we going?"

She glanced at him, noting he'd pulled on a gray denim fleece-lined coat on his way out the door. With the hoodie underneath, he looked like any other guy headed out for an active day.

"It's a surprise."

"I don't get any clue at all?"

"I already gave you one." She backed out of his driveway and headed down the road.

"You did?"

"Mmm-hmm. I told you to wear something you didn't mind getting dirty."

A cute furrow formed between his eyes. "Hiking."

She arched an eyebrow and cast a look at him askance as she pointed at the dash. "The car says it's twenty-five degrees. No."

"Okay. Cooking classes?"

Piper laughed. "Creative, but no."

He continued to guess, using clues from their route—which was taking them toward Asheville—until, finally, he tossed his hands up in defeat. "I don't know."

She chuckled again. "We'll be there soon."

True to her word, five minutes later, she made the turn down a country road.

"Logging."

Another laugh burst free. "That's a good one, but no." She slowed as she saw the sign.

"Paintball?" He twisted to stare out his window at the sign as she turned onto the stone driveway leading to the large barn that hosted Mountain Valley Paintball.

Pulling into the parking lot, she found a space and shut off the car. She unbuckled and cast him a wicked grin. "Ready to get dirty?"

He groaned. "I'm going to be covered in paint by the time we're done, aren't I?"

She laughed and opened her door. "Probably." There was no probably about it. Piper loved to shoot. She owned several weapons and went to the shooting range regularly. Though she hadn't been since she was shot.

A trickle of apprehension skated up her spine. Maybe this was a bad idea for other reasons besides seeing Cullen dressed in street clothes. She hadn't considered how she'd feel being targeted and shot.

Her steps slowed as they neared the door. When Cullen pulled several feet ahead of her, she sucked in a breath and mentally slapped herself. Paintball wasn't dangerous and was never meant to be. She'd played several times in the past and had fun. It had always felt like tag on steroids to her. She needed to remember that.

Quickening her pace, she caught up to Cullen as they reached the door. He opened it and held it for her, motioning for her to precede him. Smiling, she went inside.

Plywood walls beyond the stacked-log reception desk greeted them. Behind them, she could hear shrieks and laughter as well as little *pffts* as people fired their guns.

She relaxed as memories flooded back. Yeah, she was going to be just fine. Smiling, she advanced to the young man behind the desk. "Hi."

"Hello." He returned her smile. "Welcome to Mountain Valley Paintball. Do you have a reservation?"

Piper nodded. "Under Riordan."

He looked at his screen, tapping on it to search for their reservation. "Okay. I have you down for two for an hour." Spinning the screen around, he pointed at it. "If you could just enter your information in and sign the waivers, I'll get your gear ready." He turned and entered a small room to his left.

Using her finger, Piper entered her name into the form, then scrawled her signature across the bottom. Cullen did the same.

The young man returned with two white suits folded and in cellophane bags, goggles, and weapons. He laid everything on the desk. "I can take your coats."

Piper shrugged out of her coat, revealing her rusty orange Bon Jovi t-shirt. She glanced at Cullen. "You might want to give him your hoodie too. The suits get hot."

He nodded and took it off, making his t-shirt ride up and giving her a fabulous look at his sides and back. She pressed her lips together and looked away.

Taking their things, the young man laid them to the side, then picked up the two suits, handing them over. "Go ahead and put those on. There are booties in there, too, to cover your shoes."

Piper opened the bag and removed the suit and booties, moving to the bench against the wall to sit down. Cullen sat next to her.

"I feel like I'm at work." He held up the suit. "Kind of. It's a little more restrictive than an operating gown." He chuckled and worked the suit on over his feet.

"Look at it this way—you're making the mess instead of sewing one up."

He smiled. "Yeah." As quick as it came, his smile disappeared. "Are you okay doing this?"

Her expression sobered. "I think I'll be fine. I actually

thought about that on the way in here. But it's more like tag to me than anything else."

He tipped his head. "That's a good way to think of it. Just so long as you're sure you're okay with this. I'm sure you can come up with another way to get me dirty."

Her face flamed as an utterly improper way hit her. She cleared her throat and bent over. "I am." She pulled the booties over her shoes, then stood, bringing the upper half of the suit with her. "Come on. I want to kick your ass." She shoved her arms into the sleeves.

Cullen covered his shoes and rose. "Oh yeah?" A smile played with his lips.

Piper bit back one of her own, trying to look fierce. She stared up at him—which was a rarity for her. She looked down on or directly at most people. "Yeah."

His smile sprang free, along with a challenging glint in his eyes. "Bring it, Riordan."

"Oh, I will." She slid her zipper up.

After a quick run through on how the guns worked, the young man filled the hoppers on their guns, then showed them down the hall to their course.

"A buzzer will go off and the lights on the wall will flash when your time's up." He opened the door and stood back. "Have fun."

Piper breezed past him. "Thanks. Come on, Tate. Time for you to eat paint."

Giving a low laugh, Cullen entered behind her. The door closed, leaving them alone.

"So, how do we do this?"

"We walk in different directions as we count to... let's say twenty?"

He nodded.

"Then we come out shooting. Only rules I have are try not

to shoot me in the head, and keep moving. If we sit behind shelter, we'll never fire a shot."

He lowered his goggles over his eyes. "Sounds good to me. I hope whatever color these balls are is your favorite. You're gonna be wearing a lot of it."

Giggling, she backed away. "Not as much as you. One... two... three..." Lowering her goggles as she counted, she grinned, then turned and ran. She could hear him laughing as she disappeared around a wall.

Weaving deeper into the course, she found a low barrier to crouch behind that offered her a good view. She reached twenty and edged around the obstacle, looking for a flash of white in the sea of paint-spattered walls.

She didn't have to wait long. Across the room, she saw him dart between two sections of wall. Gun raised, she advanced. White flashed, and she took a shot. Neon pink paint splattered on his shoulder as he yelped.

Grinning and excited that she got the first shot, she forgot to hide. He didn't stay startled as long as she thought he would and fired back almost immediately. The paintball smacked her in the chest and green paint splattered, some of it hitting her face.

She gasped and dove for cover. Her heart hammered in her ears and her body shook. *Shit!*

The gun fell from her fingers as she fought to breathe. Panic clawed at her throat, fighting for room with the sob that wanted to break free.

"Ha!"

Another paintball smacked her back, and she screamed. Through her panic, she heard Cullen curse, then he was beside her.

"Dammit, I knew this was a bad idea." He folded her into his arms. "Shh, it's okay. It's just paint. You're okay, I swear."

Logically, she knew he was right, but her brain couldn't compute that fact. Hyperventilating, she clung to him.

"Piper. Piper, look at me. You need to slow your breathing or you're going to pass out."

She knew that. She did. But it didn't make a lick of difference. Blackness crowded the edges of her vision.

ELEVEN

Cullen tapped Piper's cheek, trying to break the spell holding her mind hostage. "Piper. Honey, concentrate on me."

Eyes wide and staring at nothing, her breathing continued to saw in and out. Whether she heard his voice or not, it didn't matter. Her mind was locked in the past. She was going to faint.

Her eyelids fluttered, eyes rolling up. Wanting to save her from the confusion of waking up afterward, and possibly even having another panic attack as she processed what happened, he sat down and scooped her onto his lap, cradling her close.

"Piper, listen to my voice. Come back to me, honey." He leaned down, pressing his cheek to hers as he continued to murmur in her ear. Stroking her hair, he rocked her gently.

Almost immediately, her breathing slowed. He pulled back to look at her face, afraid she'd passed out. Wide, mossy green eyes stared up at him, no longer focused on nothing.

"Hey. Are you okay?"

Her lower lip trembled. She sucked it between her teeth

and pushed against him. He let her go and she sat up, but didn't move off his lap.

"I'm sorry. I really thought I could handle this." She ran a hand over her face.

"Don't apologize, Piper. Some things run deeper than we realize."

She sniffed and nodded, eyes downcast. "I was good until the paint hit me in the face. When I—when Brett shot me, blood splattered on my face. That's the one thing still etched into my mind. The feel of my blood hitting me in the face. Not the pain, or the shock. The feel of warm wetness splattering on my cheek and lips." She shuddered. "It still haunts my dreams."

Cullen's heart tripped. He wished he could look inside her mind and take away that memory. "I'm sorry."

A quick tilt raised one side of her mouth as she looked at him. "Why are you sorry? You put me back together. Saved me from having that be the last thing I felt on this earth."

He lifted one shoulder. "Still. I'm sorry you had to go through that. I wish you didn't."

"Me too. But I'm not entirely sorry I did."

"Why the hell not?" The words were out before he could even think about them.

The tilt to her mouth slid higher. "It brought me here."

Fierce satisfaction roared through Cullen's veins that she was happy to be here with him.

"I never would have moved down here if it weren't for that."

Disappointment quickly chased his elation. He'd been too quick to react. He kept his face carefully blank as she continued.

"Going home wounded and unable to do much of anything for myself—" She shook her head. "I don't think I'd have realized how utterly alone I was otherwise. Sure, I had friends there. A few of them were kind enough to help me out the first couple of weeks, but once I could get out and move around on my own, they quit inquiring about me. Mackenzie called me every day. Did you know that?"

He shook his head.

"Even with Jake so seriously injured, she called to make sure I was all right. I got texts too. She even sent me an ice cream and hot chocolate delivery a couple of times because she thought I needed a pick-me-up. Anyone else who did things for me, it was because I asked." She fluttered her hands before folding them into her lap. "I guess it helped me see what was important. The life I had before—that wasn't it. I'm happy now. In a way I wasn't before."

Cullen smiled, pleased that some good had come from the trauma. "I'm glad."

She returned his smile, and his breath caught in his lungs. It transformed her entire face and made him think of angels and pure loveliness. He cleared his throat and blinked, breaking the spell. "You know, ice cream and hot chocolate sound nice. How about we get some of that and ditch the paint suits?"

Her grin spread wider. "I know just the place." She scrambled off his lap, then held out a hand.

He took it and stood. "Where?"

"It's a surprise."

"Another one?" He bent over and picked up her gun, then motioned her toward the exit.

"Oh, come on. Surprises are fun. You must not get surprised enough." She glanced at him over her shoulder, eyes twinkling and all traces of her panic attack gone.

"I guess it depends on the surprise. My family came to visit this past year on my birthday without telling me they were coming. That was nice."

She let them out of the room. "Well, forty's a big milestone. That's great that they did something grand. Did they all come, or was it just your parents?"

"All of them, including my niece and nephew."

"Wow."

"Yeah. I had a houseful." A smile teased his lips, and he shook his head. "I didn't get much work done that weekend."

"And as well you shouldn't have. Did you have fun?"

"I did, yes. But I was happy to have my house back. It was chaos."

"I bet. All those people not in their familiar space, living out of suitcases? Especially the kids? It's stressful."

They exited the hallway and entered the reception area. The man behind the desk frowned when he saw them.

"Everything okay?"

Cullen nodded, stepping forward with the guns. "We're good. What do we do with our suits?"

Still frowning, the man took the weapons and laid them on the counter, then pointed at the laundry bin in the corner. "You can put them in there. Are you sure you don't want to play longer? You've only been back there ten minutes."

"We're sure." Cullen unzipped his suit and shrugged out of it. Piper did the same. Once they had their coats, they headed outside to the car.

"I still don't get a clue about where you're taking me?" Cullen asked as he got into the passenger seat of her Jeep.

She grinned and shook her head, starting the car. "Nope."

He huffed a soft laugh. "Life will be full of surprises with you, won't it?"

"Always." She laughed.

Cullen watched the scenery as she steered them north. They made light conversation as she drove and were soon back in Foggy Mountain. He sat straighter as she entered a residential neighborhood, weaving through the maze of streets to pull into the shared driveway of a duplex. The garage door rose, and she drove inside.

"Is this your house?"

She glanced at him and giggled. "I can't believe you didn't guess where we were going. Where else would we get ice cream and hot chocolate in the same place?" She turned off the car and lowered the garage door.

He didn't know, but the thought of going to her home never occurred to him. "Are you sure?"

"About coming here?"

He nodded.

"Of course. I wouldn't have brought you here otherwise." She opened her door and got out.

Cullen followed. She'd said the same thing about paintball. He said nothing, though, as they entered the house through the door to the left.

"Excuse the mess. I'm still unpacking." She motioned around them as they entered the kitchen.

Bright, open space met Cullen's gaze as he surveyed her home. White cabinets and white walls reflected light off the marbled white granite counters and gleaming blonde-wood floors. Open-concept, the kitchen opened to a large living room, also painted white. Curtainless windows overlooking the backyard framed a fireplace on the rear wall. Boxes sat scattered amongst the furniture arranged around a blue and white Persian rug.

"This is nice. And very white." He wrinkled his nose.

She grinned. "You don't like the white?"

"I like some white," he hedged. Cream was better. White was too sterile.

Piper laughed as she set her purse on the counter. "I plan to paint. Probably gray. Or a very pale blue."

"Either of those would look great with your rug. Did you

bring that from New York, or did you buy it here?" It went well with the décor she had.

"I bought it here. My apartment there had carpet. Take your coat off and make yourself at home." She gestured for him to remove his coat, then unzipped hers.

Cullen shrugged out of his jacket and hung it on a hook by the door. Hers joined it a moment later.

"All right." She clapped her hands, then rubbed them together. "What do you want first? Ice cream or hot chocolate?"

"How about both? I'll dish up the ice cream while you make the hot chocolate."

She nodded once. "Sounds like a plan. Bowls are up there." She pointed to a cabinet by the fridge. "Spoons and the scoop are in the drawer by the stove."

They made quick work of readying their treats, then went to the living room and sat. Piper curled up in one corner of the couch while Cullen took the matching recliner. He lifted his mug to his lips and took a sip. The flavors of cocoa and cinnamon burst over his tongue.

"Hey, that's good." He glanced at her. "What did you put in this?"

"It's just cocoa, sugar, milk, and some cinnamon." She took a sip.

"I've never thought to put cinnamon in hot chocolate before. Peppermint, yes, but not cinnamon." But to be fair, he'd never made it from scratch, either. She'd heated milk on the stove and added things to it while he scooped up two bowls of the chocolate brownie ice cream.

"It's how my mom always made it."

"Well, it's good."

She smiled. "Thanks." Setting her mug down, she gathered a bite of ice cream. "So, since our fun got derailed, what should we do?" She slid the spoon between her lips, then withdrew it.

Cullen swallowed hard and looked down at his bowl with the pretense of getting his own spoonful. He could think of some things she could do with that mouth that would be a lot of fun. "I thought this was it."

"Hmm, no. This is a snack. My plan was to annihilate you at paintball, then take you someplace for food to appease your wounded pride. We skipped the first part."

A laugh rumbled free of his chest. "So you need to make that up, is that it?"

She grinned, nodding. "You're getting the idea, yes."

"How about a game?"

"What kind of game?"

"Chess?"

"Ack, no. That's boring." She stuffed another spoonful of ice cream in her mouth.

"No, it's not. It's stimulating."

"Maybe for you, boy-genius. We could do checkers, though. That's simpler, but still requires some strategy. I'd at least have a chance at winning."

He tipped his head. "Okay, sure." She wouldn't, but he wasn't about to burst her bubble.

She hopped up, setting her bowl on the end table. "Now I just have to find the board." She went to the stack of boxes in the corner and opened the top one, rummaging through it. "Nope, not that one." Picking up the box to move it, she staggered a bit under its weight.

Cullen shot to his feet, setting his bowl on the end table. "Here. Let me move them. You just tell me where." He reached out, wrapping his long arms around it.

"Oh." She relinquished the box. "Okay. Anywhere is fine."

Turning, he glanced around quickly, looking for a place to put it so it was out of the way. A spot closer to the fireplace caught his eye. He carried it over and set it down before turning back to her.

He froze, now confronted with her perfect ass. She'd bent over to reach for something behind the boxes. He didn't know what and didn't really care. He hoped it took her a while to find it.

Damn. She had a perfect butt. Heart-shaped with a generous curve to it. Enough for him to span his hands around and hold on tight.

His Adam's apple bobbed as that thought took hold. He swelled behind the fly of his jeans. Closing his eyes, he drew in a breath through his nose. He needed to get control of himself. What was wrong with him? He wasn't some horny kid. It had been years—many, many years—since he'd had such a visceral response to a woman.

When he opened his eyes, she was still bent over. Cursing under his breath, he looked out the window. "Do you need some help?"

"No. I dropped a stack of index cards when I pulled them out of the box. I've almost got them all." No sooner did she finish speaking than she straightened, holding the pile of white cards. "Got them." She waved the stack.

His head bobbed once. "Good. Did you find the checker board?"

Her smile did a quick downturn. "No." She turned back to the box. "It's over here somewhere. All this stuff came out of the built-ins in my old place. It's where I kept my stash of games."

"You kept index cards in a built-in cabinet? Why not a desk?"

"I use them to keep score. Those little scorecard tablets they give you don't last very long." She leaned down, wrapping her arms around the box.

"Ah, let me." He stepped up to her side.

"Right. Sorry. I'm not used to having someone around to help."

He hefted the box and carried it over to the other one. "You're fine. I just don't want you to hurt yourself."

"They're not really heavy. Just awkward. But I appreciate the sentiment." She tore off the packing tape on the third box and opened the flaps. "Aha! We have a winner." Pieces rattled as she removed several board games from the box, then stood, holding the checkers game. "Grab your snack." Tucking the game under her arm, she walked over to the coffee table and sank to the floor.

Cullen snagged his mug and bowl from the table by the chair and sat down across from her.

"What color do you want to be?" She lifted the game board from the box, exposing the red and black pieces.

"Whichever."

"You can have black. I want red, because I'm gonna light this board on fire." She gave him a wicked grin and scooted the black circles toward him.

Laughing, he picked them up and began arranging them on the board. "I'm sure you'll try."

She scoffed. "You're going down, Tate. I didn't get to kick your sexy butt earlier, but I am now. Mom and I played this a lot. She's the only person who's beaten me in a long time."

Cullen pressed his lips together, holding in his mirth. This could be interesting. "Wanna wager?"

Her hand paused over the board. "Ooo, a betting man. Okay, I'll bite. What's the wager?"

"Hmm, let's see." The words had popped free before he could think about them. That seemed to be happening a lot around her. Now that she'd accepted his offer, though, he had to think of something that would make it worthwhile for them both. He didn't want or need her money. No, whatever it was needed to be something she could do for him.

Scandalous thoughts ran through his mind. Strip checkers was not appropriate at this junction, no matter how much he wanted to see what she wore beneath that old, faded shirt.

He shifted as his body heated, then forced his mind back to the task at hand. An idea much more appropriate, but no less fun, struck him. "If I win, you have to bid on me at that Valentine's auction."

Her eyes sparkled. "I was planning to, anyway."

Startled, he blinked. "You were?"

"Of course. I won't win, but I can't let you go off with some rich man-eater without a little bit of a fight." She laid her checkers on the board as she talked.

"What if I give you the cash to outbid everyone else?"

Her hand froze over the board again, and she turned surprised eyes on him. "What? Why would you do that?"

"Because I honestly don't want to go out with some stranger, no matter how good the cause is. If I thought Gemma would let me, I'd write a generous check to the center and withdraw my name from the auction." His mouth flattened. "Knowing her, though, she'd insist I go through with it, because, one, my bio is already in the program, and two, she'd tell me it would be fun and I need to live a little."

Piper gave a soft laugh. "She's not wrong."

"So you keep telling me. But what do you say? Will you win me?"

She cocked her head and stared at him for a long moment. "Maybe. What do I get if I win our game?" She tipped a finger down at the board.

"What do you want?"

A slow smile spread over her face, and a devilish gleam entered her eyes. Cullen's breath faltered. He wasn't sure he wanted to know what was going on in that beautiful head of hers.

"If I win, you have to plan a second date for us."

"A second date? When do we have our first?"

She held her palms up, then gestured to the table.

"Now? This is our first date?"

"What would you call it?"

"Hanging out with a friend?"

She giggled. "Do you always stare at your friends' asses when they bend over?"

Heat tracked up his neck to turn his cheeks to what he was sure was a delightful shade of tomato red. "I apologize. I don't know what came over me."

"Oh, don't apologize. I've been staring at your ass in those jeans every chance I get."

His face flamed hotter.

Piper's giggles increased. "Sorry. I'll stop." She waved a hand and turned her attention back to the board.

Cullen cleared his throat. "It's okay. I've just never been very good at flirting."

"Stick around, honey. You'll learn." She flashed him a bright smile, making him laugh.

Piper was a breath of fresh air. She made him think of things besides work. Things that rarely got even a fraction of his brainpower. He was shocked to discover he was having a lot of fun. Even more than their impromptu dinner the other night.

He picked up his hot chocolate and took a drink. Swallowing the delicious brew, he set the mug down with a soft thunk, then picked up an extra checker and twirled it between his fingers. "You ready?" He lifted a brow and a crafty smile spread over his face.

Her eyes widened, her gaze fixed on the checker spinning effortlessly through his fingers. "Oh, I'm in trouble."

Smile growing, he leaned forward. "Get that bid hand ready, pretty lady."

Her laughter echoed through the room. "Don't get too cocky, Tate. Game's not over yet. You better start the wheels turning for our second date."

The joke was on her. She was getting a second date whether she won their checker game or not.

Twelve

Piper stared at the checker board, tongue poking out as she tried to decide where to move next. He had her boxed into a corner.

"It's not that difficult of a decision. You either move here" —Cullen pointed to a space—"and let me jump you, or here" —he pointed to another space—"and let me jump you. Either way, you're getting jumped."

She knew that. What she was trying to work out was how to mitigate the damage said jump would do by figuring out what her next moves would be. The variable was Cullen. His mind worked in ways she didn't understand. Like he could see the future. From the beginning, he'd owned the board. She was clinging now by the skin of her teeth. There was no way she'd be able to turn this around and beat him, but she wasn't going to roll over and just let him win, either.

"Piper."

Shooting him a look, she put a finger on top of the double-stacked pieces and slid it, watching his face as she did so. A gleam leapt to life in his eyes, and she pulled it back.

"You can't go backward."

"I never took my finger off of it." She slid it the other way. The gleam stayed silent, and she lifted her finger.

He jumped her, reaching the end of the board. She couldn't king him, since she'd done that eons ago. The checkers clinked as he picked hers up and added them to the growing pile in front of him.

"Your turn. Again." He grinned.

She rolled her eyes and slid her lone checker forward from its spot. He came after her. She did some artful dodging and managed to jump one of his kings, but on the next turn, he boxed her in again.

"Checkmate."

Piper let out a soft snort. "It's not chess."

"Close enough. So, do you want to sacrifice yourself, or should we call it?"

"To the end, pal." She slid the checker forward.

He picked up the closest king and jumped it, clearing the board. Holding her checker high, he dropped it into the pile and grinned. "Perfect. Now I don't have to date a stranger."

Laughing, she shook her head. "I hope you have deep pockets. The women are going to eat you up."

"I will pay whatever it takes to keep myself in your lovely hands."

"Good. I don't like to share." She looked him in the eye, telegraphing her intentions. The time she'd spent with him the last few days had been some of the best she'd ever had with a man. He made her laugh. And think. And feel. God, how he made her feel. She didn't care how their acquaintance started out. He wasn't her doctor now, and unless he unequivocally told her he wasn't interested, she intended to explore this insane attraction.

His eyes heated, and the color bloomed on his cheeks again, but this time it wasn't from embarrassment.

"Tell me something." His low voice rumbled over her nerve-endings, and she fought back a shiver.

"What?"

"Do you kiss on a first date?"

Shock rendered her lungs immobile for a long moment. But not her eyes. They grew as round as saucers.

He rose to his knees and leaned over the table, cupping the side of her face in his palm. "Piper Riordan speechless? I didn't know that was possible."

His words, as well as the warm puff of his breath against her face, pulled her out of her stupor. She grabbed his face. "Oh, shut up and kiss me."

Rockets left their launchpads inside her mind when his lips touched hers. Firm but supple, his mouth moved over hers. For a man who claimed to never date, he sure knew how to kiss. But she still wanted more. She wanted his hands on her body. Under her clothes. She wanted them touching, skin-to-skin.

The ferocity with which those thoughts and feelings struck jolted her back to her senses. She broke the kiss to lean back and fix a wide-eyed stare on him. Moisture glistened on his lips and desire shone in his now steely green eyes.

"That was, um, nice." God! She sounded like an idiot.

He settled on his haunches, his luscious mouth slashed upward. "Indeed."

Piper swallowed, holding his gaze another moment before looking away and inhaling a breath. "So, are you up for another game, or are you ready to go home?"

She felt his eyes on her and glanced over to see him studying her.

"Is it wise for us to play another game?"

"Probably not." She'd make no promises not to jump him and demand another kiss. Not when they left her feeling like molten silver, all fluid and hot.

"Too bad."

Piper's heart sank. She really wanted him to stay.

"I guess we'll tempt fate."

Her gaze shot to his. "What?"

He stood and walked toward the stack of boxes. "What other games do you have?"

"Wait. You're staying?"

The glance he sent her over his shoulder fanned the flames of heat she'd just banked. It was full of promise. "I'm staying."

A slow smile spread over her face as something unspoken passed between them. Whatever this was flaring to life between them, they weren't ignoring it. She unfolded herself from the floor. "Okay."

Thirteen

The box cutter made a low buzzing sound as Piper cut through the tape to open the next box of the pharmaceutical shipment. She was getting sick of inventory. After doing it all last week and now logging in this shipment, she was ready for sick and angry customers.

Opening the flaps, she found the packing slip and unfolded it, checking it against the contents in the box. Satisfied it was correct, she picked up her tablet and logged the medications into the system.

"Piper."

She glanced up as Kylie Stoss, another of the technicians, called her name. "Hey."

"Wanna switch? I'm tired of being grumped at."

Like it was hot, Piper pushed the box away and stood. "Have at it." Logging out of the inventory system, she handed over the tablet. "I will gladly deal with people." She was a people person and didn't mind dealing with the public. Even irate members.

Kylie giggled and took the device. "And I'd much rather be back here all day."

"Well, have fun, then." Smiling, she walked away.

Mood lifting as she entered the front of the pharmacy, she stepped up to the counter and logged into a computer, then beckoned the first person forward.

During a lull, she went to the filling station and picked up a basket. Reading the script, she fetched the medicine and returned to dispense the correct dose.

"You're a natural with the customers."

Piper glanced over at the pharmacist on duty, Tyler Reid. "Oh, thanks. I like people." She shrugged and turned her eyes back to the pill bottle in her hand.

"It shows. I've been watching you. That one woman, I thought she was going to come over the counter. But you stayed calm and helped her understand what was going on. I don't think she was satisfied, but she at least understood it wasn't our fault."

"There's no sense in me getting riled up too. And besides, she was upset that her child wasn't getting what he needed." She shook her head. "Insurance companies suck."

Tyler chuckled. "That they do. The whole pharmaceutical industry needs an overhaul."

She agreed. But that was well above her paygrade, so she did what she could to help people within the system.

"So, are you liking it here?"

Piper nodded. "It's been nice. Everyone here is great. Much better than my previous job. My old boss was a nightmare."

"I'm sorry to hear that, but I'm glad we're not mirroring her. Tillie's pretty great. We're lucky to have her." He worked as he talked, picking up a scanner to input the barcode on the script into the system and double-check it.

"Yeah. She's been wonderful. And a great teacher." Piper put the lid on the pill bottle and set it in the basket, then put the basket on the bottom of the stack in front of him. She reached for another, but several people walked in, so she went to help the third tech on duty, Brit Hauser.

"Hello." Piper smiled at the woman who walked forward. She wore a tight-fitting, pale pink hat over her hairless head. Dark circles shone bright under her eyes, but a smile sat on her face, reaching her silvery-blue eyes.

"Hi. I have a prescription to pick up. It's for Sarah Bailey."

Piper typed the name into the computer, then asked for her birthday. The woman rattled it off.

"Okay. I have one ready for you. Give me just a moment." She noted the bin number on the screen, then turned to the wall of bins. Rifling through the bags, she found the woman's medication. Back at the counter, she scanned the barcode. "Twenty-five dollars, please."

Inserting her card in the machine, the woman typed in her pin code. The printer spit out her receipt, and Piper handed it to her along with the bag.

"Thank you. Have a nice day."

With a soft smile, she turned away. Piper greeted the next customer in line, a young, harried-looking man with a toddler. The little boy eyed her with glassy blue eyes as he sucked his thumb, his head on his father's shoulder. After taking the child's information, she found the boy's prescription—an antibiotic that needed reconstituted. She held the bottle under Tyler's nose.

"This needs filled quick." She tipped her head toward the man at the register.

Tyler took it with a nod and went to the dispenser. Piper snagged a medicine spoon from the box and dropped it in the bag.

"Excuse me."

Glancing up, Piper frowned as the same woman from before stood off to the side. "Yes?"

"Hi, sorry. I checked my medication before I left, and it doesn't look the same as usual. Some of them do, but not all."

Her frown deepening, Piper took the pill bottle the woman held out and opened it. Sure enough, there were two different sizes of pills. The difference was slight, but noticeable if you were looking. "It's probably just a difference in manufacturer, but I'll have Dr. Reid check it again as soon as he finishes with the script he's working on."

"Okay, great. I'm glad I checked. I had one that was wrong a few months ago. My doctor noticed when I came in for an appointment. Now I always look before I leave."

Alarm bells went off in Piper's head. "You've gotten the wrong pills before?"

The woman nodded. "My Iclusig was mixed with ibuprofen." She shook her head. "It was scary. If my platelets had been lower, I could have been in a lot of trouble."

For sure. Ibuprofen and cancer patients didn't mix. "I'll get this to him right away."

"Thank you."

Spinning around, she practically ran into Tyler as he came up behind her.

"Oh, sorry."

He smiled. "It's all right. Here." He held out the antibiotic.

"Thanks." She took it, then held up Mrs. Bailey's pill bottle. "Can you check this one again? She said she's received the wrong medication in the past, and there's two different size pills in here."

"Sure. It's probably just a different manufacturer." He took it.

"That's what I told her, but there's no harm in double-checking."

"Nope." He spun on his heel.

Piper turned back to the register, looking at Mrs. Bailey. "He's looking into it."

She smiled and nodded.

Turning her attention to the young father, she smiled. "Okay. We're all set now." She put the bottle in the bag, then scanned the barcode on the paper attached to it. "Three seventy-eight."

He handed her a five-dollar bill. She made change, then handed it to him along with the bag and the receipt. "I hope you get to feeling better, little man."

The father glanced at his son and smiled. "Me too. Thanks." He turned and left.

"Piper."

She looked at Tyler as he called her name, her expectant look turning to a curious frown at the fierce downturn to his face. He tipped his head, asking her to come over to his workstation.

Locking her computer, she walked around the counter to him. "What's wrong?"

"You said she told you she'd gotten the wrong medication once before?" he asked, voice low.

Piper nodded. "She said she got a mix of ibuprofen and Iclusig."

"That's what this is." He lifted the bottle, then set it back down.

"What? How did that happen again?"

"I don't know. I didn't fill her script. Go get the open bottle of Iclusig."

Piper hurried into the stacks and found the bottle, then returned. Tyler opened it and poured it into a tray.

"It's the wrong medicine."

"In the bottle?"

He nodded, then let out a soft groan. "I've heard of pharmacies being sent counterfeit medications, but I've never had it happen. Go get the rest of them with this batch number." He showed her the number on the bottle.

She wrote it on her hand. "On it." In the stacks, she found three more with the same number. She also grabbed one that was different, then went back out front. "These three are the same lot number. I brought this one so we can hopefully fill Mrs. Bailey's prescription with the right stuff."

"Smart thinking." He opened the three bottles from the same batch first.

Piper frowned as each one was the correct medication.

"What the hell is going on?" Tyler frowned. "Reason says these should all be wrong." He sighed. "I'm going to hold these back for now. We probably need to get them tested and make sure they really are the right thing." He reached for the fourth bottle she brought up and opened it. Counting out the dosage, he put it into Mrs. Bailey's prescription bottle. "There. Give her that. I'll take care of the rest of these."

She turned, taking a step, then paused. "Wait. What about the ones that were right?"

His forehead wrinkled in question.

"In her original prescription? It was mixed. Where did the good ones come from?"

"Probably another bottle." He picked up the tray full of counterfeit pills and counted them, then counted the counterfeit ones from Mrs. Bailey's original prescription. "Yeah. It's from two bottles."

"Okay. Good." She turned away, heading back to the register and Mrs. Bailey. "Hi, sorry it took so long. We got it figured out." She held out the bottle. "You're all set now."

"It was the wrong stuff, wasn't it?" The woman took the bottle, frowning, anger flashing in her eyes.

Unsure what all she should say, Piper just nodded.

"Why does this keep happening?"

"I don't know, but we're looking into it. Thank you for bringing it to our attention."

Mrs. Bailey raised the bottle and gave it a quick shake. "You all need to do better. Once is a mistake. Twice? If it didn't cost me an arm and a leg to go elsewhere, I would."

"I'm sorry, Mrs. Bailey. I can promise you the problem will be dealt with."

"Good." With a short nod, she spun around and marched out.

Blowing out a soft breath, Piper closed her eyes for a moment and tried to reset her emotions. She couldn't do anything else about the pills. Tyler said he'd handle it, so she had to trust that he would.

Opening her eyes, she pasted a smile on her face and logged into the computer again, and motioned the next person in line forward.

FOURTEEN

Whistling under his breath, Cullen rounded a corner, and the pharmacy came into view. His step quickened, and he rolled his eyes at himself. He was acting like a love-struck teenager again, all eager to see his beloved.

That wasn't far off, though. He was eager to see her. They'd parted ways Saturday at his house without any real plans, except to spend time together when they could. He had to work all week, as per usual, and they both had to work this coming weekend. Cullen wasn't going to be picky about how they spent time together, so long as they did. She'd stirred something within him—besides his desire—and he liked it. She made the world feel brighter.

The woman at the register smiled at him. "Hello, how can I help you?"

"Hi. I'm looking for Piper."

"Cullen?"

He glanced past the woman at the counter to see Piper's blonde head peeking over the stack of prescription baskets. A broad smile spread over his face. "Hey."

She came around, smiling. "Hey, yourself. What are you doing here?"

"I came to see when your dinner break is."

"Oh." She looked at her watch. "In about fifteen minutes."

"Perfect. Would you care to join me in our classiest establishment, the cafeteria?"

She giggled. "I'd love to."

"Great. I'll let you get back to work. See you soon." He lifted a hand and backed away, suddenly feeling awkward as he noticed her colleagues staring at them.

Smile sweet, she nodded.

With a final wave, he turned and left, resisting the urge to look back.

Having some time to kill, he wandered over to the coffee shop and bought a coffee, then sat down in the atrium to check his email. When he had just a few minutes left until he was supposed to meet her, he headed down to the cafeteria and took up a spot on the wall to wait.

She didn't keep him waiting. Two minutes later, she strolled up with a bright smile.

"Hey, you." Standing on her toes, she kissed his cheek.

Cullen felt it like a brand. He wanted to turn his head and give her a proper kiss, but they were in public. That would have to wait. "Hey, yourself." He pushed away from the wall. "Hungry?"

"Starving."

Together, they entered the cafeteria and grabbed trays. Cullen looked up at the overhead menus at each station, trying to decide what he wanted.

"Ooo, they have ramen." Piper wandered away, eyes locked on a station to her right.

Chuckling, Cullen followed her.

"Back home, there was this place in Buffalo that I would go to every so often when I got a craving for it. They had the best ramen. And sushi. I need to find a place around here."

"There's a pretty good place in Asheville."

"Yeah?" She glanced at him, then picked up a ramen bowl.

He nodded, grabbing his own bowl. "We'll have to go. Hey, that can be our second date."

"Nuh-uh." She waggled a finger. "Third. This is the second. And for the record, as dates go, this isn't very impressive." A smile bloomed on her face, along with a teasing light in her eyes.

Cullen grinned. "Hey, you got ramen, so it has some redeeming qualities."

Piper laughed. "True."

"And I get points for spontaneity."

"Oh, definitely. I was not expecting to have such an enjoyable dinner break."

He was glad. It was enjoyable for him too.

They moved down the line, going to the drink station. Cullen grabbed a water, and Piper got a bottle of tea. After paying for their food, they found a table in the corner and sat down.

"So, how's your day been?" she asked, taking the lid off her ramen bowl.

"Busy. I wasn't sure I was going to get down here for your break, but things calmed down in the E.R. Hopefully, I don't have to run out."

"You don't have clinic in Foggy Mountain today?"

He shook his head. "It's Thursday and Friday this week. Next week it's Monday and Thursday."

"I don't know how you keep it all straight."

"My assistant keeps me on track. But the days are routine enough, I know where I'm supposed to be. Usually." He opened his ramen and picked up his fork. "So, how about you? How's your day been?"

Her face clouded over. "Weird."

"How so?" He twirled noodles and lifted them to his mouth.

She shrugged. "Something strange is going on at the pharmacy."

"What do you mean?"

"I'm not sure. There have been some medication mix-ups."

Cullen lowered his fork. She had his full attention now. As a physician, he relied on not just his skills, but on medications to heal his patients. Mix-ups could be deadly. "What kind of mix-ups?"

Her brows dipped lower momentarily. "Last week, I was doing inventory and I noticed two open bottles of ephedrine. Not that big of a deal. The one was behind the medication next to it. I figured it got shoved back there by accident and no one saw it. But it also wasn't marked with the date it was opened, which is a no-no. Then, when I got to the *T*s, there was an entire case of single-dose testosterone missing."

His eyebrows shot up. "That's a lot of medicine."

She nodded. "But the thing is, the inventory system was correct for what was on the shelf. The only reason I know there's a case missing is because I helped with the shipment the day it came in. There were two boxes of testosterone ampules, but only one was on the shelf, and the computer told me we only received one."

"Did you log two?"

"I wasn't logging things. One of my colleagues was. I was just reading the labels and checking them against the packing slips, then telling her what we received."

"I'd say it's possible she hit the wrong number when she entered it, but then what happened to the box?"

"Exactly." Her frown returned, and she looked out over the cafeteria, her eyes unfocused.

"There's more, isn't there?"

"Yeah." She looked down at her bowl and twirled her fork through the noodles, but didn't raise it to take a bite. "Earlier, I had a woman fill a prescription for a cancer drug. She checked the medication before she left and noticed there were two different size pills in her bottle and asked about them. I showed our pharmacist, and he discovered some of them were ibuprofen."

Cullen's eyes widened. "Cancer patients can't have ibuprofen. It's a bleeding risk."

Piper nodded. "I know. She said it happened once before, too, which is why she always checks now. Dr. Reid had me grab the lot, thinking we just got a counterfeit batch, but only the open bottle was ibuprofen. The rest were fine."

"He didn't dispense them, though, did he? They need to be tested."

"No. We gave her pills with a different batch number. It just doesn't make sense, though. One, how could this happen to the same woman twice? And two, why wasn't the whole lot counterfeit?"

Cullen sat back, mind spinning. "That's a good question. What was the drug that was fake?"

"Iclusig."

Something niggled in Cullen's mind, but he couldn't put his finger on what. It would come to him, eventually. But until then, it would bug the hell out of him. "What's being done about it?"

"Dr. Reid was going to have the bottles tested and talk to Tillie, our pharmacy manager. What she'll do with it, I don't know." She picked up her forkful of noodles. "It's just weird."

He agreed. "What do you think is going on?" He had his suspicions, but he wanted to hear her thoughts.

She chewed up the bite she just took and glanced out over the cafeteria, a thoughtful look on her face. "Honestly? That someone's stealing medication. I hope it's just a bunch of lax errors and a counterfeit shipment, but that just feels like too much of a coincidence."

Again, he agreed. "Well, just watch yourself. Make sure you follow all the protocols and don't leave a computer logged in with your credentials. If someone is stealing, you don't want them to try to pin it on you."

She nodded. "I'm very careful about that. My last job, the boss was anal. If we walked away from a screen and left ourselves logged in, she put us through a mandatory refresher course on IT security, then gave us shit-jobs for a week. I learned real quick to always log out."

"Good." Cullen scooped up another bite of ramen. "If there's anything I can do, let me know. I can bend some ears if need be."

Her head bobbed. "I will. Thanks."

He smiled, but it didn't quite reach his eyes. That nagging feeling was still there. And now, so was a concern for Piper's safety. There were more ways the thief—if there indeed was one—could hurt her than just getting her fired or arrested.

"Promise me you'll let your boss investigate?" he said.

A chagrined smile stretched over her face. "Am I that transparent?"

"No. But I know you well enough to know you won't let this go."

She shrugged. "How about, so long as she does, and nothing else strange happens, I'll leave it to her?"

Cullen's mouth flattened. He'd prefer she left it alone entirely. But, as he said, he knew her well enough to know she wouldn't. "Just be careful."

"I will."

He hoped so. The thought of something happening to her —again—left him with a bad taste in his mouth and a heaviness on his heart. She'd come to mean a lot to him in a short amount of time. He didn't want to lose her.

FIFTEEN

"No. No. No." Piper sighed as she rifled through her closet, attempting to find something to wear on her date with Cullen tonight. Before he dropped her at the pharmacy again—with a chaste kiss on her cheek—he'd asked if she wanted to try the Japanese restaurant in Asheville Friday night after he finished at his clinic. Of course, she said yes. But now she wished she'd thought about her wardrobe sooner. Nothing fit, because she'd lost so much weight. Or it was entirely inappropriate for this kind of outing. She was sure he'd love her short miniskirts and cleavage-baring tops, but those were for dancing at nightclubs. Not a classy dinner with a doctor.

Heaving a sigh, she took her phone from her pocket. Scrolling through her contacts, she called Mack. It rang twice in her ear before her friend answered.

"Hey, what's up?"

Piper sighed and flounced onto her bed. "Are you busy?"

"I'm just working on my applications for school. Nothing I can't take a break from. Why?"

"I need some help. Can you come over?"

"Sure. What do you need help with?"

"Picking out an outfit."

Silence stretched. Piper pulled the phone away from her ear. The call was still active. She put it back. "Hello?"

"I'm sorry. Did you say *you* need help picking out clothes?"

Piper chuckled. "I know, right? But I can't find anything to wear. I think I just need another set of eyes."

"What's this for?"

"I have a date tonight."

"What? With who?"

"Cullen."

"Cullen? As in your doctor, Cullen Tate?"

"He's not my doctor anymore."

"True. When did this happen?"

"I ran into him at the hospital—quite literally. Then we were both on the scene of a car accident."

"What? Girl, it hasn't been that long since we talked."

"I know. And I promise to fill you in. If you come over." She wasn't above bribery. She needed Mack's help.

"I'll be there in ten minutes."

"Great! See you soon."

"Yep. Bye." Mackenzie hung up.

Piper put the phone down and went back to her closet. Maybe something would jump out at her she hadn't seen yet.

True to her word, Mackenzie breezed in the door ten minutes later.

"Okay, spill. I want all the details," she said as she entered the bedroom.

Laughing at the fierce frown on Mack's face, Piper gave her a quick rundown of the last couple of weeks.

"And so, you're going on date three tonight. Which you're freaking out about. Got it." Mackenzie moved toward the closet. "Let's see what we can find."

Soon, clothes covered Piper's bed as they laid things out, mixing and matching.

"I don't understand why you're so nervous. You never get nervous around men." Mackenzie carried a pencil skirt out of the closet and laid it in the skirt pile for Piper to try on.

"Yeah, well, I guess I don't really date much. I go out dancing and clubbing. I don't date much more than Cullen does, honestly." Which was true. She hadn't had a real boyfriend in years. She preferred going out and just having fun more than going through the motions of dating. It wasn't like any of the men she'd met recently tickled her fancy enough for her to want to give them a chance at a relationship. They were all just looking to score. And she didn't sleep around. Once in a great while, she engaged in casual sex, but only after going on a handful of dates with the guy. With Cullen, she could see there being more than a few dates. A lot more.

"You really like him, don't you?"

Piper nodded. "I do. He's interesting and funny. And sexy."

Mackenzie giggled. "If you say so. He's too old for me."

Rolling her eyes, Piper picked up a red dress with a plunging neckline, then put it down. It was too daring for where they were going. "You're not that much younger than me."

"No, but it's enough. Thirteen years is a lot. So is ten, but it's not thirteen."

"True." She didn't feel the age gap, though. Sure, she saw it in his face, in the extra lines around his mouth and the crinkles around his eyes, but he was still young at heart. Even if he was mature beyond his years. She liked the experience he brought to their relationship. His big brain was sexy.

"So, what about this?" She held up the mustard yellow leather pencil skirt and a white cotton, long-sleeved top.

Mackenzie wrinkled her nose. "Too stuffy. It looks like

something you'd wear to the office. I like the skirt, though." She tipped her head. "Hang on. I saw something." Spinning around, she hurried into the closet and returned a moment later with a top Piper forgot she had.

"Oh, I forgot about that one." She reached out and fingered the green sateen. The top was long-sleeved, which she liked. It was cold out. The neckline was low, but it had two strips of fabric coming out of the collar meant to be worn like a tie that would cover some of her cleavage. It was classy, yet sexy.

"Go put that on." Mackenzie flicked a finger toward the outfit, then motioned to the bathroom.

"Yes, ma'am." Smiling, Piper scurried into her en suite and shut the door. She stripped out of her t-shirt and jeans and shimmied into the skirt. It wasn't as tight as it used to be, but it wasn't falling off her ass, either. Slipping on the shirt, she tucked it into the skirt and exited the bathroom.

Mackenzie let out a low whistle. "You're going to knock him dead."

Piper glanced down at herself, then walked over to her full-length mirror to study her outfit.

"You look amazing." Mackenzie walked up to stand beside her. "Classy, but with a hint of the rebel hiding inside."

"Yeah?"

"Mmm-hmm." She lifted a hand, pointing a finger and waving it. "You need shoes. Something your feet won't freeze in." She bit the corner of her mouth and walked away, back into the closet.

Soft thuds reached Piper's ears as Mackenzie rooted through boxes she'd yet to unpack.

"Aha! Victory!" A moment later, Mackenzie emerged, holding a pair of black ankle boots with a killer heel. "Put these on."

Piper took the shoes and slipped them on her feet. "It's

good the ice melted. I'd break my neck in these if the sidewalks were slick."

"But you'd look good doing it." Mackenzie stood back and surveyed Piper's look.

"Well?"

"Perfect. That shirt really sets off your eyes."

Piper glanced in the mirror again. They did pop. All in all, she was happy with the look. She turned. "Thank you for coming over to help. I probably would have ended up in a simple black dress if not for you."

Mackenzie waved a hand. "I doubt that. You're too bold for basic black and would have found something. But I'm glad I could help."

Piper reached out and wrapped her friend in a tight hug. "I'm so glad we're together again. I've missed you."

"I've missed you too. Missed having girl time." She pulled back and looked up at Piper with a mischievous grin. "I smuggled cocoa in my purse. Want some?"

Laughing, Piper let her go. "Why did you have to smuggle it?"

"I've drunk almost an entire container this week. Jake threatened to hide it if I drank anymore. Said it was too much caffeine." She waved a hand, then rested it over the slight swell of her belly. "I don't drink coffee much now, so a cup of hot cocoa a day isn't going to hurt."

"Have you had any today?"

"Nope." Grinning, she headed for the door. "I'll go make it while you change back into your other clothes."

"Sounds good." Tugging her shirt free of her waistband, she walked into the bathroom, excited about tonight.

Sixteen

Cullen hurried up the walkway to Piper's house, a little later than he wanted to be. There had been a minor emergency at the clinic, which put him behind, and he'd finished forty-five minutes later than expected. After the fastest shower on record, he'd thrown on some clothes and run out the door.

The doorbell chimed inside as he pushed the button. Through the beveled glass framing the door, he saw a tall, colorful figure heading toward him.

Nothing could have prepared him for the vision that presented itself when she opened the door, though. Nearly his height in three-inch black ankle boots, her legs looked like they were ten miles long beneath the tight yellow skirt. The shiny green top she wore hugged her generous curves and showed him just a hint of what was hiding beneath. The color set off her eyes, making them the highlight of her entire ensemble.

"Wow." His eyes roved over her again. "You look incredible."

She smiled. "Thanks. You don't look so bad yourself."

He was glad she thought so. After rushing like he had, he

wasn't entirely sure what he'd put on. Most of his clothes went together, so he just grabbed the first thing he saw, which was a pair of charcoal trousers and a black shirt.

"Are you ready to go?"

"Yes. I just need to put my coat on." She stepped back so he could enter, then opened the coat closet and removed a long black wool coat.

Cullen took it from her and held it out, so she could slip her arms inside.

"Thank you." She glanced at him over her shoulder and their eyes connected.

He stilled, her scent wafting toward him. It was something light, with a hint of vanilla and spice. Her tongue darted out to touch her bottom lip. Cullen ground his teeth together and took a step back. If he didn't, he was going to kiss her. And kiss her, and kiss her.

"You're welcome." His voice came out as a low rasp.

A pretty flush to her cheeks told him she was just as affected by their nearness as he was. This date was going to be torture.

She picked up a royal purple handbag from the entryway table. "Okay, I'm all set."

He motioned her to precede him, then pulled the door shut as they exited. At his car, he held open her door and helped her inside, then went around the hood and slid into the buttery-soft, tan leather seat.

"Did I mention the other day that I love your car?"

He smiled as he started the engine. It growled to life. He liked his car too. "No."

"Well, I do. I like my Jeep, but this thing is a whole other level of awesome." She stroked the armrest and grinned.

"I don't splurge on many things, but I did on this. And my house. Though I bought that more for the privacy all the land offered. I like my space." He pulled out of her drive, heading for Asheville.

"You deserve to splurge a bit. You work hard."

He did. And while he liked the luxury, the main reason he bought the fancy car was simple—he didn't want to worry about his vehicle breaking down. As for his house, the place had been in good shape when he bought it, but he'd upgraded the appliances and furnace when he moved in. At the end of the day, he just wanted to go home and unwind, and not worry about whether something worked properly.

"So, I take it you had a long day since you're late?" Her soft voice filled the car.

He glanced at her, stiffening at her words, but didn't see any anger on her face. Just curiosity. Relaxing, he nodded. "A minor emergency at the clinic put me behind."

"Oh, no. Is everyone okay?"

"Yes. Well, he will be with treatment and time."

Her brow furrowed.

"Bad wound infection. I had to admit him."

"Oh. That's no fun."

Cullen shook his head. "So, how about you? You've been off the last couple of days. What have you been up to?"

"Nothing much. Unpacking, mostly. Mackenzie came over this afternoon and we hung out for a bit." She shrugged. "It's been blissfully boring."

"That's good?"

She nodded. "Very good."

"You hear any more about the medication mix-ups at the pharmacy?"

Her mouth turned down. "No. I assume Tillie's handling it. There haven't been any others, though, as far as I know."

"I'm glad. I hope it was just an anomaly." It had been on his mind lately. That nagging feeling he was missing something was still there.

"Same here."

Her dismal tone told him she held little hope of that. "You think it was deliberate, don't you?"

"Yeah, unfortunately. I just can't see there being so many sloppy errors no one else noticed."

"Unless they're all lax, and as the new girl on the block, you're noticing all their mistakes."

Her head waved side-to-side. "Maybe. I guess we'll find out once Tillie investigates."

He hoped her investigation uncovered some answers. It bugged him that patients weren't getting what they needed, even if there were only a few.

"So, tell me more about this auction." A saucy smile spread over her face.

Cullen groaned.

Piper giggled. "Did you plan a date?"

"Yes."

"What is it?"

"I'm not telling you." He shook his head once. "You'll find out at the auction, like everyone else."

She shifted in her seat, angling toward him. "I thought you had to put it in the brochure?"

"I told the PR lady that I needed more time, so she just put some blurb about a fun, exciting evening." A grin overtook his face. "I didn't lie, but I could have come up with something in time. Mostly, I didn't want to give away my plans to my assistant."

"Your assistant? Why?"

"Levi got roped into the auction as well. He vowed to outdo me. If he doesn't know what I'm planning, he can't change his plans."

Piper laughed, the melodic sound filling the car. "That's hilarious. You two are like a couple of teenagers trying to be the best at the game."

Cullen chuckled. "It's all in good fun."

She gasped and put a hand over her chest. "Cullen Tate. Did you just say you're having *fun*?"

He groaned again. "Don't tell Levi I said that."

Laughing, she covered her mouth as a soft snort escaped.

A low chuckle rumbled from Cullen's chest. "I am having fun." He reached across the console and took her hand, smoothing his thumb over her knuckles. "I'm glad you moved down here. Life has more color now." He hadn't realized how boring his life had become until she entered it. He'd laughed more and thought about work less than he had in years —decades.

Cullen liked his new perspective. There was a balance now that had been missing before. Sure, it still felt strange—like he was living someone else's life. But slowly, he was beginning to see what life could be like. That there was more to life—to his life—than being a doctor. For years, he'd operated on the assumption that his big brain needed to be devoted solely to others. That it was a gift he couldn't keep to himself. He still believed the latter. But now he saw he was doing himself a disservice by burying himself in his work. Piper had opened his eyes to a life he never considered. And it was only just beginning.

SEVENTEEN

The heels of Piper's boots echoed through the chilly night air as she moved up the walkway to her front door, Cullen at her back. Dinner was fabulous. Not just the food, but the company. Relaxed Cullen was a sight to behold. The stiff, awkward man he seemed to think he was on dates was nowhere to be found. Sure, he talked about intellectual things —it's who he was. But it wasn't boring. In fact, Piper found it fascinating. She'd peppered him with questions, vowing to subscribe to some of these journals before the weekend ended.

Keys jingling, she found the one for the front door and inserted it in the lock. Twisting it, she unlocked the door and pushed it open. "Would you like to come in?" She prayed he said yes. She wasn't ready for the night to end just yet.

He hesitated only a moment. But in that moment, Piper watched a dozen emotions cross his face. The only ones she could decipher were trepidation and a quick flash of desire. Her body echoed the latter as he followed her inside.

She put her keys and purse on the entryway table, then shrugged out of her coat. Opening the closet door, she removed a hanger and put her coat on it. "I can take your coat."

"Oh, right."

Piper tried not to stare as he removed it. The action showed off every inch of his broad chest. It pushed against the dark fabric of his shirt. She wanted to grab the front and rip it open. Buttons would ping against the floor, never to be seen again. But, oh, the sight she'd get in return. It might even lead to seeing other parts of him.

Heat coiled low in her belly, making her flush. She took his coat and turned away, grateful for the momentary reprieve. As much as she'd like to find out what he hid beneath his suave attire, that wasn't why she invited him inside. She simply wanted to spend more time with him.

Coats hung, she closed the closet door, only glancing at him as she walked deeper into the house. "Do you want some coffee or something?"

"How about some more of that hot chocolate?"

"Sure. You want to play another game?" She waved a finger at him as she headed for the kitchen. "Not checkers."

He laughed and followed her. "Trivial Pursuit?"

"That depends." She shot him a look over her shoulder as she opened the fridge to get the milk. "How much history and modern trivia do you know?"

He made a so-so gesture with his hand. "Some. You probably have a bit of an advantage, though, because I'm guessing you've played the game a lot and have heard most of the questions before."

"Yeah, but that doesn't mean I can recall the answers quickly." A smile bloomed on her face. "We should save that for a night when we double date with Jake and Mackenzie or your friends, the sheriff and his wife. We can team up against them and kick their butts." She dug a pan out of the bottom cupboard near the stove and set it on a burner, then uncapped the milk.

Chuckling, he crossed to the pantry cabinet and took out the cocoa and cinnamon. "I like that idea. Gemma's a pistol. The competition would be fierce. We'll have to wait a bit for them, though. They just had a baby a couple weeks ago. But you should talk to your friend."

"Yeah?" She glanced up after pouring two mugs' worth of milk into the saucepan, then set the jug down, turning on the stove.

He walked over and set the cocoa and cinnamon on the counter beside her. "Yeah."

Piper's heart skipped a beat at his nearness and at the look in his eyes. Amusement and something deeper—satisfaction?—lingered in his gaze. She swayed toward him, raising a hand to his face. "I like this." She rubbed the scruff on his jaw. It was slightly darker than his hair, but had more silver to it. Although it aged him some, she found she didn't mind. The beard just made him sexier.

He raised a hand to touch the other side of his jaw. "I ran out of razors and haven't been able to get to the store for more."

Piper shuffled closer. "Leave them off your list." She framed his face and rose onto her toes to press her mouth to his.

Long arms wrapped around her waist, pulling her close. She clutched his shoulders, feeling the silky softness of his hair at the back of his neck. He let one hand drift down her backside to curve over her butt. An ache settled in her core. She moaned, the sound cut short as he took advantage of her open mouth to thrust his tongue inside.

The ache intensified. Piper tipped her hips forward, wanting to get closer. What she got was a solid idea of what hid behind his fly. She moaned again.

Cullen broke the kiss. Piper's eyes flew open, her hand sliding back to his jaw as they stared at each other, panting for breath.

"I think we should slow down." Cullen's voice was a low rumble, barely audible even in the quiet kitchen. "As much as I want to unwrap you—" He paused, swallowing hard as his fingers toyed with the tie at her neck. "I don't want to move too fast. I've never had a real relationship, and I don't want to screw it up or make it all about sex. Because it's—you're—not."

The ache in her core moved north to her heart. Her desire morphed along with it. She still wanted to jump his bones and rip off his shirt, but now she also wanted to hold the kind, golden heart beating beneath. "Are you sure you're not trying to get laid?"

He laughed and covered her hand with his, removing it from his face. "I'm sure. There will be a time for us, Piper. But it's not tonight."

She bit her lip, knowing he was right. What was growing between them was too fresh and new still. Maturity would make intimacy that much more powerful. Though she wasn't sure she'd be able to handle it if they waited. He'd barely touched her, and already, she was ready to pop like a cork.

But she nodded and turned back to the stove as he stepped away. She picked up a wooden spoon from the crock on the counter.

"Maybe I should go."

She glanced at him, wanting to scream no. "Stay. At least for your hot chocolate. We can sit and talk. Or find a game. Cards, maybe."

He studied her for a long moment. "Are you sure?"

Piper nodded, picking up the cocoa powder to spoon some into the hot milk. "We're both adults, Cullen. I can handle some sexual frustration." She eyed him through her lashes. "Just don't make me wait too long."

Heat flared in his hazel eyes. "Don't worry. My body will overrule my brain soon enough." He shook his head. "I've never lost control, but I came damn close tonight."

Feminine power surged through Piper's blood, and she smiled. "That's good to know."

He groaned, closing his eyes for a second. "I probably should have kept that tidbit to myself."

She giggled, grabbing the cinnamon. "Probably. But trust me, honey, women have a way of knowing what works on their men. You won't last long, even without that admission."

He hummed. "Maybe."

Piper grinned, adding sugar to the mix on the stove. "You might best me in a battle of wits, but my wiles will always win."

Laughing, he leaned in and pecked a kiss on her cheek. "Oh, I have no doubt."

Eighteen

D ead on her feet, Piper let herself in through the garage door. Her purse hit the kitchen counter with a thud. The keys in her hand clinked on the granite surface as she set them down. She sighed as she stepped out of her shoes and flexed her toes. The pharmacy had been hopping today. From the minute her shift started, she'd been thrust into the fire and hadn't stopped moving except for a couple of breaks all day. To make matters worse, Tillie was out. The pharmacist on duty, Dr. Henry, said she called in sick. Piper hadn't realized how much they relied on Tillie to make things run smoothly. She was the grease in their cogs, and things were a little sticky without her.

But she was done for the night. Piper's plan now was to find some dinner she didn't have to cook, soak in her bathtub to relieve the ache in her side, then go to sleep.

Taking off her coat, she hung it over a bar stool, then padded over to the fridge. She'd made a large pot of mine-strone soup yesterday, knowing she wouldn't want to cook the next couple of nights.

After ladling a portion into a bowl, she put it in the

microwave to warm up. While she waited, she went to the front door and picked up the mail that had come in through the mail slot earlier in the day. She liked not having a mailbox. It meant she didn't have to open the door and let in a bunch of cold air.

Leafing through the envelopes, she separated them. Most were junk, but there was a bill and another piece she wasn't sure about. The microwave beeped, and she spun on her heel. She tucked all but the mystery envelope under her arm and walked back to the kitchen. Sliding her finger beneath the flap, she opened it and pulled out the single sheet of paper.

The doorbell pealed, and she looked up with a frown. Setting the mail on the counter, she reversed course.

Piper peered through the beveled glass, trying to determine who was on the other side. She flipped on the porch light, then peered through the peephole. Her heart skipped as she saw Cullen's tall form.

With a smile, she threw open the door. "Hey. What are you doing here?"

He returned her smile and held up a white paper sack. "I heard through the grapevine you had a busy day, so I brought you dinner."

Smile widening even as her brow dipped with curiosity, she stepped back to let him in. "Thank you. How'd you hear that? Don't you have coroner duties on Wednesdays?" They headed for the kitchen.

He nodded. "Levi called to tell me to check my email about a prescription question. I only ever get email questions from the pharmacy when Tillie's not there. She always just calls, gets the answer she needs, then types up a confirmation email and sends it. I figured things were probably a bit harried there without her."

Piper let out a soft snort and opened the bag he set on the counter, peering inside. Her mouth watered as she saw containers of sushi from the restaurant they went to last Saturday. "I sat down for lunch and to pee. My feet do not like me right now." She lifted an arm to reach into the bag and winced. "Neither does my side."

Cullen frowned as he removed his coat and set it over the back of a chair. He came around to stand beside her. "Are you all right?"

She nodded. "Yeah. Just a little achy from standing all day. Nothing a hot bath and some sleep won't fix."

"You're sure?"

"Yes." She waved him toward the cabinets. "Find some plates for this stuff."

With one more long glance, he shifted to open the plate cabinet. Piper took the food out of the bag.

"You already made food?"

"What?" She glanced up.

He pointed at the microwave. The word "End" flashed on the screen.

"Oh, that. I made a pot of minestrone last night and heated some up." She waved a hand. "It can be lunch tomorrow. This is infinitely better." She took the lid off one of the sushi containers, grinning. "I can't believe you drove into Asheville to get me sushi for dinner."

He shrugged, setting two plates on the counter. "You enjoyed it the other night. I thought it might be a nice mid-week pick-me-up."

"It's perfect." She turned, standing on her toes to press a kiss to his bearded cheek. "Thank you."

"You're welcome." His arm curved around her waist, holding her steady as he leaned down to press a quick kiss to her lips.

Piper's appetite waned as a different sort of hunger reared. She fought it back, knowing tonight wasn't the night for more than a few delicious kisses.

They split the food onto the plates, then sat at the bar. She speared a sushi roll with her chopstick and popped it in her mouth, moaning as the flavors burst over her tongue. "Oh, that's so good." She picked up a salmon roll, dipping it in wasabi, then soy sauce. Every bit as hungry as she thought she was, she polished off her food in minutes. "That was delicious, thank you." She got up to take her plate to the sink.

Cullen smiled and ate his last tuna roll. She deposited her plate in the sink with the other dishes she needed to wash, then turned. He stood, picking up his plate. His rolled-up shirtsleeve caught on the mail Piper put on the counter and knocked off the top letter.

"Oh, sorry." He bent, picking it up, then froze. "Who sent this?"

Her forehead creased. "The letter? I don't know. I haven't looked at it yet. Why?" She walked over.

He held it up to show it to her, a fierce frown on his face. "Because this isn't a nice letter. I wasn't trying to be nosy. The words just caught my eye when I picked it up."

Frown deepening, she took the paper to read it. Her breath hitched as the single line of text stared back at her.

Mind your own business, or you're next.

Wide-eyed, she looked at Cullen. "I don't know what this means. Or who would send it. What does it mean, I'll be next? Who was first?"

"I don't know. But I think we need to call the police."

She laid the letter down and hugged her arms around herself. "Yeah. Okay."

Cullen took his phone from his pocket. Piper closed her eyes and pressed a hand to her forehead as she listened to him talk to the dispatcher. So much for her relaxing evening.

Nineteen

The lock clicked as Cullen turned the latch behind the officer who had just left. He closed his eyes and inhaled a breath through his nose to settle his emotions before he turned around. Why didn't he feel any better? He thought turning the letter over to the police, making a report, would help take away some of his worry about the situation. Even with the officer's promise that he would turn the missive over to the detectives and have it processed for forensic evidence, Cullen didn't feel any better; he was still just as worried. Without a suspect to match it to, there was nothing they could do, even if they found something on it.

Blowing out his breath, he turned around. Piper stood near the window in the far corner of the living room, looking out over her darkened yard. He walked up behind her and curled his hands over her shoulders. She leaned back into his chest.

"You okay?"

She fluttered a hand, then rested her elbow on the arm wrapped around her waist and propped her chin in her hand. "I'm fine."

"Hmm. Why don't I believe you?"

She sighed. "I don't know what I am. Numb, I guess. It's just weird. If this is about the pharmacy, all I did was notice some discrepancies. So, I'm just supposed to look the other way? I could lose my job if I ignore that stuff."

"You've made someone nervous—someone you work with."

"So you said to the cop. I just don't know who."

"No one sticks out?"

She shook her head. "They've all been nice. No one looks at me funny or avoids me." She sighed again and rubbed her forehead. "I have a headache." Dropping her hands, she pushed away from him, marching out of the room.

"Where are you going?" Cullen went after her as she disappeared into her bedroom. When she entered the bathroom, he paused.

"I just need some painkillers." She came back out a moment later, pills in her hand.

Cullen sighed, then took her free hand and led her from the room. In the kitchen, he poured her a glass of water. After she swallowed the medicine, he walked up behind her and started kneading her shoulders.

"Oh," she groaned. "That feels wonderful."

Her muscles were tighter than he thought they'd be. Hard knots resisted his touch. It was no wonder both her head and her side hurt.

He worked her shoulders and upper back until the muscles were pliable under his fingertips. "Feel better?" Gently, he turned her to face him.

She tipped her head, a soft smile on her pretty face. "Much. Thank you."

Cullen raised a hand, brushing her silky blonde hair back from her face. "I'm glad. You should get some rest now."

The nod she gave told him she agreed, but the slight stiffening of her spine put him on alert, and it hit him what the problem was. "Do you want me to stay?"

A flash of relief blipped through her gaze before she shook her head. "No. I'll be okay. You don't need to babysit me. I'm a big girl."

"I never said you weren't. Sometimes we just need other people around. I don't mind staying." He glanced toward the living room and the couch. "Your couch is comfortable enough. I'll be fine sleeping there."

She rolled her eyes and let out a little snicker. "Your feet will hang over the side."

He shrugged. "Maybe."

"No, not maybe. My feet end up on the opposite armrest. You're four inches taller than me."

"I still don't mind. I won't sleep well at home, knowing you're here alone and afraid to fall asleep."

With a huff, she shifted her balance. "Why do you have to use logic at a time like this?"

He kept his expression carefully blank, but feared his eyes gave away his mirth at her consternation. "Because it's logical?"

Her giggle made him grin. He wrapped his arms around her and tugged her close. "Would you rather I be all macho and take charge instead?"

Giggling more, she raised an eyebrow. "What do you mean?"

Cullen straightened, deciding that showing her would be easier. He let her go except for her hand. "Come on." He tugged, moving toward her bedroom.

Her smile died and something else—something that looked like pure want—crossed her face. "What?"

"You're going to take a shower. Or a bath. I don't care which. Then you're going to crawl into bed and not worry about me out here. I'll clean up the kitchen, then bunk down on the couch."

"Cullen—"

He stopped in the doorway to her room and covered her lips with one finger. "No. Let me take care of you."

She huffed again. "Fine."

"Thank you." He let his smile loose, amused by how perturbed she seemed at giving in.

"But I don't want to hear it tomorrow when your neck is stiff and your knees hurt from being curled up on the too short couch all night." She shook a finger in his face.

His smile grew. "I'll be fine." He turned her around and gave her a gentle push into the bedroom. "Go. Shower, sleep. I'll see you in the morning."

The sweet smile that appeared on her face told Cullen he made the right decision. The apprehension in her eyes was gone.

"Okay. Thank you."

"Anytime, beautiful." He reached for the door. "Goodnight."

"Goodnight."

Cullen stepped back, pulling the door with him.

"Oh, wait."

He paused, stepping into the doorway again.

"There's a blanket on the back of the couch, but you need a pillow." She walked to the bed and pulled back the covers, removing one from the stack. "Is one enough?"

"Should be." He took the pillow. Her scent wafted up to him from the gray cotton pillowcase, and he bit back a moan. Now he'd be the one lucky to get any sleep. Having her scent in his nose all night but not having her beside him would be torture. "Thanks." Giving her what he hoped was a pleasant smile and not a grimace through his clenched teeth, he backed out of the room and shut the door.

Crossing the room, he tossed the pillow onto the couch and went to the window, needing to get away from her enticing scent. It was no use, though. The light fragrance was in his nostrils now; it wasn't going anywhere. He growled at himself for his self-inflicted sexual frustration, then went to the kitchen and cleaned up, hoping the process would ease some of the tension in his muscles—and elsewhere.

Once he had everything washed and put away, he'd relaxed somewhat. Enough to lie down and go to sleep.

Cullen made a quick circuit of the house, making sure all the doors and windows were locked, then shut the lights off. Untucking his shirt and toeing off his shoes, he laid down on the couch and spread the blanket draped on the back over his body. Piper's scent surrounded him again, but this time, it helped lull him to sleep.

When the alarm on his phone went off at five a.m., Cullen woke to find he actually slept well. His back was a bit stiff, but he felt rested.

Sitting up, he stretched, a yawn cracking his jaw, then pushed off the blanket and got up. Padding to the kitchen, he turned on the light and dug through Piper's cabinets until he found the coffee. He wasn't sure what time she woke up, but he'd make coffee and have a cup, then head home to shower and change before leaving for the hospital. He had morning rounds to make before his clinic hours. If she got up before he left, great. If not, she'd have coffee waiting for her and he'd call her later. He wasn't about to go wake her, though, just to say goodbye. She'd been exhausted last night.

The coffeepot gurgled, and fresh coffee dribbled into the carafe, filling the kitchen with its rich aroma. He normally didn't drink any until after his workout, but today was not normal. There would be no workout, and he wanted to be awake for the drive out to his house.

Lifting the carafe, he poured himself a mug, then set it

back on the warming plate to let it finish brewing. While he sipped the hot liquid, he opened drawers, searching for a notepad and a pen so he could leave Piper a note. Finding what he wanted, he scrawled out a quick message, then stuck the note to the counter in front of the coffeepot.

Cullen went to the living room and folded the blanket, putting it on the back of the sofa, then donned his shoes. Knowing he needed to get going so he wouldn't be late, he gulped down the rest of his hot coffee, ignoring the heat. He'd long since become immune to hot liquids, having slammed back more than his share of scalding hot drinks in the last twenty years. Setting his mug in the sink, he put on his coat and left, locking the door behind him.

Fat snowflakes drifted from the sky as he got in his car. The forecast called for more snow this afternoon. He hoped he made it back to Foggy Mountain before it started up. Then it would just be a short drive home from the clinic. No more than it was from Piper's to his house.

Backing out of her driveway, he meandered through the deserted streets and exited the city. A mile outside of town, he turned down the country lane that led to his house. There, he pulled into his garage and went inside.

Cullen hurried through his morning routine and was soon back in the car and on his way to Asheville. Parking in the doctors' lot, he went inside.

As soon as he stepped into the E.R., he noticed the buzz going through the staff. Normally, this early, the E.R. staff were more subdued. But today, they were wide awake, talking animatedly.

He walked up to the one of the attendings on duty, Dr. Brewer. "Hey, Devon. What's going on?"

"We had some excitement overnight. Ambulance crew brought in the pharmacy manager, Tillie Trufant. Her husband found her in the garage in her car with the motor running."

"What? Is she still alive?"

He nodded. "She's critical, but we stabilized her. She just went up to the ICU about fifteen minutes ago."

"Are the police with her? Or her husband? Is he here?"

Devon frowned. "Why are you so interested?"

"Reasons. Are the cops still here?" He wasn't about to add Piper's name to the gossip mill.

"I'm not sure."

"Okay, thanks." Backing away, Cullen changed direction and headed for the staff elevators. He needed to talk to the cops on Tillie's case. If she tried to kill herself, he knew why. And if she didn't, she was still in grave danger. Piper could be too.

Punching the button to call the elevator, he willed it to hurry. He tapped his fingers on his thigh, trying to expel his nervous energy.

The doors opened to an empty car, and he stepped on, then pushed the button for the ICU. He jabbed the button that closed the doors. They slid shut, and the elevator started upward. Moments later, it stopped, and he got out, heading straight for the nurses' station.

"Dr. Tate. Good morning." One of his favorite nurses, Pam O'Brien, smiled at him from behind the desk. Fiftyish, with salt-and-pepper hair, she oozed competence. If he were ever in the ICU, he'd want her taking care of him. "You're early today."

"Dr. Brewer said Tillie Trufant was brought up here. Did the police accompany her?"

Her smile died as a frown took its place at his abrupt non-greeting. "They did, but they left with her husband just a few minutes ago."

"Do you know where they went?"

She shook her head. "Maybe check with security? I don't think they were leaving the hospital."

"Great. Thank you." He spun around, heading for the elevators again.

"What about your rounds?" She called after him.

"I'll be back later," he said over his shoulder. Reaching the elevator, he pushed the button to go down. The doors slid open, and he stepped in. It whisked him downstairs again.

Back on the first floor, he turned away from the E.R. and went down the hall to the security office. Opening the door, he stepped inside.

The officer behind the desk looked up. "Dr. Tate?"

"Hi. Do you have Tillie Trufant's husband here?"

The man frowned. "He's in the back with the police. Why?"

"I need to speak to the police handling her case. Can you let them know, please?"

Still frowning, the officer rose from his chair. "Uh, sure. Just a minute." He disappeared through the door behind him.

Cullen lifted a hand, laying it on the counter, and tapped his fingers, then stuffed it in his pocket, recognizing the nervous fidget. He took a deep breath, focusing inward. His emotions were getting the better of him, and he needed to remember he was in control. Flipping out over Piper's safety wouldn't solve anything, and could make things worse because he wasn't thinking straight.

The door behind the desk opened again, but it wasn't the security officer who stepped out.

"Ben?" Cullen frowned as his friend stepped out of the back office.

"Cullen, what's going on? Smith said you need to talk to me about Dr. Trufant."

"Why are you handling her case?"

"She lives in Ferris County, so it's my jurisdiction. Why are you here?"

"We need to talk. I'm not so sure Tillie tried to kill herself."

Another man pushed his way past Ben. What little hair he had stuck out in disheveled waves. He peered at Cullen through black-framed glasses. "What do you know? I told Sheriff Davidson Tillie would never do this. What's going on?"

"Mr. Trufant, let's take a breath and calm down." Ben held his hands up and patted the air.

"I don't want to calm down. I want to know what he knows." Mr. Trufant pointed at Cullen.

"And I will find out." Ben put a gentle hand on Mr. Trufant's shoulder. "Let's get you some coffee and a snack while I speak to Dr. Tate." Ben motioned one of the guards forward, who ushered the distraught man to the back. Shutting the door, Ben turned astute eyes on Cullen. "All right, talk. What do you know?"

"Something's going on in the pharmacy." He glanced away, knowing his next words could cause some huge headaches for the hospital. But the incident with Tillie changed the game. He had to protect Piper. Cullen looked at Ben. "I think someone has been stealing drugs."

"What? You have evidence of this?"

"Not me. Piper. Though I guess it's more what she's seen than hard proof."

"Back up. Piper Riordan? Jake's wife's friend?"

Cullen nodded. "She can give you more detail, but she's noticed some discrepancies in the inventory. Last week, she took her concerns to Tillie and one of the other pharmacists. Now Tillie's in a coma. Either she was involved in the thefts and thought suicide was the only way out, or someone did this to her. I'm betting on the latter. Piper got a letter. It told her to mind her own business or she'd be next."

Ben huffed a sigh and pressed his thumb and index finger to his eyes. "Dammit."

"We made a report to Foggy Mountain PD last night. They have the letter."

"Okay. I'll find out where they're at in processing it. Where's Piper?"

"Probably on her way in. She had to work today."

"Can you call her? Tell her to come straight to security when she gets here. I'll call the pharmacy and let them know she'll be there once we're finished."

Nodding, Cullen took his phone from his pocket and pulled up her name on the screen. It rang several times, then rolled to voicemail. "She's not answering." He hung up.

"Try again." Ben sent a quick glance at him as he lifted the guard's desk phone to his ear to call the pharmacy.

Cullen touched the screen again, but got more of the same. He let out a soft growl and lowered the phone. Ben hung up and looked at him. Cullen shook his head. "Still nothing. If she's driving, she might not want to answer. Her Jeep is a little older, so she might not be able to connect her phone to her car."

"Okay. I'll post someone at the pharmacy staff entrance and intercept her." Ben lifted his cell from the cargo pocket of his pants.

"Sounds good. I need to do rounds, but I'm going to look at Tillie's chart. See what tests were run on her and talk to her attending." He wanted to know if they'd looked for sedatives. If not, he hoped there was enough blood from the previous tests left to test again. Anything they took now would be contaminated.

Ben nodded. "Let me know what you find."

"Will do." Cullen tossed a hand up in a wave as he exited the security office.

Worry and determination warred within him as he kept a brisk pace to the elevator. He wanted answers, but he also wanted to go wait with Ben's deputy and reassure Piper that everything would be okay. That they were doing everything they could to find out what happened to Tillie.

The elevator dinged as he reached it. Another doctor stepped off, and Cullen offered her a tight smile and a brief nod as she walked around him, then got on.

Muscles in his jaw worked as he hit the button to take him to the ICU, and the doors slid shut. What bothered him the most about this situation wasn't them not knowing who was behind the thefts and possibly Tillie's condition. It was knowing it was someone in the pharmacy, and that Piper had to go to work with no clue who to look out for. None of them knew who she could trust.

She was on her own.

Twenty

Sipping on the coffee Cullen so thoughtfully made before he left this morning, Piper rounded the corner of the hallway at the hospital. Her step faltered as she took in the sheriff's deputy and security guard standing outside the pharmacy staff entrance. The guard noticed her approaching.

"Ma'am, are you Piper Riordan?"

Apprehension pricked her skin. "Yes."

"We need you to come with us," the deputy said.

She frowned. "What? Why? What's going on?"

"Sheriff Davidson has some questions for you." The deputy held an arm out to the side and took a step toward her. "Please follow us?"

"Um, okay. I need to tell my boss what's going on, though."

"The sheriff already called." He gestured down the hall again. "Please?"

Curious and a little worried, she followed him and the guard through the corridors to the security office. The guard let them in, ushering her into a room in the back.

"Have a seat." The deputy motioned to the table and

chairs. "The sheriff should be in momentarily."

She sat down and watched as he pulled the door closed. Piper set her coffee, purse, and lunch bag on the table, then glanced around the room. Windowless, the gray room was devoid of any personality. The only adornment was the camera mounted in one corner.

What was going on? She was sure it had something to do with the drug discrepancies at the pharmacy, but what? Why had she been hauled into what amounted to an interrogation room? And why was Ben Davidson involved? The hospital was out of his jurisdiction.

The door swung inward, startling her. She jumped and pressed a hand to her chest.

"Sorry." Ben gave her a chagrined look as he walked in and sat down across from her. The yellow notepad he carried landed on the table with a quiet slap.

"You're fine. I'm just a little jumpy. What's going on?"

He expelled a quick breath. "Tillie Trufant is in the ICU."

Piper gasped.

"Her husband found her early this morning when he came home from a business trip. She was in her car in the garage with the door closed."

Hands flying to her face to cover her mouth, she gasped again. Why would Tillie try to kill herself? She seemed so happy. Moisture pooled in Piper's eyes.

"I have some questions for you."

Piper lowered her hands and sniffed, blinking hard. "Of course. How can I help?"

"Cullen mentioned you received a threatening letter yesterday. Can you tell me about that?"

She stared at him, trying to switch gears. "What? When did you talk to Cullen? What does the letter have to do with —" She broke off as the context of the letter hit her. *Mind your business, or you're next.*

Next.

Her eyes grew round. "Tillie didn't try to kill herself, did she?"

"The jury's still out on that. I'm looking into it. But considering the letter you received and the lack of any bodies —so far—it seems like a fair assumption that someone tried to kill her and make it look like a suicide, yes. Tell me about the letter. And what's been happening at the pharmacy. Cullen gave me a brief summary of what he suspects, but I want to hear things from you." He uncapped a pen and looked at her expectantly.

"Um." She raised a hand and ran it through her hair, gathering her thoughts. "So, I noticed some inventory errors a couple of weeks ago. There was a box of medication missing— but the inventory tracking was correct. I only noticed because I helped check it in when it arrived. Tillie had me doing an audit of the stacks, basically, to learn the inventory system and familiarize myself with the volume of medications the hospital pharmacy dispenses. Anyway, I noticed the supply on the shelf seemed low for what I remembered checking in. When I looked in the system, it only showed one case was ordered and shipped. But there were two. I know there were two."

"How did she seem when you told her?"

"As perplexed as me. I don't think she had any idea the inventory had been altered."

He tapped his pen on the paper. "Okay. What else did you notice? Cullen indicated there were multiple issues."

Piper told him about the mix-up with Mrs. Bailey's prescription as well as the extra open bottle of ephedrine she found. He wrote down the drug names and Sarah Bailey's name, then glanced up.

"Is there anything else you can think of to tell me? Anything else that seemed—off?"

She started to shake her head, then paused. "Actually,

when I told Tillie about the testosterone, she asked me not to say anything to Rosalina. She's the tech who was with me when I checked in the medicine."

He frowned. "Did she say why she didn't want you to say something?"

"No. Just that she wanted to look into things before anyone said anything to her."

His brows dipped as he processed that bit of information. "All right. I have a question about your encounter with Dr. Reid and the"—he glanced down at his notes—"Iclusig? He escalated that to Dr. Trufant, yes?"

"As far as I know. I didn't see him talk to her, and she never asked me about it."

"So, it's possible she didn't know?"

Piper frowned. "I guess so. You'd have to ask Dr. Reid if he talked to her." Though she hated to think the pharmacy manager wasn't aware of the situation. Maybe she should have followed up with Tillie.

"I will." He scooted his chair back. "I think that's all the questions I have for now. Thank you for coming down here. If I think of anything else, I'll be in touch."

Standing, she gathered her things. "Okay."

Ben moved to the door and held it open.

"Thanks." She breezed past him into the main office, but paused as a thought struck her. "Am I allowed to talk about any of this?"

"I'd prefer if you left things vague with your colleagues. You can talk to Cullen about it. I trust him not to gossip."

Piper couldn't help it—she giggled. "No. Cullen is the last person to spread gossip."

Ben flashed her a grin, then he sobered. Crossing his arms, he tipped his head. "He likes you, you know? I've never heard him talk about a woman before. He's always so serious. But he was worried about you this morning."

Warmth spread through Piper's body. "I like him too."

He gave her a quick nod. "Good. Don't hurt him."

"I won't." She had no intention of breaking Cullen's heart. She wanted it for herself and planned to hold on to it for a good long time. Smiling, she offered the sheriff a quick wave, then left the security office.

Cullen dominated her thoughts as she walked back to the pharmacy. She was both thankful and upset that he'd been gone when she woke up. The coffee and note he left were wonderful, but she would have liked to have seen his handsome face first thing. She could only imagine how delicious he'd look fresh from sleep. That thick dirty blonde hair tousled and his eyes still sleepy.

She pressed her lips together. *Whoo, boy.* That was why she was glad he'd been gone. Her sleepy brain wouldn't have stopped her body from reacting to his yummy presence. He tested her willpower when she was fully awake. But half-asleep? She didn't stand a chance.

Reaching the pharmacy, she swiped her badge over the card reader on the staff door and went inside as she rolled her eyes at herself. Who was she kidding? She didn't stand a chance, anyway. Half-asleep or not, she probably still would have planted a sloppy, hot kiss on him. It's what she planned to do the next time she saw him. She'd call it a thank you for leaving her coffee this morning.

A smile stretched over her face. She doubted he'd believe her reasoning, but he also wouldn't care. Anticipation coursed through her, and she made a mental note to call him after work. She'd order a pizza and invite him over again under the pretense of talking about the pharmacy situation.

It wouldn't be a lie, she thought as she stowed her things in her locker. She did want to talk about that. And if it led to the images running through her mind right now, well, so be it.

TWENTY-ONE

Annoyed and ready to leave, Piper tapped her toes and tried not to snap at the man at the counter. She didn't make the laws governing opiate medications. It wasn't her fault she couldn't fill his prescription early, so he had enough to take on vacation. She'd already explained she would be happy to help a pharmacy at his destination obtain the script, so he could get it filled there. He seemed to think that was too much trouble.

"Sir, I'm sorry." She lifted a hand. "I know it's inconvenient, but I can't help you any more than I have. I need to move on to the next person in line." She nodded to the five people standing behind him.

He glanced over his shoulder, then huffed. "Fine." Spinning on his heel, he marched out of the pharmacy. Piper resisted the urge to roll her eyes. Why did people have to be so petulant and insensitive? Would it kill them to be less dickish?

But she was a professional, so she plastered a smile on her face and greeted the next person in line. Thankfully, the next several customers were simple pickups and drop-offs, so she breezed through them. She glanced at the clock as the last customer in line stepped up. After this, she could go home. Finally.

It had been a week since she'd spent any time with Cullen. She'd called him after her interview with Sheriff Davidson, but he hadn't answered, so she left a message. Much later, she got a text saying he'd been called in for an emergency consult in Foggy Mountain and asked for a rain check. It was finally time for the rain check.

Handing the customer her order, Piper locked the register and stepped away. She waved to her co-workers coming on shift as she walked through the pharmacy to the back.

"Piper."

Dammit! So close! She tightened her hand on the door-knob, and for a fraction of a second, contemplated continuing through like she'd heard nothing. But she knew she couldn't do that. Her shoulders sagged, and she turned to look at her temporary boss, Dr. Steven Coombs. "Yes, sir?"

He crooked a finger. "I need to speak to you for a minute."

She let go of the doorknob and followed him into his office.

"Have a seat." He motioned to the chair in front of the desk.

Piper perched on the edge, glancing around. This was Tillie's office, but Dr. Coombs hadn't changed much. He had another office upstairs in administration. Because of the nature of the allegations against the pharmacy, the hospital put one of the administrators in charge until things were cleared up. She was glad. She didn't know who to trust.

Rounding the desk, Dr. Coombs sat down. Piper took the time to study him. He was near Cullen's age, maybe a little older. Well-groomed, he had a kind smile that put her at ease.

"So, I know you spoke to Sheriff Davidson, but the hospital has asked me to conduct an internal investigation into the workings of this pharmacy. I'm evaluating procedures and protocols to see where improvements can be made. Can you go over the discrepancies you noted?"

Piper sighed. So much for pizza night. "Yes. Do you mind if I send a text quick? I was supposed to have dinner with someone. I need to let him know we need to reschedule." *Again.*

"Of course. Go ahead."

Taking her phone from her scrubs pocket, she texted Cullen, then turned off the ringer and put it away. "Okay. I'm ready. Ask away."

"Start at the beginning." He uncapped a pen and pulled a notepad closer.

Piper recounted everything she knew, responding as he asked pointed questions about Tillie, Dr. Reid, and Rosalina. It took nearly an hour before he was satisfied. At that point, her stomach felt like it could gnaw its way out through her abdominal wall. Lunch was eons ago.

"Thank you for your time, Piper. I'm sorry I ruined your evening. I hope Dr. Tate understands."

She glanced at him in surprise, then narrowed her eyes. "How do you know I was having dinner with him?"

"The atmosphere of this hospital is like a small town. People talk. Especially when the handsome surgeon who never dates takes a shine to the new pharmacy technician." He smiled.

She shook her head in disbelief that their relationship would be the subject of office gossip. "I wonder if Cullen knows people are talking about him."

Dr. Coombs's smile widened. "Probably not. He's usually oblivious to most things. Which makes you very special. And it makes me happy that you're probably the one person in this pharmacy I know I can trust. And that's not based off of your word on what happened, but on the evidence I've gathered so far."

"Evidence?" Her smile quickly turned down. "Do you know who's behind the thefts?"

"I never said there were thefts."

She pinned him with a skeptical look. "Come on. You don't think all this was accidental." It wasn't a question. They both knew something more was going on.

"You're very astute. And no, I don't think this is a case of simple negligence. But I'm not at liberty to say more just yet." He rose abruptly.

Startled, Piper got to her feet.

"Thank you again for your time, Ms. Riordan. Have a good night."

Perplexed, and with more questions now than before she walked in, she headed for the door. "Goodnight, sir." Exiting his office, she went to the employee lounge and clocked out, then gathered her things. As she left the pharmacy, she opened her phone to see Cullen had replied to her message, asking her to call him when she left.

Touching the phone icon at the top of the screen, she lifted it to her ear.

"Hey. That took a while." Cullen's low voice rumbled over the line.

Piper smiled, happy to hear his voice. It instantly soothed her troubled mind. "Yeah. He had a lot of questions. I'm sorry I had to cancel."

"We're not canceling. I'm ordering pizza as soon as we hang up. I'll be waiting on your doorstep with it when you get home."

Heart soaring, her smile widened. "Really? That would be great. I've missed you this week."

"Same here. Now tell me what you want on your pizza."

Giggling, she told him what she liked as she stepped outside. A gasp stole her breath as the cold air hit her.

"Are you okay?"

"I'm fine. It's just cold this evening."

"It is. I might be in the car instead of on your doorstep."

She let out another soft laugh and hurried down the sidewalk to the parking garage. "Well, I'll drive as fast as possible, so you don't have to wait in the cold long."

"Just be careful. I want you in one piece."

"I want me in one piece too," she said, chuckling. "I'll see you soon."

"Sounds good."

They said their goodbyes and hung up. Piper stuffed the phone into her coat pocket and pulled out her keys. She was probably close enough now for her remote start to work. She hoped. Her car was on the top floor, about as far from the elevator as possible. She'd been running behind this morning, so when she arrived, there were very few employee spaces left. It was the top floor of the far parking garage or the parking lot on the other side of the hospital from the pharmacy. She pressed the button on the remote and hoped it worked.

Reaching the garage, she scurried through the doors to the elevator vestibule and breathed a sigh of relief, happy to be out of the wind. It cut right through her thin scrub pants and left her legs feeling like popsicles.

Piper reached for the call button to go up. It lit up red when she pressed it. Crossing her arms, she bounced on the balls of her feet, trying to stay warm. She might be out of the wind, but the vestibule wasn't heated.

The doors swished open behind her, and the sound of a baby screaming drew her attention. She glanced back to see a woman pushing a double stroller and carrying a young child on her hip. The stroller caught on the threshold, threatening to tip. The woman groaned and pulled on the handle, trying to manhandle it over the strip of metal. Piper hurried forward to help her get it inside.

"Thank you. I'm so done with this day." She pushed as Piper pulled, and it cleared the doorway.

"I feel you on that. Do you want some help getting to your car? You look like you've got your hands full." In addition to the child she carried and the crying baby, a toddler sat in the other stroller seat. The woman's face said she was more than done. She was exhausted, if the dark circles under her eyes were anything to go by, and nearing her wit's end.

Moisture gathered in the woman's eyes. "That would be wonderful. My husband couldn't get off work to come with me, so I've been wrangling all three by myself while the E.R. staff patched Bradley up." She jiggled the boy on her hip, who had a bandage wrapped around his forehead. "We're all just done."

Piper offered her a kind smile. She couldn't imagine keeping three kids happy through an emergency visit. Her pizza date could wait a few minutes while she helped this stressed young mom get on the road. The elevator dinged behind her. "Come on. Let's get you headed home."

"Thank you." The woman pushed the stroller forward while Piper held the elevator door open.

"What floor?"

"Six."

Pushing the button, Piper straightened and watched the doors close. The elevator rose, whisking them to the sixth floor in seconds. It dinged, and the doors slid open. She held them while the woman stepped out.

"I'm over here." Tipping her head, the woman started down the aisle and soon stopped behind a black minivan. It beeped, and the lights flashed as she unlocked it.

"What do you want me to do?" Piper paused beside the stroller.

Both the side doors slid open. The woman walked to the side nearest Piper and put Bradley in the car. She turned and looked at Piper. "Would you strap my daughter into her seat while I put the infant seat in and buckle Bradley?"

"Of course."

The woman walked past her and lifted the toddler from the stroller, then walked back to the same door and set the young girl into the car seat. Piper took her place and worked the straps around the child, who stared up at her with a curious frown and wide brown eyes.

While she did that, the woman snapped the infant seat onto the base in the car, then climbed in and buckled her son in the third row. Piper went to the stroller and removed the bags from the bottom, then folded it up.

"Oh, thank you." She pushed another button on her remote and the back hatch lifted.

Piper picked up the stroller and put it in the van. "You're welcome. I hope things calm down and you can have peace the rest of your evening."

"Me too." The woman smiled. "What's your name?"

"Piper."

"Well, Piper, I'm Jess. Thank you for your help. It's appreciated." She held out a hand.

"You're welcome." Piper took her hand and shook it. "Have a good night."

With a nod, Jess moved toward the driver's door. Piper waved and walked back to the elevator to take it to the seventh floor. She pressed the call button and waited. It arrived moments later, and she stepped inside. The doors closed, and it winged upward a floor.

Exiting the car, she huddled deeper into her coat. Up here, she was above most everything else except the hospital, and the wind was brutal. Picking up her pace, she took a couple of running steps toward her car and the warmth it offered. They'd be having hot chocolate with their pizza tonight.

A bright light burned into her retinas a nanosecond before a boom split her eardrums and a pressure wave sent her sailing through the air. The blast of heat was the last thing she felt before her world went black.

TWENTY-TWO

Cullen's phone beeped in his ear, signaling another call. He pulled it away to look at the screen and groaned as he saw the number for the hospital in Asheville on the screen. "Dammit." He put the phone back to his ear. "Cancel that order for now." He hung up on the kid at the pizza shop and answered the hospital's call. "Tate."

"Dr. Tate, this is Lindsey in the E.R. We've had an incident here and we need you to come in."

Cullen's muscles tensed at the note of hysteria just banked in her voice.

"Someone set off a bomb in the parking garage. We're not sure how many casualties yet, but part of the structure collapsed."

Cursing, Cullen stood from his seat on the couch and ran toward the garage. "I'm at home, so it'll be thirty minutes at least, but I'm on my way."

"Okay. We should have a better triage set up by then."

"Great. I'll be there as soon as I can." He hung up and reached for his coat, thrusting his arms into the sleeves. Shoving his feet into a pair of tennis shoes, he grabbed his lanyard with his hospital ID and raced out the door into the garage. The car beeped as he clicked the remote in his pocket. Cullen hopped inside and pushed the button to raise the garage door, then started the car. As soon as the door was up, he put the car in reverse and backed out of the garage.

Once he was out on the highway, he set the cruise control on his car, knowing he'd speed—a lot—if he didn't. Tapping his fingers on the steering wheel, he ran through possible injuries and treatments in his head as the miles sped by. Soon, the lights of Asheville came into view. It was then he remembered Piper.

"Shit." He pushed the button on his steering wheel to make a call. "Call Piper." This was why he didn't do relationships. Work liked to take over his brain and push everything else out.

The phone rang through the car speakers several times, then rolled to voicemail. Cullen frowned and hung up, then tried again. "Call Piper."

His frown deepened as the call rolled to voicemail once more. Unease crept up his spine. Where was she?

Leaving a message, he turned off the cruise control and drove faster. He doubted there would be any cops out here to stop him, anyway. They were all at the hospital.

He cruised down the interstate and took the exit to the hospital. Turning onto the drive, he pulled up to the cop directing traffic and rolled down his window.

"Sir, I'm sorry. You'll have to—"

"I'm a doctor. They called me in." He held up his lanyard.

The officer looked at it, then waved him forward. "Park in the first lot. We've got access blocked going any further."

Cullen nodded, rolling up his window as he drove away. He turned into the parking lot the officer indicated and pulled into the first space he found. Shutting off the vehicle, he grabbed his ID and climbed out, then sprinted toward the building, thankful he'd given thought to how much Piper liked him in jeans and changed out of his slacks and loafers. His feet would thank him later that he was in sneakers.

The emergency room door slid open, admitting him to the chaos reigning inside. Voices bounced off the walls as nurses and doctors yelled instructions over the din. Cullen went to the nurses' station and looked at the triage board.

"Oh, thank God."

He glanced over at the nurse who'd come up beside him. "Where do you need me most?"

"Trauma bay five. A chunk of the parking garage fell off the side and landed on a van exiting the building. Mom took the brunt of the impact. Dr. Colton's working on her, but she had three kids in the car, one of them only two months old."

"Jesus. Okay. Are they all in the same room?" He couldn't see how they could fit three stretchers in the same space, but crazier things had happened here.

She shook her head. "Just the middle kid. She was right behind mom. The older one and the baby seem fine. Neonatology has the baby. The four-year-old is in bay ten."

He whirled, heading for bay five. The nurse, Joy, followed him.

"Injuries?" he asked as they wove through the throng of people.

"Broken legs. She's got head trauma, too, but she's awake."

"How long has she been in here?"

"Not long. Firefighters just brought them all up. They had to extract them first."

"How long ago did this happen?"

"Maybe thirty or forty minutes? We heard a boom, and the ground shook. Then we heard another, softer boom. When we looked outside, there was all kinds of dust in the air and we could see a fire on top of the garage."

That unease from earlier came back. "Were any hospital staff injured in the blast?"

She nodded. "Not sure how many yet. They've brought in a handful so far. Mostly, though, it's been patients and visitors."

"Did they bring in a woman named Piper Riordan?"

"I'm not sure. There have been so many people. Sorry." She paused outside of trauma bay five.

"It's okay, Joy. Thanks." He shoved thoughts of Piper out of his mind. His focus needed to be on the young girl beyond the curtain.

Pushing the fabric aside, he walked into the craziness. A resident, looking frazzled, stood to the side. His eyes were wide behind his wire-framed glasses as he listened to the nurses rattle off information over the cries of his tiny patient.

Cullen let out a sharp whistle. All the talking ceased. Even the girl quieted for a brief moment. He pointed at the most experienced nurse in the room, Karl Athens. "Give me the rundown."

"Nineteen-month-old female. Driver's side passenger in a minivan that got hit with a sizeable chunk of concrete. Visible fractures to both lower extremities and a contusion above her left eye. Pupils are equal and reactive. Pulse is one-oh-five, oxygen sats are ninety-eight percent. We've been unable to get a blood pressure on her yet."

"Hang fluids and push one milligram of morphine. Let's see if we can calm her down. Where's x-ray? And has anyone contacted CT?"

"X-ray is down the hall. They're working their way through the bays. CT has a line. She's in it, but there are a couple of patients ahead of her," Karl replied.

Cullen nodded and stepped forward. "We know her name?"

"Regan."

He leaned down and smiled at the girl. "Hi, Regan. My name's Cullen. I know you're scared, but my team and I are going to make you better, okay?"

The girl hiccupped, her breath hitching on a sob. "Mo-mommy."

"I know you want your mommy, but she can't be here right now. We'll get you to her as soon as we can. I need to take a look at you, so you're going to feel my hands." He held his hands up and wiggled his fingers. Stepping back, he grabbed a pair of gloves and put them on.

Another nurse, Emily, came over with two syringes of clear liquid. "Morphine going in." She raised the IV line and attached the first syringe.

Happy the girl would soon get some relief, he leaned over her again. "Okay, darlin', here we go." He put his fingers behind her neck, feeling the vertebrae. She didn't flinch, so he moved down, going over her collarbones and down her arms. He felt her ribs and abdomen. All seemed well. Her legs, though, were another story. The debris must have landed in her lap.

Not long after the nurse finished administering the morphine and flushed the line, the x-ray technician appeared. The films revealed several breaks that would need to be set surgically. Cullen contacted orthopedics. After making sure she was stable, he moved to the next patient waiting to be seen.

He threw back the curtain on bay eight and froze. Piper laid on the bed, her eyes closed.

"Piper?"

Those jade green eyes fluttered open. He crossed the floor to her bedside and took her hand. "Where are you hurt? What happened?"

"My car blew up."

Shock made his ears ring. He opened his mouth, only to

close it again and swallow before he could speak. "Do you remember what happened?"

"Sort of. I helped some woman with her kids, then went to my car. I remember walking off the elevator, then nothing. The next thing I knew, I woke up flat on my back with people standing over me." She raised a hand and laid it over her forehead. "My head hurts."

"You probably have a concussion." He ground his molars, wanting to examine her, but knew he couldn't. "I need to go find another doctor to oversee your care." It killed him to turn her over to someone else, but ethically, he had to. He was too close to her to be objective. Already, he wanted to skip her to the front of the line for CT.

He took a step back, ready to release her and find another doctor, but she tightened her grip. "Stay. Just for a minute. I know you're busy, but I—" Her voice cut off as her lower lip trembled and tears spilled over her eyelids.

Cullen curled his fingers around hers and raised a hand to her head, stroking her hair. A fine tremor ran through his hand as it started to sink in just how close he came to losing her. How did she come to mean so much to him so quickly?

"I'm so scared, Cullen. What's going on? Why would someone blow up my car? Is this related to the pharmacy?"

"I don't know, honey. Maybe. Ben will get to the bottom of it, though. And in the meantime, you can stay with me, so you aren't alone." If she tried to fight him on that last part, he'd do whatever it took to change her mind.

But she gave him a feeble nod and inhaled a shaky breath. "Okay."

He wasn't sure whether to be happy or alarmed that she agreed so fast. Piper had an independent streak the size of Texas. She was either terrified or more injured than he thought.

"Dr. Tate?"

He glanced back as Joy poked her head in the room.

"I'm sorry. We need you in bay two."

"Okay. I'll be right there."

With a nod, she backed out.

Cullen leaned down and kissed Piper's forehead. "I'll find you later. Don't you dare leave this hospital without me."

She snorted. "How would I get home? My car's a twisted pile of burned metal."

His mouth twisted. Damn. He forgot. "Right. Sorry."

She waved a hand. "I'm fine. Go. Save someone."

For the first time in his life, he didn't want to do his duty. He wanted to stay right where he was.

Piper pulled her hand from his and nudged his arm, sensing his hesitation. "Go. I'll be fine. And I promise not to call a cab or Mackenzie to come get me."

He sucked in a breath, backing toward the door. "Okay. I'll hold you to that. Don't make me track you down." He extended an arm to point at her.

A soft smile lifted one side of her mouth. "What are you gonna do? Spank me?"

Fire ignited in his veins. "Maybe." He winked. "See you soon." Spinning around, her soft giggle followed him from the room.

TWENTY-THREE

Piper wrinkled her nose against the smell of old coffee as she raised her cup. She didn't know why she kept drinking it. It had long since gone cold. She thought about warming it up, but that meant getting up, and her head hurt too much for that. Plus, she wanted to sleep tonight. More coffee would just keep her awake.

A yawn stretched her jaw. Maybe not.

The door to the lounge where she sat opened. Piper glanced over to see Sheriff Davidson in the doorway.

"Hi, Piper."

"Hey, Sheriff." She sat up straighter, hoping he brought information on what happened. She still couldn't remember anything beyond walking off the elevator.

He crossed the room and grabbed a chair from the table, bringing it to where she sat on the couch. "Tell me what you remember," he said as he sat down and leaned forward, bracing his elbows on his knees.

"Not much, unfortunately. I walked off the elevator, then it's blank until I woke up with paramedics standing over me."

"Okay. And you know it was your car that exploded?"

She nodded, then wished she hadn't when pain lanced through her head. Wincing, she rubbed her forehead. Her fingers were cold against her face. "Yeah. They mentioned it was a Wrangler. Considering everything going on, I figured it had to be mine. From the look of things in the E.R., it must have been a good-size bomb. I don't understand how I'm not hurt worse."

"So, we've walked the scene, and the arson investigator took a cursory peek at your car. The bomb wasn't that big, but because of where you parked, it caused some structural damage to the garage. Part of the wall fell, which destabilized the floor. It collapsed under the weight of the cars. Most of the people hurt were injured from falling debris." He sat back and ran a hand through his hair. "As for you, from what we can tell, the concrete ledge between you and your Jeep saved you. It mitigated the pressure wave enough that it just knocked you off your feet. You either hit your head when you landed, or something glanced off your skull."

Piper drew in a shaky breath and wrung her hands in her lap. Her pale skin turned paler with the pressure. "I can't believe this is happening. All I did was notice some discrepancies. I was doing my job." Her voice ended on a tight whisper, and she closed her eyes, then pressed her lips together as tears threatened.

"Criminals aren't always rational. They see you as a threat. Maybe the other techs have noticed problems, but kept their mouths shut. Or maybe someone threatened them, too, and they heeded the warning. You got a letter, right?"

She nodded. "But since then, I haven't noticed anything else, so there's been nothing for me to report. Why is this guy still coming after me?"

"You've talked to me. And the hospital said they're conducting their own investigation into Dr. Trufant. You've set a ball in motion that's put him or her—or them—in danger of being exposed. I don't think this about silencing you. It's about revenge for disrupting their operation."

Her mouth flattened. "Great. So even if I refuse to cooperate with the authorities now, I still have a giant bullseye on my back." She growled and rubbed her hands over her face.

"Unfortunately, yes. But, given the escalation, you should get some police protection. I just don't know who will be providing it. My office took the initial report on Dr. Trufant's attack, and Foggy Mountain PD has the letter you received, but the pharmacy and bombing investigations belong to Asheville. I imagine they'll bring the state investigative bureau in now as well. And probably the ATF."

"Man, this is a mess." She leaned back in her chair, sliding down as she crossed her arms over her chest and closed her eyes.

"It is."

She sighed, her mind whirling before it landed on a single thought. Sitting up, she opened her eyes. "So, why did the car blow up before I was in it?"

"Not sure yet. The arson guy has only done a quick walk-through where it's safe. It's going to take some work for the crime scene unit to find all the pieces and reconstruct the device." He tipped his head. "Did you vary your routine at all?"

"A little. Dr. Coombs—the temporary pharmacy manager—asked to talk to me at the end of my shift. He wanted to hear about what I'd noticed. We talked for nearly an hour. Then, once I was in the garage, I stopped to help a mom get to her car. She had—" Piper's voice cut out. She'd heard from one of the nurses that part of the building hit a minivan as it exited the garage. A woman and her three children were inside. Piper hadn't been able to verify it was the same woman she helped, but she feared it was.

She cleared her throat and continued. "She had three kids

with her and two of the three were quite upset. I offered to help her get them in her car. She was on the floor below me." She looked down at her hands, picking at her nails, then up at him once more. "I think they were in the van that was hit. Can you tell me if the woman's name was Jess?"

Ben's expression remained stoic as he nodded.

Tears welled in her eyes. "Dammit. If I hadn't stopped to help them, she might not have been exiting then."

"Hey. You can't blame yourself. You said she parked on the sixth floor?"

Piper nodded.

"There's a lot of damage on the sixth floor. Things could have been worse for her and her kids. From what I heard, while she and her daughter have some serious injuries, they're going to be fine."

A flash of relief brought some warmth to her cold hands. "And the other two are okay?"

He nodded. "As far as I know. And no one's died."

She blew out a breath. "That's something, at least." She folded her arms around herself and rubbed her upper arms. "Have you seen Cullen? And do I need to talk to anyone else? I'm ready to get out of here."

"Are you allowed to leave?" He swirled a finger, motioning to the bandage at her hairline.

"Yeah. Amazingly, I don't have a concussion. I'm just banged up." All her muscles hurt from the blast, and she had more bruises than she could count. It really was a miracle she wasn't hurt worse.

"All right. I'll go look for Cullen. You can give your formal statement tomorrow. My notes from our chat should be enough for the investigators right now." He stood. "Hang tight a few minutes. I'll track Cullen down and make him take you home."

"Thanks, Sheriff." Her shoulders drooped. Home

sounded wonderful. She wanted to soak in a hot bath, then climb into bed.

"You're welcome." Offering her a soft smile, he left her alone.

Their conversation replayed in her head. The first tears she'd shed spilled over her eyelids as relief punched her in the gut that no one died. She knew the blast wasn't her fault, but it still felt that way. She'd been the target. No matter the rationality, she was glad no one died because of her.

TWENTY-FOUR

Cullen's tennis shoes tapped a soft thud on the hallway floor as he hurried down the corridor to the lounge where Piper waited. It hadn't taken much prodding from Ben for Cullen to hand off his patients to Dr. Brewer. Everyone was stable and the E.R. had quieted. Piper needed him more than the hospital.

He opened the lounge door, searching the dim room for her. She'd curled her tall form into one corner of the couch. The light from the hall hit her face, and he saw the tears coursing down her cheeks.

His heart lurched, and he hurried forward. "Hey. Honey, it's okay." He sat next to her and pulled her onto his lap. She curled into him, and he wrapped his arms around her, holding her tight while she cried. Rocking gently, he smoothed her hair back and placed a soft kiss on her temple. "Everything is okay. Everyone will be fine."

She sniffed and lifted her head. Dashing at the tears on her face, she took a shaky breath. "I know. These are more tears of relief than anything. And release. Today's been nuts. Can you take me home now? I just want to go to sleep."

Cullen nodded and shifted her off his lap, then stood. He held out a hand and helped her up. Piper snagged her purse from the seat beside her and they walked out of the lounge, hand-in-hand.

Rather than lead them through the staff hallways to the exit, Cullen walked straight through the E.R. and out into the waiting room so they could leave through the emergency room doors. It was a more direct shot to his car.

Piper shivered as the cold air hit her. Cullen picked up the pace, wanting to get her warm. He took his keys from his pocket and activated the remote start, giving the vehicle a head start on warming.

Crime scene tape flapped in the breeze off to their right, blocking off access to the parking garage. People in Tyvek suits still walked around, gathering evidence. They glowed bright under the lights lining the road.

He turned his gaze away, preferring not to think about what could have been. Piper was safe. No one died. That was all that mattered right now. Ben and his colleagues would find who did this.

They found his car in the sea of the visitor's lot. Once ensconced inside, Cullen cranked up the heat and turned on the seat warmers, then pulled out of his space.

The drive north was quiet. If it weren't for the fact he knew Piper was utterly exhausted, he'd be worried. But the silence wasn't awkward. It was comfortable.

He reached over and took her hand. She gave it a squeeze, but still said nothing.

At the edge of Foggy Mountain, he turned off to head for his house. She sat up as the scenery changed.

"Where are we going?"

"My house. With what happened, I figured it wouldn't be a bad idea for you to be elsewhere tonight. And call me cavemanish, but I don't want to leave you alone."

Her brow pinched, then smoothed out, and she nodded. "I don't want to be alone."

Relieved she didn't argue or press the issue, he continued down the country road to his house.

The car's tires crunched on the gravel drive as he drove into the garage. As the door whirred closed, they got out and went inside.

"Do you want anything to eat?" Cullen gestured to the stainless-steel fridge tucked into the cabinetry as they entered the kitchen.

"No. I just want to take a bath, then go to sleep. Please tell me you have a giant tub I can soak in."

A smile toyed with his face. "I do, actually." He tipped his head. "Come on." Leading her from the kitchen, he turned, going up the staircase to the master suite.

"I don't have any fancy bath stuff, but the tub is a soaker and the water's hot." He stopped in the bathroom doorway and pushed the door open.

"That's fine. I just want to soak my muscles. Everything's stiff from the fall."

Cullen could understand that. She'd been hit by quite the shockwave, plus the impact of hitting the ground. Even with the hot soak, she'd probably still feel stiff and sore in the morning. "I have some Epsom salts. You should add those to your bath water. Let me get you something to sleep in." He stepped back and went to his closet, finding a pair of flannel pants with a drawstring and a t-shirt.

"Here." He held the items out.

"Thanks." She took them and held them to her chest.

"Are you sure you don't want anything to eat? I can make something while you bathe. When was the last time you ate?"

She frowned. "I had a snack around four. But I'm fine."

He held up a hand and ticked a finger side-to-side. "Seeing as it's now one in the morning, you need to put something in your stomach. Especially if you want to take any more pain medicine. What did they give you at the hospital?"

"Tylenol."

"Do you want some ibuprofen?"

She lifted a shoulder.

Cullen frowned, not liking this quiet, stoic version of Piper. "How about some toast and a glass of milk?" And the toast would have peanut butter on it.

"I guess that's fine. But I can make it when I get out."

"Nope." He backed toward the door. "You soak. I'll wait about fifteen minutes or so, then get it ready. I'll leave it on a tray in here on the bed. You can eat it, then go to sleep."

It was her turn to frown. "Isn't this your bedroom?"

"Yes, but I can sleep in the guest room."

"I don't want to chase you out of your room, Cullen. I can sleep in the guest room."

He shook his head. "My room is more comfortable. I keep the guest room closed off, so it's chilly in there. You stay here where it's warm."

She hesitated, glancing at the bed, then at him. "Are you sure?"

"Positive." He stepped into the hallway. "Take your bath. Epsom salts are under the sink. Your food will be waiting when you're done."

Piper bit the corner of her lip. "Thank you."

Smiling, he grasped the doorknob. "You're welcome." Before she could change her mind, he pulled the door shut and went downstairs.

Twenty-Five

Feeling the weight of the last several hours, Piper exited the bathroom, drying her hair with a towel. Despite her height, she swam in Cullen's clothes, but they were clean and warm.

Her stomach grumbled, responding to the sight of the tray on the bed. True to his word, he brought her toast and a glass of milk. There was also a dish of fresh fruit.

Smiling softly, she crossed to the bed and lifted the tray, then sat down in the chair by the window to eat. The scent of peanut butter wafted to her nose, and she pulled the two slices of toast apart. He'd made her a toasted peanut butter and jelly sandwich. Squishing them back together, she took a bite. Raspberry and the nutty flavor of the peanut butter spread over her tongue, and she moaned in delight. It was still warm. In just a few bites, she polished off the sandwich, then moved onto the fruit, devouring it. She'd been hungrier than she thought. And thirsty too. The glass of milk washed down the pain medicine he left her, and she quickly finished it.

She set the tray and glass on the floor by the chair, then turned off the light, ready to go to bed. Sliding between the light gray sheets on Cullen's king-size bed, she sighed as the mattress cocooned her in its pillowy softness. Eyes drifting shut, she waited for sleep to overtake her.

And waited... and waited.

Her thoughts swirled as her brain processed the day. Groaning, she opened her eyes and rolled over. She thought she'd worked through this at the hospital. Apparently not. More of the evening's events had come back to her in the tub as her body and mind relaxed. Now her brain wanted to replay it over and over again. It was just a flash of light. Why was that so fascinating? She didn't get it.

Flipping over again, she stared at the clock on the night-stand. At least she didn't have to work tomorrow. Though she almost preferred it. There wouldn't be much relaxing going on. Instead, she'd spend her day off writing a statement for the police and calling her insurance company, then finding a rental car. Oh, and worrying about whether the person who tried to kill her would try again.

The first spark of unease since she walked into Cullen's house skated down her spine. Was she safe here? Was Cullen? Just being around her could be dangerous. She should have insisted he take her to a hotel. At least there, she was surrounded by hundreds of witnesses and security cameras.

A loud crack sounded through the house, and she jumped.

"Geez. Get a grip, Piper," she mumbled to herself. It was just the house settling. The place was ancient. It's what old farmhouses did. Especially in the colder months.

Heaving a sigh, she flopped onto her back and stared up at the ceiling, just making out the light fixture in the moonlight coming in through the window.

This was dumb. She sat up and pushed the covers back, then got out of bed. She'd go downstairs and maybe find a book. Try to get her mind to focus on something else so she could go to sleep.

Her footfalls soft, she left the bedroom and went down-stairs to the living room, where she remembered seeing book-shelves. Turning on the lamp by the couch, she wandered to the overstuffed shelves, tipping her head so she could read the titles. Spine after spine showed medical-related books and journals. She sighed, hoping he kept some fiction somewhere. Though some of the medical journals might be dry enough— or confuse her—enough, she'd fall asleep reading.

Moving to the other shelf, she found what she wanted halfway down. He had a single shelf full of fiction titles. They were mostly action-adventure spy thrillers, but that worked. The mystery would engage her mind.

Book in hand, she retreated to the couch and curled up in the corner by the lamp. Cracking it open, she read the first paragraph, then had to read it again. Her mind refused to be dissuaded from the memories playing on repeat.

With a growl, she closed the book and got up. Maybe Cullen had stuff to make hot chocolate. Perhaps cooking would reset her brain.

Footfalls a little less quiet as her anger simmered, she went down the hall to the kitchen. Slapping a hand against the wall, she found the light switch and illuminated the room. Bright white cabinets and light gray walls met her gaze. She'd given the room a cursory glance when they arrived earlier, noting its clean, simple design. But now she noticed the top-of-the-line appliances and smooth quartz countertops. It was classy and elegant, but it lacked personality, just like the rest of the house.

Shopping for gifts for Cullen would be easy. She'd just start buying artwork.

Piper shook her head and stepped further into the kitchen, heading for the cabinets. She had her doubts he'd have what she needed, but maybe there was at least some herbal tea lurking.

Deep inside the pantry, she found a box of chamomile

tea. The top was dust-covered, telling her he didn't buy it. He'd mentioned his family visited last year, and she was betting his mom or sister bought it and left it here. The date on the box told her it was still good, so she took out a tea bag and found a mug in one of the cupboards. He didn't own a teakettle, so she put water in the mug and put it in the microwave.

When it beeped, she tore open the pouch and unfurled the string, plopping the bag in the hot water. With a few minutes to kill, she turned to the large farmhouse sink and the stack of dirty dishes inside. She'd clean up while she waited for her tea to steep. Piper opened the dishwasher, only to find it full.

Rolling her eyes, she reached for the first glass on the top rack. That's why there was still a sink-load of dirty dishes.

Plates clanked and silverware clinked as she put everything away. Once the clean dishes were where they belonged, she removed the tea bag from her mug, then went back to loading the dishwasher. Absorbed in her task, her mind blocked out her earlier thoughts.

"You don't have to do my dishes."

A shriek erupted from her chest, and she spun around, laying a hand over her racing heart. "Good Lord, where did you come from?" Her gaze raked over his tall form, and her heart sped up for a different reason. Soft gray cotton clung to his broad chest and shoulders. The black lounge pants outlined some interesting tidbits, and she couldn't help but wonder if he wore anything beneath. She was betting not.

He scratched at his head near his temple and yawned. "I heard the noise down here. Can't sleep?"

Taking a deep breath, Piper willed her heart rate back under control and her eyes back to his face. "No. My brain won't shut off. You look like you were asleep, though. I'm sorry I woke you. Go back to bed. I'm fine."

"I doubt that." He walked forward and took the handful

of dirty silverware from her. "You wouldn't be down here doing dishes at two a.m. if you were fine."

"What can I say? I like a clean kitchen." She rinsed the sink and reached for the tea towel hanging on the oven door.

He straightened from depositing the silverware in the dishwasher, one side of his mouth curling up. "Sure you do." Crossing his arms, he tipped his head. "So, what's keeping you awake?"

Piper sighed, realizing he wasn't going back to bed until she talked about what was on her mind. "I remembered more while I was in the bath. Just a quick flash of light. But for some reason, my mind won't stop focusing on that." Over and over, it replayed the moment she stepped off the elevator and turned toward her car. With a quick burst of fiery light, the memory cut off.

Cullen frowned, studying her. "Is there anything else in the moment? A person or a sound?"

A frown furrowed her eyebrows as she considered that. "I don't think so."

"Close your eyes and picture it. What do you see?"

She did as he said, freezing the image in her mind. "Just a burst of fire. It started under my car."

"Can you tell where? In the front?"

"No. It was more toward the middle." She opened her eyes.

"What about sounds? Did you hear anything out of the ordinary?"

She closed her eyes and played the scene in her head. Nothing jumped out at her. "No." She opened her eyes and shrugged. "It's just the light." Blowing out a breath, she reached for her tea and took a sip. The bitterness washed over her tongue and she grimaced. "Do you have any honey?"

He uncrossed his arms and turned, disappearing into the pantry. Piper opened the fridge, hoping he hadn't used all the milk for her snack earlier. The carton sat on the shelf, and she reached for it, only to change direction as she saw a carton of cream. Even better.

"Do you want some tea?" She glanced at him as he reemerged from the pantry with the honey bottle.

"No, I'm good." He handed her the honey.

"Thanks." She flipped open the top and squirted some into her drink. After adding the cream, she grabbed a spoon and stirred it up, then took a sip. Sweetness now balanced the tea's bitterness.

"Better?"

She nodded. "Much. I don't want to keep you up. I found a book, so I'm going to take it and my tea upstairs and try to wind down. Thank you for the snack earlier, by the way. It was delicious."

That half-smile quirked his full lips again. "Peanut butter toast is hardly gourmet food."

Piper giggled. "No, but it was warm and it hit the spot."

"Good." He held out a hand. "Come on. I'll walk you back to bed."

Smiling at the chivalrous gesture, she put her hand in his and followed him from the kitchen. They stopped in the living room to get the book she picked out, then went upstairs.

At the door to his bedroom, she fiddled with the edge of her teacup, holding it and the book between them, so she wouldn't be tempted to reach out and touch the muscular chest hidden beneath his gray t-shirt. It also helped block her view of his lower half.

"Do you think you can sleep now?"

She shrugged. "I guess we'll find out."

Those luscious lips turned down. "You need to rest."

"I know, but my brain can be stubborn. I'll probably toss and turn some more, even with the tea and the book. I think I'm just trying to process the shock of it all, and there's nothing to distract me when I'm lying there in the dark."

One dark blonde eyebrow lifted. He shuffled a half-step closer. "What if you had something more interesting to think about?"

Fire erupted in her veins at the heat that flared in his eyes. She swallowed, then licked her lips. His eyes drifted to them, and the heat in his gaze burned hotter. Was he suggesting what she thought he was? Were they ready for that?

She cleared her throat. She had to ask. "Such as?"

He took another half-step closer, and his chest bumped her knuckles. She clenched her fingers around the cup, so she didn't drop it.

"This." His head dipped, but he paused a hairsbreadth from her mouth.

Her belly clenched as his warm breath puffed over her face. Her scalp pricked as need raced along her nerve-endings. His eyes searched hers, then closed as he erased the gap and kissed her.

Piper moaned at the exquisite feel of his mouth on hers. They'd kissed before, but this kiss—it was on a different level. Maybe it was the hour or the intimacy of their attire and location. She didn't know. All she knew was it was different. Something had shifted between them. Their light, flirtatious relationship had just flipped to something wholly more serious and adult.

She clutched the teacup and book in her hands, wishing she didn't have them. Her fingers itched to feel his hair slide through them and to explore the peaks and valleys of his muscular torso. Not to mention parts south.

All too soon, he drew back. A satisfied smile toyed with his lips when Piper opened her eyes.

"There. That should give your brain something else to dwell on."

Dazed from the passion clouding her mind, it took her a moment to understand his meaning. Huffing a laugh, she pushed at his chest with the back of her hand, still holding her book. "Yes, but now I'll be sleepless for a different reason."

His lopsided smile came back. "That makes two of us." The smile faded, and he lifted a hand to skim her cheek with one finger. "Goodnight, Piper."

Need clenched her stomach again. How could such a simple touch make her want so much more? She sucked in a breath and nodded. "Goodnight."

With a final, heated look, he stepped back. Piper's eyes flicked to the front of his pants. Even in the low light in the hall, she could tell he sported quite the hard-on. Heat colored her cheeks as her desire grew. *Oh my God!* He expected her to sleep after seeing that?

His smile widened and turned naughty, but he kept backing away. "Sweet dreams."

She growled as he turned and loped down the hall. They'd be something, but she surely wouldn't use the word sweet to describe them.

TWENTY-SIX

Piper glanced at the clock, the seconds inching by, as she waited for her shift to end. No one better try to talk to her once that clock hit seven. She was leaving, and nothing short of a dire emergency would stop her. She had a man to bid on. Getting held up wouldn't be such a big deal if the hospital hadn't changed their mind about hosting the auction. With the bombing, they didn't want to draw anymore press—good or otherwise.

Rather than cancel the event, Cullen told her that Sheriff Davidson's wife, Gemma, talked her boss into hosting it at the equestrian therapy center in Foggy Mountain.

That now meant Piper had to drive all the way back there and hope it wasn't Cullen's turn before she arrived. He'd promised her he would talk to the emcee and make sure he was one of the last ones on the list. She should be safe, but it didn't stop her wondering if the cop who'd been her shadow the last two days would mind if she sped—or would even give her an escort.

The minute hand on the clock ticked to seven p.m. Piper finished the prescription she was working on, set it in the stack for Dr. Reid to look at, then logged off her computer. "I'm out of here. See you all tomorrow." With a smile and a wave to her co-workers, who were also signing off, she hurried away from her station.

It only took her a minute to grab her things and exit the pharmacy. She nodded to the young State Bureau of Investigation agent, Oscar Quartermaine, keeping an eye on her as she stepped into the main corridor. He pushed off the wall and followed her to the secure parking garage, usually only reserved for the hospital's senior leadership and VIP guests. Piper was thankful Dr. Coombs let her come back to work. She didn't want to sit home, idle. It helped that it sent a message to whoever was behind the problems in the pharmacy that the hospital wasn't backing down and supported her. She was glad. It was nice to have an employer who stood behind her. Her old boss wouldn't have hesitated to put her on leave, then punish her for it later by making her work long hours.

Piper stepped into the elevator with her shadow and rode it down to the basement level to her car. She stood to the side, tapping her foot, impatient as Oscar used a mirror on a stick with a light to check her car. She understood why it was necessary, but still cursed the delay.

Finally, he deemed her car explosive-free, and she got inside. He hopped into the unmarked car across from her and followed her out of the garage.

The drive north was uneventful. Piper edged the speedometer slightly higher than what was probably wise, but her shadow didn't stop her. She'd probably hear about it once they got to town, but she didn't care. He could even give her a ticket if he wanted.

At the equestrian center, Piper turned into the lot and muttered a curse as she drove through the aisles. This place was packed. She was going to have to park on the side street. Half a block away, she finally found a space and whipped her rental into it. Grabbing her purse, she yanked open the door and jumped out, locking it as she hurried down the sidewalk to the building. She could hear Oscar's footfalls on the concrete as he rushed to keep up with her. He caught up as she reached the glass front doors and held one open so she could enter.

Muttering a thanks, she stepped inside. Music thudded through the building, drawing them toward the back. Piper walked down the hallway and pushed open the door to the arena. Her mouth dropped open as she caught sight of the spectacle taking place. A disco ball hung suspended from the rafters, reflecting the stage lights with a bright sparkle over the women below. Music thumped from the speakers on either side of the runway that backed up to a corridor at the back of the arena.

It was the crowd, though, that drew her attention. A horde of women dolled up in everything from tight jeans and crop tops to sparkly cocktail dresses crowded around the stage, waving number cards as the woman at the podium solicited bids for the man on stage who wore a light gray suit and a cocky smile.

"I'll wait back here."

She glanced back at Oscar, who hooked a thumb to the door. "You sure?" She grinned. "I bet they wouldn't mind adding another bachelor to the list."

His face colored, and he waved his hands. "Nope. I'm good. I'll keep an eye on you from the shadows. Don't leave the arena without me, please."

Chuckling, Piper nodded. "I'll behave." Wagging her fingers at him, she scampered down the walkway to the open gate. She stopped at the registration table at the edge of the fray. An auburn-haired woman smiled at her.

"Hi." Her smile slipped, turning speculative. "You're Piper, right?"

A curious frown crossed Piper's face. "Yes." The woman looked familiar.

"I'm Gemma Davidson. This is my sister-in-law, Laurel Mabley." She gestured to the petite blonde sitting next to her.

"Oh, of course. It's good to see you again." Now she remembered why they looked familiar. They'd both been at Mackenzie and Jake's wedding.

"You too. You look great." Gemma tilted her head. "Though a little underdressed."

"I came straight from work." She glanced at the stage. "They haven't sent Cullen up there yet, have they?"

"No, but it should be soon. He asked to go toward the end, so Jodie shuffled things around and ordered the guys by the bid they'd probably draw and started with the lower end of the scale." She paused and let out a little laugh. "Geez. Listen to me. It's like we're auctioning off horses and starting with the unbroken ones."

Piper and Laurel laughed with her. It was true, but it was a sad fact that the handsome successful men would draw a far larger price than the average-looking men with less than exciting jobs. She just hoped everyone had fun tonight and on their dates. And maybe someone would find love from all of this.

"Anyway," Gemma continued, "from the sound of things, they've hit that 'better stock'." She held up her hands and air-quoted. "Levi's drawing quite the bidding war." She gestured to the stage and the man hamming it up for the crowd.

Indeed, the man on stage danced to the music. Piper laughed as he peeled back the lapels of his suit jacket, shrugging it off his shoulders to show his muscular biceps straining the fabric of his shirt.

"Why Cullen hired him, I'll never know. They are exact opposites," Gemma said.

It clicked then in Piper's brain that this was the assistant

Cullen mentioned when he told her about the auction. Her eyes widened as she watched the man gyrate and strike poses, whipping the women into a frenzy. "Whoa."

Gemma giggled. "Yep." She held up a paddle with a number on it. "You better go find a place where our emcee, Jodie, can see you. Ben said Cullen told you to spare no expense." She winked. "I expect him to write me a big fat check later."

Piper took the paddle. "I hope so too." She didn't know how deep his pockets were, but like Gemma said, he told her to bid whatever it took to win. And she planned to do just that. None of those amped up women with their boobs on display and their butts practically showing were going to get their hands on her man. She didn't care if they hadn't put a label on their relationship. He was hers, dammit. Especially after that kiss Wednesday night.

She fanned herself with the paddle as she walked away from the registration table as the memory hit her. That kiss had left her tingling from head to toe even after she crawled back into bed. It took every ounce of willpower she had not to get up and wander down the hall to his room and ask for more. So much more.

Tonight, she'd at least get another mind-numbing kiss. She'd been hoping for one Thursday, but he left for work before she awakened. When she went downstairs, she found a pot of coffee, a plate of pancakes and bacon in the warming drawer of the oven, and a note, saying he hadn't wanted to wake her, but he'd be happy to take her wherever she needed to go after he finished his clinic hours. He also wrote that he understood if she needed to leave sooner. At the bottom, he'd written the number for Foggy Mountain's lone taxi service. Piper ended up calling Mackenzie—after she ate the breakfast he left for her. For a man who was never home and ate out more often than not, he sure could make some tasty pancakes and crispy bacon.

"There you are!"

Piper looked left at the sound of Mackenzie's voice. Her friend beckoned to her from the edge of the crowd. "Sorry." She hurried over. "I drove as fast as I dared. Has it been like this the entire time?"

Mackenzie lifted a shoulder. "Sort of. This guy really amped up the energy. I hope the guys that come after can deliver, or these ladies might boo them off the stage."

The bang of a gavel on the podium echoed through the arena, then the voice of the woman wielding it. "Sold to number eighty-one for thirteen hundred dollars."

Piper's eyes went wide. Thirteen hundred bucks? She was glad it was Cullen's money she was spending.

"Okay, ladies. Next up we have Carter Townsend. He's Ferris County's K-9 deputy." The emcee held out an arm, gesturing to the man emerging from behind the curtain. He held a leash attached to an all-black Belgian Malinois.

"Damn." Piper eyed the man. Close to Cullen's height, a shock of dirty blonde hair with bright sun streaks fell over his forehead. He walked forward, an easy roll to his hips. In tactical pants, combat boots, and his department polo, he looked like a romance cover model.

Mackenzie giggled. "Yeah, Carter's pretty sexy. And not shy." She tipped her head toward the stage.

Carter paused at the end of the runway and flipped his hand around, bringing it up to cup his ear, then rolled the other one, encouraging the crowd to cheer.

"Carter is accompanied by his partner, Maverick," Jodie said. "For his date, Carter has planned an evening at the zoo for a behind-the-scenes tour of the elephant exhibit. The tour also includes a paint-and-sip event with Thelma the African elephant. The event also includes dinner."

Piper glanced at Mackenzie. "That's a pretty good date."

Mackenzie nodded. "I think Ben helped him come up with it. I know he was struggling to think of something."

"So was Cullen." She still didn't know what he'd decided on. He wouldn't tell her. Said he wanted it to be a surprise. It better be a good one, or she was going to demand a do-over.

Bidding erupted in a frenzy over Carter. Finally, Jodie banged her gavel and declared him sold for twenty-one hundred dollars to a brunette in a tight leather skirt on the other side of the crowd.

Several more men paraded down the runway after Carter, each one fetching a thousand to eighteen hundred dollars. Piper shifted, wondering how many more there were to go until it was Cullen's turn. She glanced at the program Mackenzie held and realized he should be next. Mack had crossed off the men as they appeared. Cullen was the only one left.

"All right. I'm sad to say this is our last bachelor of the evening," Jodie said over the speakers.

A moan went through the crowd.

"I know. I'm sorry. This has been great fun, and we've raised a lot of money for the crisis center, so thank you!" Jodie paused as the crowd cheered, then continued. "Let's go out with a bang, shall we?" She paused for another round of cheers, chuckling at their enthusiasm. "Our last bachelor is a trauma surgeon as well as our county coroner. Please welcome, Dr. Cullen Tate."

TWENTY-SEVEN

The roar of the crowd swelled as Jodie introduced him. Cullen took a deep breath. He could do this. All the other men had gone out there and had fun. And he couldn't give Levi the satisfaction of chickening out. Running a finger under his collar, he pushed the curtain aside and stepped onto the stage.

Cheering and whistles greeted him as he plastered a smile on his face and walked down the runway. He hoped none of them could tell he was gritting his teeth behind his smile. This was his worst nightmare come to life. Only knowing Piper was out there to bid on him kept him on stage. He didn't care how good of a cause it was. If it weren't for her, he'd have probably taken one look at the crowd and done an about-face. Gemma would be content with a generous check.

"Dr. Tate's date sounds wonderful. It's also an animal experience, but this one features big cats and wolves at a local wildlife rescue. He has secured two tickets to their Valentine's fundraiser, happening Monday evening, which includes a behind-the-scenes tour of their facility and a catered, five-course meal. Let's open the bidding, shall we?" Jodie glanced over the crowd.

Several paddles shot into the air, and women called out numbers, rapidly outbidding each other. Cullen's eyes went wide as they soon reached fifteen hundred. He squinted at the crowd, looking for Piper. He hadn't heard her voice in the melee. Unease sent tingles over his scalp. She better be out there. Hopefully, she didn't get held up at work.

The sea of faces near the stage quickly faded into darkness. It was impossible to see more than a few feet because of the lights. He had to trust she was out there and in the middle of the throng.

But he grew apprehensive as the bidding got down to two women, both near the stage. He didn't want to go out with either of them. One wore entirely too much makeup, likely covering up her true age, and the other woman showed enough skin he didn't have to wonder what she had beneath her minute sparkly dress.

"We have twenty-four hundred from the woman in the red sparkles," Jodie said. "Going once. Going twice."

Sweat popped out on Cullen's forehead. *Fuck!* This was not how this was supposed to go.

"Three thousand."

Cullen's knees threatened to give way as Piper's voice rang out over the crowd.

"Oh, we have a new bidder way in the back. And with a very generous bid. Do I hear thirty-one-hundred?" Jodie looked at the woman in red.

Cullen glanced at her and glared, willing her not to bid. She flattened her lips, not looking at him. Instead, she glared daggers toward the rear of the crowd. Finally, she shook her head. He resisted the urge to fist-pump.

"Okay. Three thousand going once. Going twice."

His heart thumped in his ears as he waited for the gavel to fall.

"Sold! To number ninety-eight."

Shoulders slumping in relief, Cullen waved at the crowd, then left the stage. Jodie's voice echoed through the arena as she thanked everyone for coming and told those who won to visit the registration desk to meet their dates and pay for them, if they hadn't already, before leaving.

Cullen ignored her and went backstage, avoiding the crush. He'd find Piper once the crowd thinned.

"Hey, boss." Levi walked up and slapped him on the shoulder. "You did great. Best price of the night."

His wallet felt it. He offered his assistant a tight-lipped smile. "Yeah. The crisis center got some great donations tonight."

"They did. The women who organized this did a great job of pulling in some ladies with deep pockets."

"For sure."

"You coming out to find your date?"

"I will in a bit. I know who it was, so I'll wait for the crowd to thin."

"Oh. Is it someone you like, at least?"

A smile broke out on Cullen's face. "You could say that."

Levi blinked. Then blinked again. A smile spread over his face. "Well, well. I think I need to meet the woman who fell the mighty Dr. Cullen Tate."

"I'm sure it will happen at some point." He tipped his head toward the stage. "Go find your date. I'll see you later."

Still smiling, Levi nodded. "Have a good evening, Doc."

"You too."

The curtain swished as Levi disappeared. Cullen went over to the line of chairs set up for the bachelors and sat down. Propping his elbows on his knees, he rested his head in his hands and blew out a breath, glad the auction was over. He didn't care what anyone said to convince him otherwise; he was never doing that again. It took little effort or thought for him to run a room of residents and nurses on a trauma call or to give a lecture on the latest critical care procedures, but that? The anxiety of it all wiped him out.

"You're not being very social."

His head popped up at the sound of Piper's voice. "Hey." He stood and walked over to her, some of his energy returning at the sight of her smiling face. "I'm glad you made it. I thought I was going to end up with the woman in the red dress for a minute."

A mischievous smile stole over her face, and he squinted. "Wait. How long were you here before you started bidding?"

She lifted a shoulder, one side of her mouth lifting higher. "Your assistant really worked up the crowd. Is he that bold at work?"

Cullen's eyebrows shot up. "You deliberately let that woman almost win? I about had a heart attack, thinking I was going to get stuck with her."

Piper's low, sultry laugh dissipated some of his ire. His body tightened at the throaty sound.

"I couldn't resist. At first, I couldn't get a bid in. The women in front dominated it all, so I just let them duke it out until there were only a few left. At that point, I wanted to see how high they were willing to go." That mischievous smile returned. "Then I saw your face. The higher they went and the longer I held my tongue, the more nervous you got. I was waiting for you to run." She clicked her tongue. "But you didn't, so now you owe the crisis center three grand."

He growled and stalked closer. Her smile dipped and her eyes went wide, the pupils dilating as she caught sight of the look on his face. It promised retribution—of the naughty variety.

Cullen grabbed her hips and tugged her into his body,

lowering his head so he could speak directly into her ear. "I've never had a woman tease me quite like that. I'm not sure I liked it. Probably requires some sort of revenge." He curled his hands around the curve of her butt, bringing her pelvis into his. A fine tremor went through her body. Knowing he could affect her so with just a simple touch tightened his body further. He was glad they were alone back here.

She slid her hands up his chest, bringing her torso against his. "Bring it," she whispered.

"Whoops! Piper, I'll call you tomorrow."

Cullen lifted his head to see Mackenzie whirl around the way she came and raise a hand in farewell. He chuckled as she vanished beyond the curtain and put some space between himself and Piper. "We should probably get out of here. Have you had dinner?"

She let out an inelegant snort and met his gaze. "You get me all worked up and you want to go *eat*?" A wicked smile crossed her face. "I can think of something I'd like to munch on."

Heat suffused his cheeks. Would he ever get used to her bold personality? He hoped not. She made him laugh, and he liked not knowing what would come out of her mouth next.

But he could also give as good as he got. "Real food first."

Fire leapt to life in her eyes. "First?"

He nodded.

She pushed out of his arms and snagged his hand. "Come on. You need to pay Gemma so we can leave."

Laughing, he followed her beyond the curtain.

TWENTY-EIGHT

A fine hum ran through Piper's body, making her feel like she was attached to an electrical wire. Cullen's statement had her feeling like she could run to the moon. She was quite confident he'd take her there later. Probably beyond that, actually.

A quick shiver went through her. Yep. They needed to leave.

Nearing the registration table, she groaned as she saw the line. Why hadn't these women paid for their dates as soon as they won?

"You know what? We're going to skip the line. I'll drop a check off at Ben and Gemma's tomorrow." Cullen changed course around the crowd and took his phone from his pocket. He sent a quick text and led her toward the door.

"Who'd you text?"

"Gemma, so she knows we didn't just skip out on her." He put his phone away. "Come on. How does Jester's sound?"

"Too slow."

He chuckled. "Tough. I'm hungry."

Yeah, well, so was she, but a different hunger rumbled

louder in her belly. "Can we get it to go?" If she got him back to his house, she was sure she could make him forget he hadn't eaten dinner yet.

He lifted an eyebrow. "Will I get to eat it?"

Piper giggled and bit her bottom lip.

Cullen groaned and tugged her closer, pressing a hard kiss to her mouth. "Fuel first."

She huffed. "Fine."

On their way out the door, she caught the eye of her bodyguard and tipped her head toward the entrance to let him know they were leaving. He pushed off the wall and followed, catching up as they neared the door.

Cullen did a double-take as the man walked up to them, calling Piper's name.

"He's my shadow from the police." She laid a hand on his arm as she explained the man's presence, then turned and offered the officer a smile. "Hi, Oscar."

"Ma'am." He nodded in greeting. "The area outside is clear. My partner's been watching the venue. Are you headed home now?"

"No. We're going to Jester's to get some dinner, then probably back to Cullen's." She glanced up at him. "Although, it might not be a bad idea to stop at my house so I can get some clothes. Then I don't have to rush out in the morning."

"We can stay at your place if you'd rather."

She wrinkled her nose. "I'm still living out of boxes."

"The next day off we have together, we need to remedy that."

Piper rolled her eyes. "Because that's what I want to do when we have an entire day together."

He grinned. "It could be fun."

"Only if you did it shirtless." She frowned and glanced away as she envisioned what he'd look like sans shirt. "But then we'd get nothing done. Or at least I wouldn't, anyway." She'd be much too busy watching his muscles flex as he lifted things to do anything else. Not to mention struck dumb by the sight.

Chuckling, Cullen looked at the agent. "Sorry. Anyway, we're getting food to go, then stopping to get some things for her, then going to my house."

The man nodded, his face carefully blank, but Piper could see the amusement in his eyes.

"I'll let my partner know. We'll check out both residences."

"Thanks."

Piper echoed Cullen's gratitude, then followed Oscar out the door.

The night air hit her face, reminding her it was February. The arena had been warm from the crush of bodies and stage lights. She also felt more vulnerable out here. This was the first she'd been anywhere besides work, her house, or Cullen's since the bombing. Any time she left one of those places, she always hustled to her car, her head on a swivel. It helped to know she had someone looking out for her, but it was still nerve-wracking to be out in the open. She knew she could stay home, but there was no telling how long it would take before the police caught the person responsible. It wasn't feasible to put her life on hold indefinitely.

She also knew she wouldn't have police protection forever. If this case grew cold, they'd yank her guards away. That's when she'd be truly nervous.

But she wasn't going to think about that right now. Worry didn't solve anything. It only stole today's peace.

"Where did you park?" Cullen asked, drawing her out of her thoughts.

"Down the block." She rolled her eyes. "I might have arrived in time to bid on you, but I was still late to the party."

"Do you want a ride to your car? Mine's right there." He pointed to his SUV parked twenty feet away.

A thought struck her. "Actually, you could get our food while I go get my clothes, and we could meet at your house." She didn't know why she hadn't thought of that until now.

He lifted a shoulder. "Oh, okay. What do you want? The same thing as last time?"

"That works."

"Wait." Oscar held up a hand. "We're changing the plan?"

"Is that all right?" Piper asked.

"It's fine. One stop is better than two."

"Okay, then. Yes, we're changing the plan."

"Sounds good." Cullen leaned over and kissed her cheek. "I'll see you at home. Be careful."

"You too."

He lifted a hand and jogged away. Piper watched him go and sighed. She couldn't wait to see that ass naked later.

Tipping her head, she looked at Oscar. "Come on. I'm ready to get tucked in for the night. It's been a long day."

His lips twitched, and Piper's face flamed as she realized how that sounded. Rather than sputter and backpedal, she laughed and shrugged. "That's the least embarrassing thing that will probably come out of my mouth."

Chuckling, he followed just behind her to her car, then did a quick sweep of her vehicle before letting her near it.

"Don't pull out until you see me pull in behind you."

With a nod, she got in her car and locked herself inside. Starting the engine, she let it heat up while she watched for his unmarked cruiser. When he drove up and flashed his head-lights, she pulled out and headed for her house.

The drive was quick—Foggy Mountain wasn't large. Turning into her driveway, she opened the garage door, but didn't pull inside. Oscar and his partner would sit outside, and she'd only be a few minutes.

Shutting off the engine, she hopped out and hurried inside. Dashing into her bedroom, she went into the closet and grabbed a small duffel, filling it with a clean set of scrubs for tomorrow, underwear, and her toiletries. She thought about digging into some of her unpacked boxes for her sexy lingerie, but one, she wasn't sure which box they were in, and two, she didn't plan on wearing anything for long tonight.

Bag packed, she strode from her room. Her eye caught on the pile of mail on the floor by the front door as she made the turn to go into the kitchen from the living room. Figuring she should check for bills, she changed direction.

She scooped up the envelopes and the lone padded mailer. Glimpsing through the letters, none of them were important. Junk, mostly. She tucked them under her arm, then looked at the padded envelope. Did she order something and forgot? And who would she order something from that didn't use a printed label?

Disquiet made her hesitate before opening it. She didn't order anything. And she didn't know anyone who would send her something. Only Mackenzie would ever send her a package, and now that they lived in the same town, she wouldn't mail it. She'd just bring it over.

Not sure what it was, and not wanting to take chances, she laid it on the floor, then flung open the front door and dashed outside, waving her arms to get Oscar's attention.

He opened his door and got out, coming around the front of his car. "What? What's wrong?"

"I got a package. I didn't order anything, and there's no return address on it. Or postage, now that I think about it."

His blue gaze sharpened. "Where is it?"

"I left it on the floor in the foyer."

He lifted the radio from his belt and called his partner, who was stationed down the block, and told him to come up to the house.

"Go get in the back of my car." He pointed at the beige

sedan, then lifted the radio again, not waiting for her to comply.

Piper wasn't about to argue, though. She scurried past him and climbed into the backseat, then reached over the driver's seat to lock the doors. No one was getting in without some serious effort.

Scooting to the middle of the seat, she peered through the windshield as Oscar loped up the walkway and disappeared inside. He reemerged a few moments later, holding the package by the corner. Piper's heart thudded in her ears as he laid it on the hood of the car.

"What are you doing?" Her voice sounded shrill in the confines of the car as she yelled at him. "What if it explodes?"

He came around and pulled on the door handle, his mouth flattening as he realized she'd locked the doors. Reaching into his pocket, he used the key fob to unlock them, then opened her door and bent down so he could see her. "It's much too small to be an explosive device. I called the bomb squad, though, anyway. They have a portable x-ray machine so we can get a better idea of what's inside. I don't want to open it and get a face full of some chemical."

"Oh." She hadn't thought about that. Her mind immediately went to the bomb in her car and thought someone was trying again. "So what do we do until they get here?"

"We wait."

TWENTY-NINE

Cullen's heart triple-timed as he turned onto Piper's street and saw the enormous police response. Red and blue lights reflected off the houses, giving the shadows an eerie look. Neighbors stood on their porches and in their front lawns, staring down the road.

When Piper called and told him about the package she received, he'd been on the way to his house. One quick U-turn in the middle of the road sent him to hers. He hadn't expected such a large police response, though. Whatever was in that package had the cops worried.

He parked outside the crime scene tape, then walked up to the officer manning the perimeter.

"Can I get through? That's my girlfriend's house." He pointed to Piper's duplex down the street.

"What's your name?" Frowning, the officer lifted his radio off his shoulder.

"Cullen Tate."

The man relayed the information to someone at the house. A moment later, the tinny voice told the officer to let him through.

"She's in the sedan in the driveway." The officer lifted the tape.

Cullen ducked and passed under it. "Thanks." He jogged up the street to the beige car parked in the driveway. Through the rear window, he could see the back of her head. His long legs ate up the ground, and he rapped his knuckles on the passenger window.

She let out a little shriek, laying a hand over her heart as her shoulders sagged when she recognized him. With one finger, she unlocked the door. Cullen yanked it open and climbed inside, folding her into his arms.

"Are you okay?"

She nodded against his chest. "Yeah. Why does this keep happening?"

He hugged her tighter, not answering. Voicing that it was because someone was a greedy bastard and she was in their way wouldn't help soothe her nerves. "What do we know so far?"

"Not much. The bomb squad is on the way. Not because they're worried it will explode, but so they can x-ray it and see what's inside." She shuddered. "I'm glad I didn't open it. Agent Quartermaine said it could be some sort of chemical."

His heart flip-flopped at the thought of her opening something that could harm her. "You're not staying alone until they catch this guy. Either I'm moving in, or you're moving in with me."

She lifted her head to look at him, raising an eyebrow. "I have a police guard."

"Not the same." She could have a whole squadron watching over her, but it wouldn't change the fact that he wanted to be the one to stand between her and the evil on her doorstep.

"What about the times our schedules are different? Or you get called to an emergency?"

Cullen knew there were gaps in his plan, but it didn't

change how he felt. "Maybe you can hang out at Mackenzie's until I get home. And come with me when I get called to the hospital."

She dipped her chin and looked at him through her lashes. "Or I could rely on the police, who are already there, to keep me safe."

Oh, this side of her stubbornness he didn't like. Instead of giving in, though, he hummed and glanced out at the police activity beyond the cocoon of the car. "Maybe."

Thankfully, she dropped the subject and snuggled deeper into his side, wrapping her arms around his waist and laying her head on his chest again. He held her like that, watching the hive of activity until the bomb squad arrived a half hour later.

"You know, I think it might be best for you to stay at my house." He stared at the armored vehicle rolling up the street to stop at the end of her driveway. The neighbors would never leave her alone after this. He felt bad for the woman living in the other side of the duplex. He could see her sitting in her living room, watching out the front window. Piper certainly wasn't making any friends in her new neighborhood.

Piper groaned. "People are going to think I'm some sort of criminal. Or trouble magnet."

A low chuckle rumbled in his chest. "You'll win them over again with your personality, eventually."

"After the bomb squad is at my house? Yeah, no."

Cullen's muscles tightened, and he sat up straighter as a bomb technician approached with a small machine and a flat, white rectangle about an inch thick. He set the plate on the ground, then with gloved hands, picked up the padded mailer from the hood of the car and laid it on the plate. Standing over it, he held the small box-like machine above the envelope, then retreated to the armored vehicle.

"That was it?" Piper turned, watching him walk away.

"It's an x-ray. They only take a moment."

"How long will it take for them to read the images?"

"They probably already have it. Most of them transmit wirelessly to a program installed on a laptop." He shifted, so he could see out the rear window, and willed the technician—or anyone—to come out and give them an update.

Several people went up to the vehicle, but none came out and came their way.

Piper growled. "Why is this taking so long?"

Minutes ticked by, making Cullen more concerned about what they saw on the x-ray. Finally, an officer approached and picked up the mailer, taking it to the armored car.

"Seriously? They can't open it here? Or at least tell us what they saw?"

"Maybe it's hazardous, so they want to put it in a box and have a robot open it."

"Wouldn't they just roll the robot up to it, then?"

Cullen shrugged. "No clue."

She sighed and continued to watch the activity behind them. Cullen ran a hand over her back, soothing them both.

While they watched, news vans showed up, the media having gotten wind of the call. Ben also arrived, going straight to the armored car. He reemerged five minutes later and loped toward them. Cullen unlocked the car as he approached. Opening the driver's door, Ben got in, then turned to face them as he pulled the door shut.

"What was in the package?" Piper wasted no time getting to the point. Cullen was fine with that. He wanted to know too.

Ben opened his mouth, closed it and glanced away, then tried again. "A severed finger."

Cullen's eyes went wide. Piper's breath left her with a whoosh.

"A severed finger?" Cullen was the first to get his voice back. "Whose?"

"Don't know. It looks like a woman's. Anyone call into work sick or not show up?" Ben asked Piper.

"Not on my shift. I don't know about the others."

His head bobbed once. "I'll look into it. You notice anything out of the ordinary when you got home?"

She shook her head. "No. My porch light was on and nothing inside seemed out of place. I didn't look that closely, though."

"Okay. We'll have you do a walk-through once forensics finishes with the foyer." He opened the door. "Hang tight. I'll be back." Not waiting for a response, he got out and shut the door.

Piper sagged into Cullen. He held her close, needing to feel her presence as much as she needed him. That was not what he'd been expecting.

"Why would someone shove a severed finger through my mail slot?" She glanced up at him. "And what does it mean?"

"I don't know, honey. It's a warning of some kind."

"Well, yeah, but why? They tried to kill me. Why send me a finger after that? Why not just try to kill me again?"

"I'm not sure, but hopefully, Ben will get us some answers soon."

She exhaled a long breath. "Yeah." Closing her eyes, she leaned her head back. "I get the feeling they're going to put me on lockdown now."

Cullen was okay with that. He'd prefer it. If he didn't have a full week, he'd go on lockdown with her. He might, anyway. There were several doctors he could call to fill in for him. Many who owed him favors. It might be time to cash in a few.

THIRTY

Bone-weary and starving, Piper trudged through the door from Cullen's garage. She kicked off her shoes and set her purse and overnight bag on the counter before removing her coat. "I'm really glad you got our food before I called you. I don't want to cook. Not even a sandwich."

He offered her a tired smile and set the bag on the counter. "Me, either. Can you get some plates out?" Tipping his chin toward the cupboard, he shrugged out of his coat.

"Yep." She handed him her jacket, then turned away. The white plates clanked as she removed them from the cabinet. Grabbing silverware, she set everything next to the food. "It still smells good, even if it is cold now."

"It'll reheat well, trust me." With a crooked smile, he tipped a mountain of brisket onto his plate.

After nuking their food, they each grabbed a bottle of water and sat down at the bar to eat. Piper shoveled her food in, not tasting it until she got near the end. She'd been too hungry to care what she put in her mouth. With her plate clean, she rinsed it off and put her dishes in the dishwasher. "I'm going to take a shower." She straightened from loading her dishes, then headed for the door, but paused at the threshold.

Should she? Biting her lip, she debated for half a second. It wasn't a hard decision. "Care to join me?"

Startled hazel eyes met hers. They darkened as need leapt to life in their depths. "Are you sure? You've had a traumatic evening."

"We were heading this direction before the day took a crap, right?"

His lips twitched, but he nodded.

"Then hell yes, I'm sure."

Cullen stood abruptly, leaving his plate on the bar, and stalked toward her. Piper's heart sped up. Tingles raced through her body, making all the fine hairs stand on end.

He brought a hand up, tracing her cheekbone with one finger. "My brain says we need to slow down, but my body won't let me."

She grabbed the lapels of his suit jacket and pulled him close. "Good." Standing on her toes, she sealed her mouth to his. She was done listening to her brain. It was a mess right now, with the chaos going on in her life. Her body, though—it knew what it wanted. This man. And it was telling her brain to shut up. Who was she to deny it?

Strong arms wrapped around her waist, bringing her body flush against his. That hard ridge she felt the other night pressed into her belly, sending a flood of warmth to her core. They wouldn't make it to the shower—or the bed—if she didn't call a halt to this now.

Tearing her mouth from his, she took his hand and pulled him toward the stairs. With quiet footsteps, they ascended to the second story. In the dark, they moved down the hall into the master bedroom. Cullen slapped at the wall and turned on the light as she tugged him toward the en suite. The tingle he started earlier had progressed to a full-fledged hum.

She let go and reached for the tap in the shower, needing a moment to gather herself. This intense desire wasn't something she was used to. No one else had ever unsettled her so.

Water running, she turned back to him, suddenly nervous. Already, she knew being with Cullen would be different from being with any other man. With a look and a touch, he set her body aflame. She'd probably combust and turn to a pile of ash once he got her naked.

But the burn would be fabulous.

It was that thought that wiped away her nerves. She wanted this. Wanted to feel the pleasure—and the connection —making love to Cullen would bring. Grasping the bottom of her scrub top, she peeled it over her head.

"Damn, Piper. You don't waste time."

She gave him a sweet but sultry smile. "Life's too short not to grab it by the horns." Her hand went to the drawstring on her pants.

He stepped forward, stopping her. "It's also too short to rush things." He bent his head, his lips skimming the shell of her ear. "I want to memorize every inch of you."

Need curled her toes. Her eyelids fluttered, and her lips parted on a sigh. "Okay." He could do whatever he wanted to do to her so long as he kept talking like that—low and sexy.

A haze over her vision, she blinked when he pulled back. More warmth rushed south as he took off his suit jacket and loosened his tie, pulling it from his collar. Button by button, he unfastened his shirt, revealing tanned, hair-roughened skin an inch at a time. By the time he reached the bottom, she was ready to yank the fabric from his body so she could see all of him.

He didn't make her wait, though. Once he had his shirt unbuttoned, he peeled it off his shoulders and down his arms. Piper's mouth went dry as all the moisture headed to her core. He was magnificent.

Sinewy, ropey muscles defined his arms and chest. And his abs... she could bounce a quarter off those things.

Her eyes traveled lower to the bulge in his pants. With a mind of its own, her hand raised, reaching for his belt.

He batted it away. "If you touch me now, we'll never make it into the shower."

She raised one shoulder, a sly smile on her face. "So?" The giggle building in her throat died when he reached for her and kissed her again.

Cool air touched her back as he unfastened her bra. She didn't care what he thought about going slow; she needed to be naked now. Wedging a hand between them, she plucked at the drawstring on her pants, managing to get it undone. The fabric loosened. Cullen took full advantage and slid his palms inside and over the curve of her butt.

Piper moaned against his lips at the feel of his hands on her bare flesh. He needed to go just a little further down.

Like he read her mind, his hands followed her curves lower until his fingers teased the junction of her thighs through her underwear. A fiery zing of pleasure ripped through her, and she broke their kiss with a gasp.

"You okay?" His voice was a thick rasp.

Her head bobbed with short, jerky movements. "Perfect."

A wicked smile crossed his face. "Good." His hand moved lower still, sliding along the thin cotton, teasing her.

She shook her bra straps free of her arms and clutched his shoulders, sure she was going to go off like a rocket before he ever even truly touched her.

The pleasure abruptly ebbed when he removed his hand. She huffed and glared up at him. "Why did you stop?"

That smile slashed higher. "No rush, remember?"

Piper growled.

He laughed, then whisked her pants down her legs. "Maybe a little bit of a rush."

She framed his face with her hands. "Yep." Kissing him, she swayed forward, pressing her breasts to his chest. The rough hair teased her nipples, adding to the need pulsing through her body.

Cullen walked her backward to the shower, then lifted his head. "Get in."

"You're coming, too, right?" She hooked her fingers in the waistband of her panties and quirked an eyebrow.

His gaze heated as it drifted to her hands. "Yeah."

Grinning at the glazed look in his eyes, she pulled the fabric away from her body and slowly tugged it lower.

"Jesus, Piper. You're killing me."

"You're the one who said no rush." She inched the cotton lower.

"I think I regret that now."

The underwear slid over her butt, but still shielded most of her. "I don't know. This tease thing is kinda fun."

Hazel eyes met hers; they carried a flash of impatience. Piper smiled and lowered her panties another inch, exposing the thatch of neatly trimmed blonde hair hidden by the fabric. His eyes darkened, and she kept going. Free of her hips, they slid to the floor. She stepped out of them and into the shower.

"You coming? Or are you just going to stand there and stare at me?" She tipped her head into the hot spray, but turned her eyes to look at him.

He reached for his fly. Piper stilled, letting the water rain over her as she watched him lower the zipper. She bit her lip as his slacks fell to the floor, leaving him in just his boxer-briefs. She gulped as she took in the tent he sported. Moisture that had nothing to do with the shower flooded her core.

Take it off, baby. Take it all off.

Thankfully, he didn't make her wait. Hooking his thumbs in the waistband, the dark blue fabric joined his pants on the floor.

A soft moan escaped her, and she bit her lip. Long and thick, his erection jutted away from his body, ready for her. She was ready for him, too. So very ready.

He stepped into the shower, crowding her into the corner. Piper didn't care. His shaft bumped her belly, so she did the only logical thing. "We need more space." Wrapping her arms around his neck, she did a soft hop and anchored her legs around his waist.

Groaning, he stumbled forward, pinning her to the wall. He pressed his forehead to hers, breathing hard. "I don't know why I agreed to this. I forgot I don't have any protection. This isn't something I do regularly."

Piper's heart melted at his admission. It still blew her mind that a man who looked like him and was as successful as he was didn't have someone special—or a few someones.

But he did now. "I'm on the pill. And I doubt either of us has anything to worry about when it comes to disease."

He shook his head. "No."

"Then I say do your worst. Or best. I don't really care, so long as you make me scream your name." She loved that he lived in the country. The neighbors wouldn't hear her voicing her pleasure. She planned to be loud.

With a harsh groan, his mouth crashed down onto hers. Piper latched on and gave as good as she got. She didn't even mind that the tile was cold on her back. It held her up, freeing his hands to roam over her body.

Up her thighs and over her hips. Around her ribcage to cup her breasts and tweak her nipples. Everywhere his hands traveled, fire erupted until she felt like she was burning from the inside out. Ashes wouldn't be fine enough for how she'd end up after this. She'd be nothing more than dust in the air.

Squirming against him, she tried to line up their bodies. She wanted to feel him at her entrance, then deep inside her.

He pulled back to look at her. "Impatient again?"

She snorted inelegantly. "Aren't you?"

"Maybe." He reached between them and grasped his shaft, aligning it with her entrance.

Piper's eyes rolled back as his slick head moved through her folds. With a gentle push, he dipped inside.

"Yes." The word hissed out through her teeth.

Cullen's hips moved between her thighs in gentle waves, pushing him deeper with each thrust. She pulsed around him, which sent zings of electricity to every erogenous zone in her body. Even her scalp prickled as the need spread like wildfire. "Cullen."

"That wasn't loud enough." He pulled back and thrust again.

Piper let out a soft shout, then moaned. "Do that again."

He did, but this time he didn't stop and rocked into her time and time again. He leaned down and nipped the tops of her breasts, then her neck. Sensation built, piling up, giving her footholds on the climb up the mountain until her feet took flight and she soared over the top.

Her climax broke over her in a deluge. She yelled his name, the sound echoing off the shower walls. His fingers dug into the flesh of her hips, and he growled, thrusting harder until his growls turned to raspy moans and he stilled.

Breath coming in rough pants, Piper lost all muscle tone in her legs, and they fell away from his hips. Only the wall and his arms kept her from sliding into a pile of satisfied woman on the shower floor.

She'd been right. Nothing compared to this.

THIRTY-ONE

The doorbell echoed through Piper's house. She paused, elbow deep in a box, and glanced toward the bedroom door. Who could that be? With a frown, she got up, reaching for her phone on the nightstand, and called Oscar, who stood guard outside.

"It's Mackenzie," he said in lieu of greeting.

"What, you're a damn mind reader too?" She shook her head, leaving the bedroom to answer the door.

He chuckled. "Something like that. Jake's here, too, so I'm going to take a dinner break. I'll check in when I get back."

"Okay. Thanks, Ozzie."

A long sigh came over the phone. She could almost hear the eye roll. He hated the nickname she'd given him.

"Yep. Be back soon."

The line clicked in her ear. Smiling, she shoved the device in her pocket and opened the door. "Hey." She stepped back so her friend could enter, then glanced behind her. "Where's Jake? Ozzie said he was here."

"He decided to stay in the car. Give us some alone time." Mackenzie walked in and unzipped her coat.

"Oh. Great." She needed some girl time. Cullen had her tied in knots, and she could use a sounding board. "You want some hot chocolate?"

Mackenzie's face fell. "I already had some today. But I wouldn't be opposed to some decaf coffee."

"Sure." Piper led her friend into the kitchen and set about making a pot of decaf.

"So, you had an exciting weekend."

"You could say that, yes."

Mackenzie perched on a stool at the counter. "Spill. I know there are a million thoughts running through your mind."

Piper sighed and turned, leaning against the granite countertop. She drummed her fingers against the stone and twisted her lips. "I don't know where to start. A lot happened. And not just with the pharmacy thing."

Mackenzie's eyes rounded. "Oh? How about we start with that, then? Something happened between you and Cullen?"

Heat suffused Piper's cheeks as her thoughts traveled to her weekend.

"Oh, I know that look." A smile lifted the corners of Mackenzie's mouth. "So how was it? Though I'm not sure I need to ask."

Piper giggled. "Yeah. It was pretty great." Understatement of the century, but telling her friend she'd been screwed to within an inch of her life wasn't the most couth thing to say.

"I'm glad. So why do you look so conflicted? Is it work?"

"No. Not entirely." She chewed on the corner of her lip. "It just feels too good to be true, you know? I've gone through my adulthood without any really serious relationships and he just sort of fell into my lap. Things are great between us. We get along. He's funny and kind." She shrugged. "I guess I'm just not used to having something come to me so easily, you know?"

Mackenzie nodded. "I do. That's how I felt about Jake. At first, I didn't feel like I deserved him. Then I didn't want to put him in danger. Once I got past that, it just felt like a fairytale. It still does. But I'm learning to embrace my happiness. And to not take it for granted."

Piper hummed. "I guess that's my issue. I need to embrace it." She grimaced. "Though we haven't talked about where this is going." She chuckled. "That conversation probably should have happened before we jumped each other's bones in the shower."

Mackenzie laughed. "Maybe. Today's Valentine's Day. Perhaps that should be on the agenda for tonight. You do have a date with him, right?"

"Yeah. Though not what he had originally planned. We were supposed to do the auction date, but with everything going on in my life, the police asked me to limit my movements. Home, work, Cullen's house. I'm not even supposed to go grocery shopping. I give Ozzie a list and he sends someone to get it."

"Hey, that sounds kinda nice. I'd have to be pretty specific, though. I sent Jake to get shredded cheese for dinner one night and he came back with the expensive, fancy stuff. I just wanted plain old shredded cheddar." Mackenzie giggled.

Piper joined in. "Yeah, I'm learning that. They just grab. Thankfully, there haven't been too many oddities. I ordered in last night, though. I didn't feel like cooking."

"Does Cullen cook?"

"Some. He had to work, though." Her nose wrinkled. That was the one dark spot in dating a doctor. His work schedule could be unpredictable. He was supposed to be off, but got called in to consult on a case. He left just before dinner and didn't get back until she was ready for bed. Though that hadn't stopped them from enjoying each other's company before falling asleep.

"That look says he didn't work all night."

Piper's face reddened. Why was she blushing? She was an adult. And she wasn't shy. But the things he did to her would make anyone blush. "No. No, he did not." She spun around, searching for coffee mugs to hide her flaming face. The man had a wicked tongue and some talented hands.

Mackenzie's giggles filled the room. "Maybe you should drink ice water instead of coffee."

"Probably. Who knew the shy, quiet surgeon had a naughty side?"

"It's always the quiet ones."

Yep. And she wasn't complaining. He'd been keen to try things and explore her body. She'd returned the favor.

"So, enough about my sex life. How are you feeling?"

"Pretty good. Most of the nausea has passed. I'm going to need to go shopping for clothes soon, though. My pants are getting tight. This drug, explosion thing needs to get resolved soon so you can go with me."

Piper's face pulled. "Trust me, I want it to be over too." She poured two mugs of coffee and handed one to her friend. "It's just a waiting game right now. I don't think they can do much until they get results on the evidence they've gathered."

Mackenzie blew on her coffee, then took a sip. "Have you heard anything? Jake won't say much. Just that they're working on things. I think the ATF has wrested control away from the locals."

"Yeah. Ozzie doesn't know anything. Cullen talked to Ben and hasn't gotten much, either. But they don't know much yet." She sighed. "Part of me wants whoever's behind this to come after me again. Then, at least, maybe we'd find out who it is."

"Maybe." Mackenzie ran her thumb along the rim of her cup. "Or it could cost you your life. That's not acceptable."

"No. But I'm just frustrated. I moved here to make a

change and start a new life. I have that within my reach, but it's on hold because someone got greedy." She waved a hand. "I don't know why I'm complaining, especially to you. You've been through far worse than me."

"Yes, but I'm also living proof that things don't always stay bad." Mackenzie covered Piper's hand with one of her own. "Just try to have some patience. Things will work out."

Piper let out a quick bark of laughter. "Have you met me? Patience is not my thing."

Giggling, Mackenzie squeezed her hand, then let go. "Use Cullen as a distraction. I'm sure he'll be amenable to that."

A flush of heat crept over her. Piper quite liked that idea. "Good plan." Smiling, she raised her mug and took a drink, already thinking about her first distraction.

THIRTY-TWO

Juggling his briefcase, a bouquet of roses, and dinner, Cullen let himself into Piper's house. Soft music met his ears, but Piper was nowhere in sight. "Honey?" He moved toward the kitchen to deposit their food, taking in the atmosphere in the living room. She had candles on every available surface, their glow the only light.

His pulse kicked up a notch. Seems he wasn't the only one with romantic plans for Valentine's Day.

Long legs eating up the ground, he crossed to the kitchen and set everything on the counter. Curious about where she was hiding, he left it all there and wandered into the living room. "Piper?"

The bedroom door opened, and Cullen forgot to breathe. The soft light from the candles cast a golden glow over her skin—of which there was a lot showing. Clad only in a teal lace bustier and a short brown leather skirt, she looked like some sort of Amazonian sex goddess come to life. He swallowed to alleviate the dryness in his throat and just stared. "You look stunning."

A slow, sexy smile spread over her face. "Thanks." She

sauntered forward, and he noticed the black stiletto heels on her feet. They made her already long legs look miles longer.

He bit back a groan, wanting to feel them wrapped around his waist. "I brought dinner." He hooked a thumb toward the kitchen.

Her smile and direction didn't change. "Great." She stopped inches away. "Will it keep?"

"Does it matter?" Reaching out, he grabbed her, yanking her to him.

"No." Voice airy, she wrapped her arms around his neck and kissed him.

Cullen tightened his arms and lifted, carrying her into the bedroom. He broke the kiss as they tumbled onto the bed. "I like your outfit. How do I take it off?"

With a giggle, she shoved at his shoulders. "It has a zipper in the back."

He sat back on his heels, letting her up. She rose onto her knees and turned her back to him. Cullen found the zipper and drew it down. The bustier parted, exposing her back. She held it to her front with one hand.

Walking forward on his knees, he pressed against her, smoothing his hands over the creamy expanse of skin he exposed. His fingers bumped the ridge of scar tissue left behind from her wounds. It didn't bother him like he thought it might. Instead, it was a reminder of Piper's resiliency, and her will to live.

Cullen pushed his hands beneath the sides of her top. She let it drop, leaving her open to his touch. He cupped her full breasts, teasing the tips and eliciting short, breathy whimpers with each flick of his fingers. Dipping his head, he nipped at her neck, then trailed a hand down her abdomen and over the top of her thigh to dip under her short skirt.

His fingers met bare flesh, and he froze. "Oh, you're naughty."

"Figured I'd save us some time."

"You just like it when I get too eager to go slow."

"Yes—oh..." Her words cut off with a low moan as he slid a finger into her channel.

With his other hand, he unfastened his pants and freed himself. Tipping her forward, he lined his aching member up with her entrance and thrust inside.

Cullen lost himself in her body. In the sensations caused by her tight walls and breathy shouts of pleasure. Clutching her hips, he pounded into her and sent them both flying into orbit.

Collapsing on top of her, he sucked in lungfuls of air, then rolled to the side, taking her with him. He stroked her soft breasts as they came down from their high and their breathing slowed.

"I need to dig deeper into my lingerie box if that's the response I get when I wear it."

Cullen groaned. "I'm not sure I'll survive that box."

She turned her head, a wicked grin on her pretty face. "But it'll be fun to try."

Of that, he had no doubt.

Piper rolled in his arms and snuggled into his chest. "We should probably go eat before the food gets too cold."

He hummed. Moving was not something he wanted to do right now. He'd much rather strip them both naked and go for round two.

She giggled and made some space between their hips as he stirred. "Aren't men in their forties supposed to take longer to recover from sex?"

"I'm a young forty."

Her laugh echoed around them. "I'm glad."

"Good." He leaned in for a kiss, but she put a finger over his lips. Cullen sighed. "You really want to eat first?"

"And talk." Some of the merriment slipped out of her eyes, but she didn't look worried.

Curious now, he nodded. "Okay. Do you want to talk while we eat?"

She lifted a shoulder. "We can talk here." Her eyes strayed to his neck, and she toyed with his collar.

He put a finger under her chin and tipped her face up. "What's on your mind, honey?"

She sucked in a quick breath through her nose. "Where are we going with this?" She waved a finger between them.

"Our relationship, you mean?"

"Yeah."

"I see us having what our friends have. I want what Ben's got with Gemma. What your friend has with her husband." He raised a hand and smoothed it through her hair on the side of her head, smiling at her wide-eyed expression. "I never envisioned that for myself until you came along. Now, I can't imagine life without you in it. I don't think about work all the time anymore. You were right. I needed a balance. And I like the way it feels."

"Me too," she whispered.

"I know it's too soon to make this permanent. That neither of us has fully worked out how we feel. But I'm not waiting long."

A slow, beautiful smile blossomed on her face. "Good."

Cullen flexed his arm, bringing her face to his for a long kiss. It sparked a different kind of desire than he felt when he walked in earlier. This was deeper, more soulful.

Yeah, he liked this a lot.

Thirty-Three

Cullen's soft whistle bounced off the hallway walls as he walked from the E.R. to the staff elevator. The case he'd been called in for was resolved, and the patient was doing well. He was headed home just in time to make dinner before Piper returned from her shift.

Things had been quiet this week. No more mysterious packages or severed body parts had arrived. He and Piper had settled into a bit of a routine. On the days she worked, she came to his house, and he made or ordered dinner. On her days off, he went to her place, and they did the same. Soon, he was going to suggest she break her lease and move in with him. Going back and forth between was already growing tiresome—he was a person who liked stability. Plus, he liked the idea of her being around all the time. Of her mixing her things with his and turning his plain house into a home. Their home.

The elevator doors swished open. Cullen's whistle cut off as he spotted Ben inside. "Hey. What are you doing here?" His heart thudded in his chest as a thought struck him. "Piper?" He stepped back, ready to run to the pharmacy. He hadn't heard an emergency page come over the speakers, but he'd been holed up in an operating theater for two hours.

"She's fine, as far as I know." Ben stepped off the elevator. "I'm here to interview Tillie Trufant. She's awake."

"What? When did that happen?"

"Early this morning, I guess. She's groggy, but coherent."

"Can I come?"

"You can wait outside until I'm done, then I'll give you an update." He tipped his head toward the empty corridor. "Come on."

The two men strode down the hall in silence. Cullen's mind whirled with the possibilities Tillie's interview would bring. Was she involved? Did she know the person who tried to kill her? Or were they wrong and she did it to herself? Whatever the reason and whatever she revealed, at least they'd have something new to go on.

They rode the public elevator to the ICU. Ben flashed his badge at the nurses sitting at the desk. One pointed to a room to her left.

"Wait here." Ben pierced Cullen with a look before striding away.

With a low grumble, Cullen leaned against the desk. "You guys have any patients that need checking?"

The same nurse who pointed Ben to Tillie's room shook her head and offered him a commiserating smile. "Sorry, Dr. Tate. It's been pretty—" She stopped and waved a hand, wrinkling her nose.

Cullen bit back a smile. He appreciated her reluctance to say the word "quiet." It always heralded chaos.

"Well, the doctors have everything under control," she continued. "But if that changes, I'll let them know you're here and available."

"Thanks." He gave a short nod, then pushed away from the desk, wandering down the hall to look out the window.

The last few leaves held over from fall skittered across the parking lot along with a few food wrappers. Leaden clouds lined the sky. It was supposed to snow again tonight.

Tapping his fingers against his thigh, he turned away and took out his phone. He'd check his email while he waited. Levi told him there were some that needed his attention today, and he hadn't gotten to them yet.

Twenty minutes later, he'd answered a few and deleted a bunch more when Ben emerged from Tillie's room. Cullen pushed away from the wall. "Well?"

"Walk with me."

Frowning at both the tone of his voice and the pinched look to his face, Cullen put his phone away and followed Ben to the staff lounge at the end of the hall. The door snicked shut behind them.

"Someone tried to kill her."

"Did she see who?"

Ben's mouth flattened. "No. Just a shape in the dark. She said she thinks it was a man, but couldn't be sure. She remembered a smaller shape too."

"A woman did this?" Cullen had a hard time believing a woman could get Tillie Trufant through her house and into her car. She was petite, but she was on the heavy side.

"It could be a team. What's going on in the pharmacy probably involves at least two people. I've been looking into the pharmacists and the technicians, hoping something would pop."

"And? Do you have any leads?"

"A couple of them have some outstanding debts—more than just a mortgage or a car payment—but nothing that's not payable with time." He shook his head. "I'm missing something. There's another piece to this I haven't figured out yet."

"What else did she tell you?" Cullen crossed his arms. "Does she know what this is about?"

"She said she didn't at first, but there was something in her eyes—more than just the confusion from waking up. It was a hesitation that said she knew more than she was telling. I finally got her to open up, and she said she was looking into the discrepancies Piper found and had started questioning staff about whether they'd noticed anything else."

"Did she learn anything?"

"Nothing concrete. She said she got a feeling some of them were lying to her, but she couldn't prove it."

"Who?" Cullen wanted to know, so he knew who to look out for.

"I can't tell you that. It's an active investigation."

A scowl darkened Cullen's face. He crossed his arms and glared at Ben.

"Don't give me that look. I can't tell you. We don't know that any of the people she talked to are directly involved. Just that they might know who is. I have to investigate more."

Cullen's brows dipped, and he sighed, knowing Ben was right. "Do you think these people will talk to you?"

Ben shrugged. "Maybe. Depends on how scared they are of the person behind this."

Pursing his lips, Cullen nodded. He could understand that. "Didn't you guys seize her computers after the attack?"

Ben nodded. "Yeah. And the ATF took them. The only reason they let me interview her is because this was my case first and I have an FBI background." He scoffed. "Agent Porter called it a courtesy. There are days I miss my federal badge." He held up a hand. "And I never told you any of this. Even what I've said is probably more than I should have."

"Got it. Has their investigation turned up anything about the bomb in Piper's car? Or who the finger belongs to?"

"They recovered the detonator, and from what they've pieced together of the device, it looks like it was a timed device.

Her deviation from her routine saved her life. It also looks like something they've seen in cartel hits."

"Cartel? As in drug cartel?"

"Yeah. I think there's more at play here than an employee stealing drugs from the pharmacy. Something bigger. My guess is they're after Piper because she opened the can of worms that brought the authorities in. Someone not only wants to silence her before she can uncover any more, they want revenge, hence the finger. This is about terrorizing her just as much as silencing her."

Cullen swiped his hands over his face. His beard rasped beneath his palms. "So, she's still in danger, isn't she? Will she ever not be?"

"I hope so, but I'm not sure. She doesn't know anything, so my guess is that once we find the people working for the cartel and dismantle their little ring here, the threat will go away. They won't want to continue to draw attention to themselves and threaten exposing their identities. But in the meantime, she's keeping her guard and limited mobility. Now that Tillie's awake, I might recommend restricting it further. We'll have to see how things play out."

"Play out? You mean see if there's another incident? The next one could kill her, Ben." Cullen's voice rose with every word.

Ben patted the air. "I know. And I don't intend to put her in danger. But if she's anything like my wife or my sister-in-law —or hell, even Jake's wife—she won't willingly go into hiding. I don't want to force it unless it's necessary. Things have been quiet. She's following the rules. We'll see."

Cullen blew out a breath. "Fine. But I think I'll talk to her tonight about asking for a leave of absence. I don't think the hospital would object."

"Probably not. I'm amazed they haven't put her on one already."

"It's damage control. They don't want it to look like they have a problem. Or set themselves up for a libel suit. If they put her on leave, it will inevitably leak to the press, who will then think she's the one behind it all. It would ruin her reputation—and possibly mine by association. Trust me, they're very aware of what they're doing."

Ben's head bobbed. "Politicking at its finest. Okay, well, just keep me posted. I'd love it if she stayed in one place. It'd make keeping her safe easier. But I get it if she declines. Imprisonment—even voluntary and in your own home—can be too much for a lot of people."

A plan took shape in Cullen's mind as they left the lounge. Maybe he could sweeten the pot and get her to agree. He still had those favors to cash in.

Thirty-Four

Piper's stomach growled, sounding loud in the quiet hallway at the back of the pharmacy. She hoped Cullen had dinner ready when she got to his house. She was starving. It had been busy today—again. An outbreak of strep sent more people than usual to the urgent care located adjacent to the E.R., so they'd had an influx of patients all needing antibiotics. She felt bad for the kids. Some of them looked downright miserable.

"I can't do that, Peter. There's too much scrutiny on the pharmacy right now. Dr. Coombs is checking every shipment himself."

Piper paused as a woman's voice drifted out of an office. The doors in the pharmacy weren't very soundproof, she'd noticed.

"We don't have a choice, Kylie. They've got my wife. The only reason they don't have my kids is because I sent them away. I put the order in, but I need you to snag the extra boxes when the shipment arrives in the morning. I'll fix the invoice tonight."

Piper covered her mouth, stifling a gasp. That was Dr.

Henry. He and Kylie were the ones stealing drugs? And who were the "they" he was talking about? She sidled closer to the door, staying out of view. The glass panel was frosted, but that didn't mean they wouldn't see her shadow.

"How am I supposed to do that? I don't work tomorrow."

Piper heard him growl. "Call Rosalina. Remind her it would be terrible if something happened to her son."

"Peter—"

"No. You're in this as deep as I am. We have to do this or they'll kill Brenda, then they'll come after us. I don't like involving others, but Rosalina already knows about our operation. It won't hurt to remind her what's at stake."

A long pause met his proclamation before Kylie spoke again. Piper strained to make out the words.

"All right. But if I get caught, I'm singing like a bird. I won't go down alone."

A shift in color behind the frosted pane was Piper's only warning before the door swung open. She jerked away from the wall and started walking, glancing back as they stepped out. "Oh, hi, guys. I thought I was the only one from our shift still here." Which was true. She'd been with a customer when their shift ended. She'd seen Kylie and Dr. Henry go to the back as their relief arrived.

She kept walking and waved. "Have a good night." Quickening her step, she continued down the hall and entered the employee lounge, practically running to her locker.

"Piper."

Crap! So close! She stopped with her hand on the lock. A quick rush of fear and adrenaline spiked her heart rate. She closed her eyes for a brief moment and sucked in a breath, then turned around. "Yes?" Hot damn, that almost sounded normal, which was a minor miracle. The cold, angry look on Dr. Henry's face sent ice water through her veins.

He walked closer. Piper held her ground, though she wanted to turn and run.

"What did you hear?"

She feigned confusion. "What do you mean?"

"Don't play dumb. We all know you don't fit the blonde bimbo cliché. The doors in the pharmacy are thin. What. Did. You. Hear?"

Piper swallowed, her eyes darting to Kylie, who fidgeted just inside the doorway. The other woman worried her lip between her teeth as she picked at her fingernails.

"Hey," Piper held up her hands, "I don't know either of you well or your families. I won't say anything about your affair. The secret is safe with me." She mimed zipping her lips, praying they fell for her line of bull about an affair.

His gaze narrowed, and he studied her. Piper held his gaze. *Don't flinch, don't flinch, don't flinch.*

He shook his head. "I don't believe you."

"What?" Her eyes went as round as saucers. "When I make a promise, I don't break it. I won't tell anyone about the two of you."

"Cut the crap. We aren't having an affair, and you know it." He snagged her arm.

Piper gasped. "Wh-what are you talking about?" She fought to put some confusion in her voice, but her terror overrode it and it rang false.

"You have terrible timing, you know that, right?"

Anger replaced some of her fear. He was blaming her for this? "I'm not the one discussing my criminal enterprise in a place with paper-thin doors."

The cold look on his face morphed into fury, turning his cheeks red. "Get your coat. We're leaving."

She lifted an eyebrow, some of her backbone returning. "Yeah? And how do you plan to get away with kidnapping me? There might not be any cameras in here, but there are in the hallway we just walked through and all over the hospital outside of the pharmacy. Plus, I have an escort. He's been sitting right outside the pharmacy all day. The police will know we walked out together. One will even follow us."

"She's got a point, Peter." Kylie's quiet voice intruded.

"It doesn't matter. This has all gone to shit. Once I get my wife back, I'm getting far away from here. I've been squirreling most of my money away, knowing it would one day come to this. I'll go to Africa and help the people I started out trying to treat."

Piper frowned. "What?" What on earth was he talking about? Who was he trying to treat? And for what?

He ignored her and kept talking to Kylie. "What you do is up to you, but I'm not coming back." His head turned. "Get your coat, Piper. It's time to go."

Acknowledging the thread of steel in his voice, Piper opened her locker and took out her things. She'd have to signal her guard or something on their way out, or try to overpower him.

Dr. Henry snagged her purse as she withdrew it from the locker.

"Hey!"

"Where's your phone?" He tossed the bag to Kylie. "Search that."

"It's not in there." She knew he'd search her next when he didn't find it in her bag, and she didn't want his hands roaming over her body. Reaching into the cargo pocket of her scrub pants, she took out the device. "Here."

"Wise woman. I want you to call your guard. Tell him you had to run a medication upstairs to the oncology unit on your way out and he can meet you at the staff elevators on the first floor."

Piper tucked her tongue into her cheek and stared at the phone.

He shook the device. "Do it, or I will call my friends and tell them to go after your friend Mackenzie and Dr. Tate."

The fear from a moment ago returned. Her hand shook as she took the phone. Finding Ozzie's number in her contacts, she called him.

"Hey." His low voice rumbled over the line. "You about ready? Your shift ended ten minutes ago."

"Um, yes." She cleared her throat. "Sorry, I'm thirsty. I had to run a medication up to oncology. Can you meet me by the staff elevators near the cafeteria in about five minutes?"

"Wait. You left the pharmacy? Why didn't I see you?"

"I don't know. I thought you did. I waved, but then I got to the elevator and realized you hadn't followed me. I just need to get one of the nurses to sign for this, then I'll be ready to go. I have my stuff."

"Okay. Next time, though, make sure I see you."

"I will. See you soon." She pulled the phone away and hung up.

"Good job. That was believable." Dr. Henry took her phone and threw it in her locker. "Put your watch in there." He pointed to the Bluetooth watch on her wrist.

Dammit. She'd been hoping he wouldn't notice it. Unfastening the strap, she laid it on the shelf in the locker.

He slammed the door shut and let her go. "Put your coat on."

Piper did as she was told, mind spinning a thousand miles an hour. Dr. Henry took her purse from Kylie and thrust it at her.

"We're going to walk out of here like one big happy family. Don't forget, if you draw attention to us..." He let his words trail off and raised an eyebrow.

She nodded. "I know."

"Good." He grabbed her arm again and led her out the door into the main hospital.

"You want to tell me why you did all this? You seem like a nice person, not a criminal. Kylie, the same goes for you. Why did you do it?" She looked back and forth between them. Kylie kept her eyes straight ahead and refused to engage. Dr. Henry glanced at her, his expression stern.

"It started out as a way to help people in disadvantaged countries." He kept his voice low as they walked. "I discovered a flaw in the pharmacy's ordering system. It allowed me to place orders, then change them later and then create invoices for training courses or office supplies to cover the costs." His mouth flattened, then he shook his head. "We were sending vital medicines to people who couldn't otherwise afford them. But it was just getting too expensive to continue without help. My contact in South America put me in touch with a man who has ties to a Colombian cartel. The next thing I knew, cancer drugs and antibiotics weren't the only things we were smuggling out of the pharmacy."

He paused as they nearly ran into a group of nurses when they turned a corner. Nodding a greeting at them, he hurried her past, and his voice dropped even lower. "Anyway, it's all gone to shit, and I'm done. Now, no more questions."

Piper's eyes bounced off people's faces as she tried to process what he told her. She both wanted someone to notice he held her against her will and wanted them to completely ignore her. Knowing what she did now, she knew without a doubt he would do as he said and send his Colombian friends after Cullen and Mackenzie. So, she kept her mouth shut and let him lead her out of the hospital to the doctors' parking lot, praying the entire way the police could track them down before she met Dr. Henry's friends.

THIRTY-FIVE

The microwave clock stared back at Cullen like a neon sign in Vegas, teasing him. With each minute that ticked by, his anticipation that Piper would be home grew. She should have been back thirty minutes ago. He'd given her the benefit of the doubt, knowing sometimes she got waylaid by a patient or her boss. But he was ready to call now and find out where she was.

He thumbed open his phone and found her name. The soft burr of the ringer filled his ear, then rolled to voicemail. Cullen frowned and tried again. When it went to voicemail a second time, he called her escort, Agent Quartermaine.

That call, too, rolled to voicemail.

Growling, he stabbed at the screen. "Why won't anyone answer their phones?" He called Quartermaine again, who picked up.

"I can't talk right now, Dr. Tate."

"Where's Piper?"

The hesitation coming over the line told Cullen all he needed to know. "What happened?"

"Still trying to piece that together. She left the hospital

with two other pharmacy employees about thirty minutes ago. I'm trying to coordinate things, so I don't have time to give you the details."

"That's fine. I'm on my way." Cullen hung up on the man before he could tell him to stay home. They'd have to tie him down to get him to stay put.

Swiping his keys off the counter, he ran for the door, snagging his coat from the hook. He was in his car and on the road in less than a minute.

The miles ticked by slowly, even though he pushed his car over the speed limit—just a little. Getting pulled over would hold him up more than keeping it reasonable.

Halfway to the hospital, his phone rang. On the infotainment display, Ben's name flashed. Cullen pushed the button on his steering wheel to answer.

"Did you find her?"

"No. Quartermaine said you're on your way to Asheville. Go home. There's nothing you can do here."

Cullen growled. "I can't just sit at home. I'll go nuts. Where are you? Are you there?"

"Yes. Quartermaine called in the task force when she didn't appear where she said she would."

"Appear where—what do you mean?" He frowned at the display, confused.

"She called him and told him to meet her at the staff elevators. Said she was up in oncology, delivering a medication, but that she was ready to go as soon as the nurse signed for it. But then she never showed to meet him. I haven't seen the security footage yet, but Quartermaine has. That's how we know she left with two pharmacy employees. We're working on identifying them. That's all I know. Go home, Cullen. I'll call you when I know more."

Grinding his molars together, Cullen clenched the steering wheel.

"I mean it. You'll go just as crazy here and take us all with you. Catch up on paperwork to distract yourself. I know you have plenty of that."

A muffled voice came over the line, then Cullen heard Ben reply that he'd be right there.

"Look, I have to go. Turn around. I'll call you later." The line clicked before Cullen could reply.

Growling again, Cullen's mind spun, weighing his choices. He let out a soft curse and slowed. Ben was right. No matter where he was, he'd be restless. At the hospital, he'd feel useless. But he could go to his office and get some work done. It was better than wearing a hole in his floors, pacing while he waited for Ben to call back.

He found a side road and turned around. It bugged him to be driving away from Piper's last known location, but he knew this was the best thing for everyone—including himself.

Once back in Foggy Mountain, he drove straight to his office. He was never caught up on his coroner duties, so he'd tackle those and make the local police happy.

Parking behind the building, he went inside, flipping on lights as he moved down the corridor. In his office, he shrugged out of his coat and tossed it on the visitor's chair, then sat down behind the desk and booted up the computer.

His mind drifted to Piper. He prayed she was safe. That whoever had her hadn't harmed her yet. He sighed, pissed off. All this over some drugs.

The list of medications Piper told him about played through his mind. He frowned, sitting straighter. That was an odd list. Some of them he could understand. There was a market—especially for the cartels—for some of the drugs. But cancer drugs like Iclusig? Few people in the U.S. would pay for black market cancer drugs when most insurance companies covered them at a fraction of their retail cost or the manufacturer offered a copay assistance program. The medicines were more likely to be sold in other countries, where medications were scarce or cost prohibitive.

A case from last month niggled his brain. Evan Dryden.

Cullen logged into the system and pulled up Evan's file. He'd died from an infection. That didn't respond to antibiotics.

His eyes widened. What if the drugs Piper found weren't the only ones being tampered with?

He sat back and ran his hands over his jaw. "God. This is a nightmare." His mind cycled through all the deaths due to infectious causes to come across his desk in the last year. He jotted down several names, then did the same for cancer deaths. This was when he appreciated his memory.

List in hand, he logged into the hospital database and found their charts, reading through the notes on the cases. Three of them shouldn't have died based on their medical and treatment history. All of them were chalked up to a failure to respond to treatment.

Cullen reached for his phone and called Ben. It rang four times before he picked up.

"I don't have any news. We're still—"

"It's not about Piper. Well, not directly. There's more to this case than just drug smuggling."

A beat of silence came over the line.

"What do you mean?"

"So, I did what you said and stopped at my office to catch up on paperwork. I couldn't concentrate and started mulling over the facts of the pharmacy case when I remembered something. A former patient of mine died last month from an infection. One that, by all counts, he should have successfully fought off. This was after his leukemia came back, for which he was undergoing treatment."

"I'm lost. Don't leukemia patients normally have weak

immune systems? Why would him dying from an infection make you suspect foul play?"

"Because he was on all the right drugs. He'd been given immunity and blood cell boosters to fight it off, his numbers were through the roof, and he didn't have a resistant strain of bacteria. There's no reason he should be dead. Unless someone switched his drugs. I also found three other similar cases."

"Wait. You think he was murdered? That all this is about killing people?" Ben groaned. "I do not need another serial killer."

"Oh, I hadn't considered that." A furrow formed between Cullen's eyebrows, and he paused. The idea had merit, but he didn't think it was right.

"What were you considering, then?"

"Huh?" Cullen snapped back to the conversation. "Oh. That someone's taking the drugs, switching them for another more innocuous one or a placebo, then selling them to patients in other countries where medicines are in short supply."

"You got all that from one patient's death?"

Cullen shrugged. "It's how my mind works."

Ben sighed. "Right. Um, I'm not sure we can prove he died from the wrong medications. He's been embalmed or cremated already, right?"

"Yes, but he might still have blood stored at the hospital. I'll have to check. My point with this, though, is to give you another angle from which to investigate. It might not all be about the cartel you guys linked to the bomb. They don't have much use for cancer meds."

"Hmm... okay. I'll put it in my case notes and mention it to the task force. See where it leads us."

Some of Cullen's adrenaline ebbed now that he'd relayed

his discovery. "Great." He paused a beat. "There's still nothing on Piper?"

"No. We've identified the man with her. Dr. Peter Henry. He's one of the pharmacists. Still working on the woman. Henry's car is missing from his space in the doctors' lot, so we think they're in that. BOLO just went out, and the SBI sent some agents to his house. That's all I can tell you so far."

Cullen propped an elbow on the desk and rubbed his forehead. "All right. I appreciate the info."

"I know this is hard, Cul. I've been in your shoes. Just try to be patient. Keep yourself busy."

"Yeah." Cullen remembered when Gemma was missing. He hadn't known Ben that well then, but knowing him now, he could imagine how much her disappearance tore him up inside. It was nice to know someone understood what he was going through.

"I need to get back to the investigation. I'll keep you updated, I promise."

"Okay. Thanks, Ben."

"Yep. Talk to you soon." The line clicked as Ben hung up.

Cullen let the phone fall onto the desk. It clattered on the wood. He dropped his face into his hands and took a steadying breath.

Blowing it out, he sat up. Distraction. He needed a distraction.

The pile of folders in his inbox loomed large. He reached for the top one.

Thirty-Six

F ine sawdust tickled Piper's nose as she shifted her feet, scattering it into the air. Her face twitched as a sneeze threatened. She was in an old wood mill deep in the forest outside of town. Dr. Henry had brought her here and tied her up in what remained of an old office high above the mill floor.

It wasn't abandoned, though. Not anymore. Down below, someone had cleared out the milling equipment and filled the space with tables and packing supplies. People of all ages—but mostly young women—wearing tattered clothes and latex gloves stuffed small bags with pills, then boxed them up. She was in some sort of illicit drug processing facility.

Flexing her wrists, she tried to loosen the rope binding her to the chair. All it did was bite into her skin and make it burn.

Dammit, she needed to get out of here. Before Dr. Henry's "friends" arrived. There were a few downstairs with the workers, but they were low-level lackeys there to keep the peace. Sure, they could hurt her, but they weren't going to unless she escaped. Even then, she didn't think they'd kill her. Their bosses probably wanted that honor.

She didn't know what made her so special. Until today,

she didn't know they were behind the drug thefts. Or why Dr. Henry and Kylie were involved. But at least if they were going to kill her, she knew exactly why now.

Piper glanced around the space, looking for anything to saw through the rope. She was in a mill, for crap's sake. There had to be something.

But all that was up here was a metal desk and its chair, and the chair she sat in. There was a pad of paper and a pen on the desk, but nothing else. No stapler or tape dispenser, and definitely no scissors.

She rolled her eyes. It's not like she'd be able to use them, anyway, with her hands tied down.

Mouth pursed, she looked around again, her gaze stopping on the desk. It had pointy corners. Maybe she could snag the rope and fray it.

Standing as much as possible, Piper duck-walked to the desk. She bent her knees, holding a squat to line her hands up with the edge, and sawed her hand back and forth. A few pitiful strands came loose.

"Come on." Growling, she sat down. Her thighs were on fire from the squat. She'd never saw through the rope before her legs gave out.

Noise from below reached her through the dusty, grimy glass. She stood and shuffled to the window to look down. It was hard to see, but it looked like several men moving through the rows of tables. One of them shouted orders in Spanish, sending several others scurrying to do his bidding. Her heart thudded in her ears as she saw him approach the stairs.

No! She wasn't free yet. Her eyes tracked around the space again, but the same paltry furnishings met her gaze.

Piper plopped her chair down in the middle of the floor, her mind spinning. She needed a new plan. One that used her brain. It was her only way out.

The door opened and a middle-aged man stepped inside.

His perfectly coiffed coal-black hair had threads of silver through it. Beneath his impeccably tailored dark gray suit, Piper sensed a lean but fit physique. If she met him on the street, she'd think him a handsome, successful man.

"Ms. Riordan. I'd say it's a pleasure to meet you, but you've caused me nothing but trouble." Legs spread slightly, he clasped his hands in front of his body.

"Sorry." She wasn't, and her tone conveyed that.

Nice, Piper. Antagonize him. She pressed her lips together, heeding her inner voice. She needed to watch her mouth.

He offered her a cold grin. "I like spunky women. They make things... interesting." He rolled a hand over, then clasped it over the other again.

"That's nice. And who are you, exactly?"

A hint of amusement entered his eyes. "Gustavo Herrera." He sauntered forward, hands still clasped. "You know, I'm glad now my attempt to—remove you from the equation failed. I think you'll make an excellent outlet for the stress that comes with relocating operations."

Sweat prickled Piper's skin as horror flooded her veins when she grasped his meaning. It only lasted a moment before anger and determination replaced it. He might get more spunk than he bargained for if he tried anything. She was no wallflower.

Eyes narrowed, she glared at him.

He laughed. "Yes, I will quite enjoy you. I must remember to thank Dr. Henry for bringing you here instead of getting rid of you himself. His weak stomach for killing is my gain."

"Don't be so sure." She jerked against her bonds, wanting to punch the smug look off his face.

Desire lit in his eyes. Piper's stomach twisted and bile rose in her throat. What a sicko. Her defiance turned him on.

But she could use that to her advantage. Not here, though. Even if he came close enough for her to lash out at him with her legs, she was still tied to this damn chair, and there were half a dozen of his men down below.

"Yes, you'll do quite nicely. But I must go see to some other business. I'll have one of my men bring you some water. Would you like a snack?"

Despite herself, her stomach growled at the mention of food.

Herrera laughed. "I'll take that as a yes." He backed toward the door, a malevolent smile on his face. "You stay put, now." Wagging a finger at her, he stepped through the doorway, pulling the door shut.

Piper let out a growl of frustration and jerked her hands up again. The rope burned her skin, but she barely felt it. She needed a plan. Because it would be a hot day in Hades before she let that man touch her.

THIRTY-SEVEN

Piper's tinkling laugh morphed into chiming bells, pulling Cullen from his dream. He sat up, having fallen asleep on his desk and winced, grabbing his neck. The bells grew louder, and he realized it was his phone. Snatching up the device, he saw Ben's name on the screen. Neck pain forgotten as a surge of adrenaline hit, he answered. "Hello?"

"You okay? You sound funny."

"I'm fine. You woke me up. What time is it?" He lifted his wrist, blinking the sleep out of his eyes.

"About one a.m. I'm surprised you fell asleep."

"Me too. I'm still at my office. At my desk. Did you find Piper?"

"No, but we found Dr. Henry's car. Forensics is processing it. Her purse was in the backseat. There's no blood, so she was likely unharmed to that point."

Cullen blew out a breath and swiped a hand through his hair. "That's good. Where was the car?"

"Abandoned off an access road in the forest. A park ranger stumbled over it. He happened to be out looking for poachers and saw it tucked into the trees. We found tire tracks to another vehicle in the snow, but not much else. They lead back the way he came."

Damn. That wasn't much to go on.

"The raid on Henry's house netted some info, though. It was empty. SBI talked to the neighbors. They haven't seen his wife or kids in over a week and said he told them she and the kids left for a trip to visit some family out of state."

"Oh, man. How much you want to bet that finger belongs to Mrs. Henry?"

"That'd be my guess. Forensics gathered some DNA from their house. There's a rush on it, but the state lab is backed up. We might solve this before we find out if it's hers."

That would be Cullen's guess too. He prayed it was. If this went on for more than a day or so, the odds of finding Piper alive dropped dramatically. He couldn't let himself think about that.

"Is there anything I can do?"

"Not really. We're playing a waiting game now until forensics processes everything. There are a few people I need to talk to, but that's it. We need more information."

Cullen clenched his fist. It boggled his mind that in this day and age, there wasn't something that could be done to track her down.

His eyes drifted, landing on his watch. Like lightning, a thought struck him. Piper wore a Bluetooth watch. "Her watch."

"What?"

"Piper wears one of those watches that connects to her phone. Don't those have GPS?"

"Yeah, but we found it and her phone in her locker."

"Dammit." Cullen sat back in his chair.

"But I didn't think about Dr. Henry. We also identified the woman with them. Kylie Stoss. She's another pharmacy technician. I'm going to look into that right now. I'll call you back when I learn something."

The phone clicked in Cullen's ear as Ben hung up. Restless, he got up and paced to the window. Snow fell, giving the world a coziness he didn't feel. There was a hole in his heart that no amount of winter wonder could fill. It left him cold. He knew he'd need more than a blanket to warm him up. If they didn't find Piper alive, he wasn't sure he'd ever feel warm again.

Thirty-Eight

Footsteps thudded up the metal stairs outside the office. Half-asleep, Piper jerked awake, sitting up as the door opened and one of the goonies from downstairs came in. Her eyes widened, and she gasped as she saw who was with him. And her condition.

"Kylie?"

"*El jefe* wanted you to have a friend." He threw her to the floor at Piper's feet. She landed in a heap and didn't move. "Though I don't think she'll last long." Laughing, he backed through the door, shutting it again.

"Oh my God. Kylie, can you hear me?" Beneath the blood covering her face and arms, deep bruises shone black. Swelling surrounded her eyes to the point Piper didn't think she could see. "What happened? Why did they do this to you?"

Kylie moaned, but stayed still.

Tears pressed into the back of Piper's eyes. She might not like what Kylie did, but that didn't mean she wished her dead. "Kylie." She nudged the woman with her foot, rolling her onto her back. One arm flopped to the floor, lifeless. If it weren't for the moan, Piper would think her already dead.

"I'm... sorry." Kylie's voice came out breathy and low. "We just... wanted... to help people."

By stealing drugs? Piper kept her thoughts to herself, though, not wanting to tax Kylie. None of that mattered right now. "Shh. Don't talk. It'll be okay."

"No. It won't." A hard cough wracked her body. Blood droplets flew from her mouth, and she gagged. Rolling to her side, her fingers dug into the wooden floor as she struggled to breathe.

"Oh, God!" Piper glanced at the windows. "Help! Somebody! Help!" She stood, feeling utterly helpless as she watched Kylie gasp for air; more blood poured from her mouth as she gaped like a fish.

Desperate, Piper searched the room. There was still nothing to help free her.

Her gaze landed on the metal desk. It couldn't fray her bonds, but maybe she could use it to break the chair.

Sidling up to the desk, she turned sideways, then swung her hips, slamming the chair into it. Pain reverberated through her arms, but the wood held. She needed to hit it harder. Turning, she swung harder, putting her entire body behind the movement.

The wood cracked.

Hope made her heart race. Ignoring the ache in her arms, she rammed the chair into the desk a third time. A leg fell off and one arm splintered enough she was able to loosen the rope. With one hand free, she attacked the binding on her other arm. The knot was too tight for her to pick with one hand.

"Dammit!" Frustrated, pissed off, and scared Kylie was dying, she turned to the desk again. Lifting what was left of the chair, she swung it like a tennis racket into the metal frame. It broke into several pieces. She was still attached to the arm, but she could move more freely.

Dropping to her knees, she lifted Kylie to a sitting position, hoping the blood was coming from her face and not her lungs. The woman sputtered, but didn't struggle. Her mouth opened, and her chest heaved, but no air moved. All Piper heard was a gurgle.

"No!" The blood was in her lungs. She was drowning.

Kylie's hand latched onto Piper's arm, the grip punishing. Legs kicking, she writhed as she suffocated.

The door flew open as she went limp. Piper looked up at the man who entered, tears flowing down her face. "What did you do? She didn't deserve this."

Another set of footsteps sounded on the stairs. The man in the doorway stepped aside, and Herrera appeared. His cold, dark eyes spotted Kylie.

"Shame. I thought she'd last longer." He shrugged. "Oh, well." He glanced at his employee. "Get rid of her."

The man nodded and stepped into the room. When he bent down to pick up Kylie's body, Piper swung an arm up, smacking him with the remnants of the chair still attached to her.

"Ow!" Lurching backward, he tripped, falling to the floor.

"Get up, you fool!" Herrera kicked him in the side.

The man stumbled to his feet, clutching his ribs, and glanced at his boss.

"Get the dead girl." He pointed to Kylie, then looked at Piper. "If you want to not end up like her, I suggest you don't do that again."

Piper glared at him, but kept her hands down when the other man moved forward and lifted Kylie's body off the floor. He retreated from the room, leaving her alone with Herrera.

"You're a monster," she spat. Hatred for the man dripped off her words, and she sent him a death glare. "What did she do to deserve that?"

"She tried to talk to the cops. Luckily, Dr. Henry called.

He's been quite loyal since I kidnapped his wife."

Her eyes grew round. "The finger. It belonged to her, didn't it?"

He nodded once. "A warning for you. That I don't like meddlesome *mujeres*."

"Tell me—how many others in the pharmacy did you intimidate into silence? I can't be the only one who noticed things."

"You're very astute, Ms. Riordan. Several of your colleagues received visits from my men after they brought discrepancies to Dr. Henry's attention. It is unfortunate that you went to Dr. Reid and Dr. Trufant instead."

She lifted a shoulder. "Sorry."

The cold, deadly look returned to his eyes. Apprehension stiffened Piper's muscles.

"Careful, *princesa*. My patience where you're concerned is running thin. Spunk will only carry you so far before I get angry."

She blinked, knowing defiance shown in her eyes, but she stayed silent.

He narrowed his gaze, then tipped his head, studying her. "Since you seem to have busted through your restraints, I guess it's time to move you to more—comfortable accommodations." A wicked gleam entered his eyes a moment before he advanced on her.

Piper scampered backward on her hands, but in the small space she couldn't get away. He cornered her against the windows and reached for the arm still tied to the chair piece.

She swung with her right, connecting with his jaw. If he took her out of this mill, she had a feeling her quality of life and subsequent chance of survival would plummet. She didn't want to die, but she'd rather die here, fighting, than let him abuse her—repeatedly—before he killed her.

Growling, he tried to snag her hand, but Piper injected her

long legs into the equation, tucking her knees and shoving her feet into his midsection. With one hard thrust, she sent him flying across the room.

She didn't wait to see where he landed. Scrambling to her feet, she lunged for the shard of chair leg in front of the desk. Her only way out was to fight. He was between her and the door.

Angry Spanish echoed through the room. Heart in her throat, she rolled as he regained his footing and came after her.

"Wrong move, *princesa*." His voice was a low growl. In a few strides, he was across the room.

Piper raised the chair leg, but it was like poking him with a feather. He batted it away and grabbed her arm, then smacked her across the face. Stars swam in her vision, growing brighter when he fisted a hand in her hair.

"I'm going to enjoy breaking you." His grated whisper sent hot breath washing over her face.

A soft whimper escaped her as his fingers tightened in her hair. She raised a hand to clutch his wrist and stood on her toes to relieve the pressure. Tears leaked from her eyes.

He yanked, pulling her toward the door.

Piper let out a screech and stumbled after him. She didn't have a choice except to follow.

Down the stairs they went and across the mill floor, then through the packers, who cast glances at her from the sides of their eyes. He twisted the doorhandle and gave the door a vicious shove. It banged against the wall outside.

When they stepped over the threshold, Piper's fear hit new heights, and her fight response kicked in. She reached out and grabbed his shirt, pulling their bodies together. It threw him off balance, and he let go of her hair. She took advantage of his surprise and thrust a hip into his middle, pushing away with her arms.

He was quick to recover, though, and snagged her arm

before she could take more than a couple of steps.

"*Princesa*, you're just making things worse." He picked her up and slung her over his shoulder.

Piper screamed and wiggled, knowing her size would make her hard to hold and walk at the same time. She toppled out of his arms, and he fell with her. Kicking at his face, she scrambled back. He grabbed her foot and crawled up her legs, pinning her to the ground.

The punch to the face stopped her frantic scramble. Stunned and dazed from the blow, she didn't protest as he hauled her to her feet and dragged her toward a car.

Her mind screamed at her to fight, but she couldn't make her muscles work now.

"Gustavo!"

Herrera turned. Through her foggy brain, Piper registered one of the goonies running toward them.

"We have a problem, *jefe*. The police know who took her." He pointed to Piper. "They raided Dr. Henry's house late last night."

"Where is he?"

"He left. Just before you got here with that other woman. Said he had some things to take care of before we relocated."

Herrera's low growl vibrated through Piper's chest. Some of her muscle function returned, but she stayed still, wanting him to think she was still dazed.

"Find him. And tell the packers to step it up. I'll go retrieve Dr. Henry's collateral right after I do something with this one." He gave Piper a shake.

A jolt of terror went through her. What did that mean? Was this it? Was he going to kill her now? She kept herself still. Now wasn't the time to fight back again. Not when he had help.

"Yes, *jefe*." The man turned and ran back to the mill.

Herrera changed direction, dragging her around the side

of the building. A small weathered shed loomed, ominous, at the back of the mill, and she could see the river flowing under the main building; the waterwheel sat idle just above its surface.

"What are you going to do?" She tried to dig her heels into the dirt and snow, but he just pulled harder.

"Ah, she speaks. I should kill you and dump you for the police to find, but I'm invested in breaking you now." They reached the shed, and he opened the door. "You can sit tight in here until I'm ready for you."

She pitched forward as he shoved her inside. Landing in the dirt, she got to her feet, but was too slow to stop the door from closing. She threw her weight into it, but he was too strong. It stayed closed, and she heard a lock click on the other side. His laughter rang through the wood, fading as he walked away.

Piper rattled the door. The knob turned freely, but it wouldn't open. He'd padlocked the door.

Letting out a frustrated groan, she turned, glancing around the shed in the small amount of light coming through the grimy window from the midday sun. Stacks of boards leaned against the walls. Animal droppings, leaves, and other detritus covered the floor. In the far corner, there was an old table saw.

She hurried over to it, hoping it still had a blade.

Peeking through the top were the rusted teeth of a circular blade.

"Yes!" The word hissed through her teeth. She raised her left arm over the blade and carefully sawed through the rope still binding the chair arm to her body. It frayed and loosened enough she was able to shake it off.

Piper rubbed her wrist and squinted at the machine, looking for a way to get the blade out. She had no clue how the saw worked, but she needed that blade.

Thirty-Nine

"Dr. Tate? There's a call for you."

Cullen glanced up from the chart he was annotating. He'd gotten another doctor to cover his shift, but restlessness drove him to work, anyway. He needed to stay busy to stay sane.

The nurse at the end of the long desk waved the phone receiver in her hand.

"What line?" He reached for the phone in front of him.

"Three."

He picked up the receiver and pressed the button to connect the call. "Dr. Tate."

"Cullen, it's Tristan Mabley. We need the coroner's van on Irvine Road, where the bridge goes over the river. Are you able to get away, or should I call your assistant?"

Cullen's heart stuttered. The emotions he'd bottled up so he didn't fall apart peeked out of their box. He slammed the lid down; if he wanted to function, they had to stay locked away.

Mind clear, his logical, rational thinking returned. If it was Piper, Ben would have shown up and told him in person. He cleared his throat, pushing the last of his anxiety back into its corner of his mind. "I can get away. Can you tell me more about the case?"

"Passersby found a woman floating in the river. She was hung up on the bridge."

"Okay. I'll get Levi gathering equipment, and we'll see you there in about forty-five minutes." Cullen went over a mental list of what they'd need for a body that had been in the river.

"Sounds good. See you soon."

He echoed Tristan's farewell and pressed the button on the phone base to disconnect the call, then dialed the colleague covering for him.

Once he had the few cases he'd taken on covered, Cullen went to his office to get his things, then left the hospital. He called Levi en route, giving him a quick rundown of the situation and a list of things to put in the van. They were going to meet there to save time.

Not for the first time, he said a prayer of thanks for his assistant. He'd lucked out when Levi applied for the job. It had been a Hail Mary when he put that ad out. He'd gone through two office assistants and kept borrowing techs from local crime labs, before he got sick of the disorganization. He wanted someone dedicated to his office. He got that in spades with Levi Chambers. Not only did he get a forensic tech who specialized in death investigation, but an office manager who kept his life running like a well-oiled machine.

It took Cullen thirty minutes to reach the scene. His headlights washed over the area, adding to the flashing blue and red bouncing off the trees and cars. He pulled in behind the coroner's van and got out, walking up to the taped off perimeter, where Tristan and Levi stood in conversation.

"Hey, boss." Levi saw him first.

"Hey. What have we got?" His eyes traveled to the yellow, tarp-covered lump on the ground.

Tristan squatted and lifted a corner. "Young woman. Probably mid-twenties. She's been badly beaten. No ID, but I think it's Kylie Stoss. Her build matches, not to mention the blonde hair and scrubs."

Bile rose in Cullen's throat as he took in her face. He swallowed and pulled his doctor persona around him like a cloak. He had a job to do and needed to forget this woman's connection to Piper, what this could mean for her.

He crouched next to Tristan and looked at her injuries more closely. He could understand why they weren't one hundred percent certain this was Kylie Stoss. Her face was unrecognizable thanks to the swelling and bruising.

"Here." Levi held out some gloves to him.

"Thanks." Cullen took them and put them on, then spread her eyelids apart as much as the swelling would allow. Small purple dots speckled the whites of her eyes. "It looks like she asphyxiated."

"Probably couldn't swim all beat up like that and drowned. Or she was unconscious." Tristan shook his head. "Someone has a rage problem. That level of beating isn't something we see—ever."

Cullen agreed.

"Any idea how long she's been in the water?" Tristan asked.

"I'd say not long. A few hours, maybe? She's got some rigor, but it's not set. And her wounds look relatively fresh. I don't see much evidence of healing. Levi, pass me the liver probe and a scalpel."

Digging in the black plastic box at his feet, Levi took out what looked like a meat thermometer and handed it to Cullen, along with a scalpel.

"Thanks." Cullen broke open the packaging on the scalpel and made a small incision on the woman's right flank just below her ribcage. He cut down through the muscle and fascia and into the abdominal cavity, then inserted the temperature probe. "What's the water temp?" He glanced up.

Levi removed an infrared thermometer from his bag and walked the few feet to the river's edge. He aimed the device at the water. A red dot marred the glassy surface, and it beeped. "Thirty-eight degrees."

Cullen withdrew the liver probe and did some quick calculations in his head based on the water temperature and her condition. "She's likely been dead about four hours, maybe a couple more."

"Dude, I love you." Tristan took out his phone. "I can work backward from that using the speed of the river and hopefully find where she was dropped into the water." He turned away, lifting his phone to his ear.

"Nice job, Doc." Levi clapped him on the shoulder.

"Yeah." Cullen blew out a breath. He just hoped it helped find Piper.

FORTY

Teeth chattering, Piper hugged her knees closer to her chest and dipped her face into the well between them, doing her best to stay warm. The shed was unheated. She was glad they never stripped her of her coat. Things would be much different if she were only wearing her scrubs.

It didn't mean she wasn't freezing, though. Her hands were stiff and numb, and the end of her nose felt like a popsicle. And her face ached where Herrera punched her. She could feel the swelling in her cheekbone. It was the only hot spot on her body.

Her lack of movement didn't help matters. She could only do so much running in place before her lungs reached their limit and she started gasping. The cold wasn't helping, either. She felt like she couldn't catch her breath.

So, here she sat, trying to ignore the cold and the ache in her face. It wasn't like there was much to explore in here, anyway. She'd managed to get into the table saw, but couldn't get the blade off without the proper tools. The only implement in the shed that came close to fitting into the screw holding the blade in place was the end of the saw's plug. But it was too fat to fit into the slot.

Once she exhausted her options to take the saw apart, she tried to pry the shed door open with one of the boards. All she succeeded in doing was giving herself splinters. They went right through her gloves.

A tear slid out of her eye and dripped onto her pants. Despair made her chest ache. She didn't want to die in here. She wanted to go home and warm up in Cullen's arms, sipping her homemade hot chocolate.

Memories of his hazel eyes, bright with amusement, filled her mind. She grabbed hold of the thought and kept it front and center. She had a lot to live for and couldn't think like she was going to die. When she got out of here, she planned to attach herself to one handsome doctor and never let go. One thing all this alone time had made her realize was that she loved that man more than anything. She loved his quiet nature and hearty laugh. The way his eyes lit up when he looked at her, and how his normally reserved attitude disappeared when they made love. Most of all, she loved his big, sexy brain and all the good he did for people.

God, she missed him.

Sniffing, she swiped her face on her pant leg and took a steadying breath. She just needed to last until someone either came for her or the cops found her. She might even try to bust out the window and squeeze through before long. Maybe once all Herrera's men left. If they left her here alone, that was. That monster could still come back.

Faint voices brought her head up. It had been hours since she heard anything other than the rumble of vehicles. Standing up, she grabbed the piece of two-by-four she found in the stack of lumber and eased toward the door to listen.

Spanish floated on the air. She made out several words, her

heart leaping into her throat as one in particular caught her attention—*policía*. Edging closer, she put her ear to the crack, straining to make out more. Herrera's voice carried to her, and she concentrated, trying to decipher the rapid-fire Spanish, thankful she hadn't forgotten all of it since high school. She heard the name Manuel mentioned and a reference to him wanting this operation wrapped up and all the cargo on the road.

Piper frowned. So, Gustavo wasn't the big boss? He sure acted like it.

The rattle of the padlock on the door made her jump. She stepped back, brandishing the two-by-four like a bat.

Light from the setting sun spilled through the doorway, blinding her. She swung, hoping she connected with whomever entered, but only got air. Blinking to force her eyes to adjust, she noted the figure coming toward her too late. Herrera grabbed her, spinning her around. He wrenched the board from her, then held her arms behind her back. Cold metal encircled her wrists, and she heard the snick of handcuffs as they tightened.

She jerked against his hold. "Let me go, you rat!"

"Sorry. Can't do that. Time to go." He tugged, pulling her off balance. She tripped over her frozen feet, and he half-dragged, half-pushed her out the door.

Getting her feet under her as they moved through the snow and dead grass, she did what she could to resist him.

He stopped, then something hard pressed into her side. "Behave, or this ends now. I don't have time to deal with your feistiness."

A clammy sweat broke out on Piper's face, prickling her scalp as she realized he held a gun to her side. Her muscles tensed, and she quit struggling.

"Good girl, *princesa*." He resumed walking, leading her to

the silver SUV parked in the gravel lot. A utility van disappeared down the drive into the trees.

Her mind spun. She had to do something. Had to get away. Leaving with him wasn't an option, but she didn't want to die, either.

She glanced around. All the other vehicles were gone, and no one else was in sight. The mill was deserted now. They were all alone. This was her chance.

But what could she do with her hands cuffed behind her back?

Something she saw online once floated through her head. It was one of those short videos intended to give women quick tips on self-defense. She'd never tried any of it, but if ever there was a time, it was now.

She waited until they stopped at the car and he was distracted. He lifted the gun away to get the keys, and Piper reacted, going limp. Her arm slid free of his grasp as she fell down. She stopped short of letting her knees hit the ground and pivoted on the balls of her feet. With a mighty yell, she sprang forward and used her shoulder to ram into him like a linebacker. His back hit the side of the SUV, and she heard the air leave his lungs with a whoosh. The gun flew from his hand.

Piper righted herself and took off running. She didn't know where she was headed, but knew she had to keep moving. Anywhere was better than here.

Herrera's angry shout echoed through the clearing. She kept going, praying she didn't get shot in the back.

The sharp retort of his pistol sounded, and she flinched, letting out a yelp. Bark splintered to her right. She prayed harder and pumped her legs faster, weaving now between the trees.

Another shot went off. She didn't see where the bullet struck. Glancing back, she caught a glimpse of him coming after her. He wasn't that far behind. With her hands tied at her back, she wasn't going to escape; she couldn't run fast enough.

The ground beneath her feet gave way. A sharp scream burst from her chest as she fell into a deep hole. Pain radiated up her legs as she crashed into the bottom amid the remnants of the rotten plywood she fell through.

Piper scrambled through the leaves, standing. She winced at the pain in her left ankle. Her head whipped from side to side as she took in her surroundings. What did she fall into? A well? She quickly discarded that thought. It wasn't deep enough. Some sort of cellar, maybe?

Rustling leaves sent her into flight mode. She searched the area for somewhere to hide, but it was just an open pit. She dove into the shadows, praying it was enough.

A low laugh emanated from above. "I can still see you, *princesa.*"

Piper's expression morphed into a severe frown. She hobbled forward and glared up at him and the gun he pointed at her. "Just shoot me and get it over with. You won't get me out of here without a fight." She'd pull him in with her if he tried to haul her out, then they'd both be stuck. And she certainly wasn't climbing out so he could hold her hostage again.

He tipped his head, studying her, then lowered the gun, clicking the safety into place. A slow, calculating smile spread over his face. "I don't need to shoot you. The elements will do you in long before anyone finds you. It's a shame, though. I was looking forward to our time together. But speed is of more importance now. Rest assured, I'll find some other woman to take your place." His smile turned evil, and he turned away. The leaves rustled again as he walked back the way they came.

His footsteps faded, and soon the only sound was the

wind blowing through the bare trees and her heart thudding in her ears.

She sagged against the dirt wall as the reality of her situation hit her. She was all alone, exposed to the elements in the middle of the forest, and handcuffed.

Well, shit.

Forty-One

Cullen's gloves snapped as he took them off and tossed them in the biohazard bin in the morgue. The task force asked him to do a cursory exam on Kylie Stoss to see if she offered any further clues. He'd done what he could, short of a full autopsy, including putting a bronchoscope down her trachea. She'd drowned, but not in the river. Her lungs were full of blood.

With a quick tug on his paper smock, he broke the ties. He couldn't imagine the pain she'd gone through leading to her death. The x-rays revealed multiple rib fractures and a broken sternum, as well as numerous facial fractures. Someone used her like a punching bag.

He exited the exam suite and headed for the morgue office to get his coat and car keys, ready to go home. Despite the churning in his stomach from worrying about Piper, his gritty eyes and heavy limbs told him he needed to sleep. He'd call the agent in charge on his way home and let him know what he found.

Shrugging into his jacket, he turned out the lights and left, making his way up one floor to the ground level. In the main hospital, he walked through the staff hallway with his head down, not wanting to talk to anyone. He pushed through the staff exit, steeling himself against the bitter wind, and headed for the doctors' lot.

The car beeped as he unlocked it, and he climbed inside, happy to be out of the wind. He reached for the seatbelt, but his phone rang before he could fasten it. Lifting a hip, he removed the device from his pocket. It was Ben.

His heart pounded in his chest, warming him despite the cold air in the car. He slid his thumb over the screen and lifted it to his ear. "Hello?"

"Hey. Tristan found a likely location where Kylie Stoss was dumped. It's an old abandoned mill a few miles from the bridge. I just got here and there's evidence of recent activity. We're still searching, but no sign of Piper yet. I just wanted to call and keep you updated."

Cullen started the engine, his fatigue forgotten. He wanted to be there to help search. "I'm coming. Don't try to talk me out of it."

A beat of silence passed. "Fine. But you have to do as I say. Did you learn anything from Stoss' body? I haven't heard from Agent Porter."

"I just finished examining her and was going to call him on my way home. She drowned in her own blood. Someone beat her to death."

"You're sure she was dead before she went in the river?"

"Completely. The blood in her lungs wasn't diluted." His hand shook as he raised it to rest on the steering wheel. Saying the words out loud broke through the barrier he'd erected around his feelings. Piper could be in the same predicament as Kylie. They could find her body next.

Ben's voice droned in his ear, but he missed what he said. "Sorry, say that again."

Another beat of silence came over the line. "I said I'd pass that along to Porter. Hey, don't lose hope, okay? We haven't found anything to indicate she's been harmed."

Cullen swallowed around the lump in his throat and shoved his thoughts back into their cage. The walls were see-through now, though. "I know. It's just wearing on me. It's been a full day. So much could have happened in that time."

"Don't let that genius brain of yours think up all the bad stuff. Focus on other things."

"I'm trying." And he was, but the fatigue plaguing him made it damn hard.

"Try harder. And get your ass out here. I'll put you on the search."

"Yeah."

"Okay. See you soon."

Cullen hummed a goodbye and hung up. He set the phone in the center console and backed out of his space, heading north to the bridge where Kylie Stoss washed up. He knew where that mill was. It used to be a hot spot for teenagers until some foreign company bought it and changed the locks. Before that, they got several kids a year into the E.R. who drank themselves sick at parties there.

Despite the adrenaline in his system, he yawned. He hadn't slept, other than a catnap here and there, since Piper disappeared. Rolling his window down, he let the bitter air hit him in the face. The chill was just enough to keep him awake as he drove up the winding mountain road to the mill.

He saw the flashing red and blue lights before the cars. Breaking through the trees, he came to a halt behind a county cruiser. Cullen scanned the scene, but didn't see much other than the lone deputy manning the perimeter. He cut the engine and got out.

"Dr. Tate? What are you doing here? No one called down and said they found a body." The deputy frowned as he approached.

"I know. But I talked to Sheriff Davidson. He told me to come up and join the search for Piper."

"Oh, okay. Let me radio up there and see where he wants you to go."

Cullen rocked on his heels as he waited for the deputy to contact Ben. He studied the mill just visible through the trees, illuminated by saltpeter lights. They must have found something to justify hauling all that equipment out here.

Ben's voice crackled over the radio. "Send him up to the mill."

Giving the deputy a tight smile, Cullen jogged past him and up the lane. On the other side of the trees, the activity increased. Men and women in uniform came and went from the mill, some carrying boxes full of evidence bags.

"Things have escalated since we talked." Ben stepped out of the mill, black gloves on his hands and a serious expression on his face.

"I see that. What did you find?" *Please let it be something that tells us where Piper is.*

"Evidence of a drug operation. And blood."

Cullen's heart did a two-step. "How much?"

"Enough, but not so much that someone could die from blood loss. It might be Kylie's. We found parts of a broken chair, some bloody rope, and skid marks in the dust in the office. There was quite the scuffle up there."

A frown turned down Cullen's eyebrows. "There weren't any ligature marks on Kylie's body."

"Hmm." Ben pressed his lips together, his expression turning contemplative. "That's interesting. Dosting."

"Did you find anything to indicate Piper was here?"

"Possibly. Forensics is still processing the office, but they found some blonde hairs. They could be Kylie's too. But if she wasn't tied up, then there's a possibility someone else was up there and they aren't hers."

The first stirrings of hope lit in Cullen's chest. "Okay. Is there a search going? You mentioned one. Where do I start?" If she was anywhere near the mill, he wanted to find her. Even if—even if it wasn't the outcome he wanted.

"Hang on, I wasn't finished." Ben held up a hand. "Quartermaine and his partner found an open shed behind the mill. It, too, showed signs of a struggle. There are footprints interspersed with drag marks leading out of it, then two sets of footprints heading into the woods."

"Why didn't you lead with that?" Irritated that there could be a solid lead on Piper's whereabouts, he glared at his friend, then took a step to the side to head out back.

Ben held up a hand again. "There's only one set returning from the woods, Cullen. They're too large to be a woman's."

His heart skipped several beats. He blinked, his mind blank, unable to process what that meant. When his brain started working again, a fierce need to search for her sent his feet moving toward the trees.

"Cullen."

Ben's voice carried after him, but he didn't stop.

"Cullen, wait!"

Cullen ignored him, breaking into a run. He didn't know where he'd start searching, just that he had to.

A firm hand clamped onto his forearm, spinning him around.

"Cullen—"

"Let me go, Ben. I have to—" His voice broke off with a choked sob. The glass prison walls holding back his emotions shattered. He sucked in a breath. "She can't—she can't be dead." He turned bleak eyes on his friend. "Please, Ben. We have to find her." Knees like gelatin, he stumbled a few feet to his left and leaned against a tree.

Ben's hand landed on his back. "Remember what I said

earlier—don't lose hope. I'll do everything I can to bring her back alive."

Cullen's head bobbed, his eyes trained on the forest floor. "I'm trying not to." He ground his teeth together, doing his damnedest to reconstruct the prison in his mind and shove his feelings back inside. Closing his eyes, he focused on reining them in.

Once he felt more in control, he glanced at Ben. "How do we find her in all this?" He swept an arm out, gesturing to the sea of trees. "And in the dark?"

"I have a K-9 on the way. Carter and Maverick should be here any time. They would have been here sooner, but they were on the other side of the county on a call." Ben touched Cullen's shoulder. "Come back to the mill. Maverick will have better luck than any of the rest of us. If she's out here, he'll find her."

"Yeah." Cullen scrubbed his hands over his face as a bone-deep weariness took hold. He wasn't used to this riot of emotions, and it was wearing him down.

Ben led them back to the bright lights in the mill yard. Commotion from the drive drew their attention as they reached the building.

"It's Carter."

Cullen's adrenaline spiked again. He tamped down the hope, knowing the outcome could be heartbreaking.

The deputy and his K-9 partner jogged up the lane. Ben headed their direction. Cullen followed closely behind.

"Sorry, Ben. It took me a bit to hike back to my car." Carter's mouth slashed down as Ben and Cullen approached. "Dr. Tate." Confusion lit in his gray eyes. "Did you guys find a body?"

Ben shook his head. "Our missing victim is Cullen's girlfriend."

Understanding dawned on Carter's face, and his expression turned sympathetic. "Oh. Got it." His mouth twisted. "Sorry, man. We'll do our best to locate her."

"Thanks. It's appreciated." Cullen gave him a quick nod.

Carter turned to Ben. "Where do you want us to start?"

"By the shed." Ben pivoted and jogged toward the mill. "We found two sets of prints leading from there into the forest and signs of a struggle." He paused at his cruiser and opened the front passenger door, removing an evidence bag. "I brought Piper's purse for Maverick to scent from."

"Perfect. Let's start at the shed and see if he gets a read."

The three of them and the dog trotted around to the small shed. Its weathered door hung open, shifting slightly in the wind.

Ben opened the evidence bag and handed it to Carter.

"Mav, scent." Carter held the purse to the dog's nose. Maverick buried his face in the bag for a moment before his handler pulled it away. "Seek, Mav."

The dog barked once and took off toward the trees, quickly reaching the end of his leash. Carter ran behind him, flicking on his flashlight as he went. Cullen glanced at Ben, who tipped his head toward the duo, and the two of them took off in pursuit.

Ben's flashlight bobbed in the darkness, illuminating a small swath of forest in front of them.

Cullen tripped on a root, stumbling forward, but caught himself before he hit the ground. He wished he had a flashlight of his own.

Sidling closer to Ben, he did his best not to trip over anything else as they ran after the dog. The animal took a crazy path through the trees, weaving between the trunks. When he started barking and straining at the end of his leash, the hope Cullen had stuffed down deep arose.

Carter barked out some commands as the dog paced near

an area twenty feet ahead. He stared at the ground, ignoring Carter's commands to quiet.

It didn't matter. They reached him in moments. Carter and Ben aimed their lights at the ground, illuminating a ten-by-ten hole that was about the same depth. Piper laid at the bottom, motionless.

Cullen didn't wait for the others to do something. He dropped to his butt on the forest floor and slid over the edge.

"Piper!" He landed beside her and reached for her, afraid of what he'd find. She was curled up half on her side, her hood low over her face. Grabbing her shoulder to turn her onto her back, he noticed her arms were cuffed behind her back. "Honey, can you hear me?" He nudged her hood back and brushed her hair away from her face. She was ice cold. Her eyelids fluttered and she let out a soft moan. He glanced up. "Get a medical crew here. Tell them to have warm saline, heat packs, and blankets ready when we reach the ambulance. And I need a handcuff key."

Above, he heard Ben relay the information over Maverick's whines, then he called down to Cullen. In the glint of the flashlights, Cullen saw a flash of metal in Ben's hand.

"Catch."

The small object hit him in the chest, and he trapped it against his body. It was a handcuff key.

He turned Piper over to get to her hands, unlocking the cuffs mostly by feel. "Piper." He gave her a soft shake as they came off. "Honey, it's me, Cullen. Wake up for me."

Her lashes fluttered again as he rolled her back over, and her eyes opened, but they weren't focused. He clenched his teeth, holding back a growl. She was delirious. He glanced up again. "Find me a way to get her out of here. Fast." Turning back to her, he gently laid her out so he could better examine her, then reached his hands under her coat, feeling for injuries to her torso. Her ribs felt fine, and she didn't flinch when he pressed on her abdomen.

Moving down her legs, her left ankle was swollen, and when he peeled back the sock, he could see dark purple bruising. He left her shoe on for now, and checked her arms and head, but found no further obvious injuries.

Maverick barked, then whined. Cullen looked up to see him staring at something beyond them in the trees. A moment later, he heard voices and leaves rustling and could see more flashlights bouncing off the tree branches.

"Help is here," Ben said.

Several faces appeared at the rim of the hole.

"What do you need, Dr. Tate?"

Cullen squinted up into the light, recognizing Maurice. "A backboard, some restraints, a foot splint, and a stethoscope and blood pressure cuff. I want to check her vitals before we move her." Her semi-conscious state worried him. He hoped it was just a result of hypothermia and not from a closed head injury.

The stethoscope and blood pressure cuff came first. He eased her arm out of her coat. She opened her eyes again and tried to pull away.

"It's okay, honey. I just want to check your vitals."

She gave another weak tug, then closed her eyes again.

Cullen didn't waste time. He applied the cuff and quickly took the measurement. It was low. He pressed two fingers to her neck and counted. So was her pulse.

Maurice dropped into the hole beside him.

"How's she doing?"

"Not great. We need to get her out of here and start warming her up. I'm guessing her core temperature is in the mid-eighties."

The paramedic looked up, signaling to the others above. "Pass everything down."

As equipment came over the edge, Cullen applied it to Piper's body, starting with the foot splint. Once her ankle was stable, he and Maurice loaded her onto the backboard. They tied her down, then attached ropes to the board and threw them to the others. Ben jumped in to help them hoist her up and keep her level while the rest of the group pulled her out of the hole. With her out, Carter lowered a rope down and acted as a belay so the three of them could climb out.

Cullen dusted off his hands when he reached topside and wiggled his fingers. The cold had seeped into them without his gloves on. Ahead, the other medics and police officers carried Piper toward the mill. He took off after them. Maurice and Ben weren't far behind.

Without the need to zigzag through the forest, they made it to the ambulance in a fraction of the time. Cullen hopped up inside, behind the medics.

"Get a reading on her temperature. Who's starting the IV? You warmed the saline, right?"

"And we've got heat packs." Maurice's partner, Liz, picked one up and waved it before she tucked it into Piper's armpit, then grabbed the thermometer and ran it over Piper's forehead and behind her ear. "Temp is eighty-five-point-three." She laid it down and picked up an IV kit.

Cullen stared at the scene, trying to keep himself disconnected from his emotions. They wouldn't help him now. Piper needed him clear-headed. *He* needed himself to be clear-headed to maintain his sanity.

"Are you guys good?" he asked. "Can we head to the hospital?"

Liz nodded, spreading a bandage over the IV she just placed in Piper's hand.

Maurice jumped out the rear doors. "Let's roll." They slammed shut and a moment later, the driver's door opened and closed, then the engine roared to life.

"Where you want to go, Doc?" Maurice called from the front.

"Foggy Mountain is closer." He sank into a seat opposite Liz as the ambulance bumped down the driveway.

"Foggy Mountain it is."

Cullen braced his elbows on his knees and folded his hands, propping his chin on top. He watched Liz put ECG electrodes on Piper's chest. The wave form that appeared on the screen told him her body was fighting for survival. A sliver of fear that she wouldn't make it escaped its prison. He closed his eyes and pressed his lips together. She had to live.

FORTY-TWO

Shards of pain throbbed through Piper's fingers and toes, stabbing her in time with her heartbeat. The buzz in her ears gradually faded and the sound of muffled voices alongside a quiet whir penetrated her foggy brain. She opened her eyes, blinking against the harsh overhead lights, and raised a hand to block them out.

A clear tube snaked out from beneath a bandage on the back of her hand. She turned her head, following the tube and found the source of the whir; an IV pump pushed fluids into her veins.

"Welcome back."

Cullen's deep voice came from her other side, and she turned her head. Seated next to the bed, he leaned his elbows on his knees, a delighted smile toying with his full lips beneath his short beard as he stared at her.

"Hi." Her voice came out raspy, and she cleared her throat.

He got up and walked to the end of the bed, picking up a small cup of water and a wrapped sponge on a stick. Opening the sponge, he dipped it in the water, then handed it to her.

"Suck on that. I'll have the nurses bring you some water soon."

Piper tried to take the sponge, but she couldn't make her fingers work. Cullen lifted it to her mouth, and she parted her lips, letting him slip it inside. The moisture hit her tongue, making her want more, but it was enough for now.

"How do you feel?" He tossed the sponge into the trash can by the door, then sat down and took her hand.

"Stiff. And my hands and toes hurt. How long ago did you find me?" She glanced at the window, seeing the early morning sunshine lighting up the world outside.

"About seven hours ago. You were severely hypothermic. We measured your temp at just over eighty-five degrees in the ambulance."

Her breath hitched. She was lucky to be alive.

"You have a little frostbite on your face and hands, but so far, it looks mild. Pulling your hood so low and sitting on your hands kept it from being too severe. And you were out of the wind down in that hole."

She raised her free hand to her face, feeling her cheeks. There were small numb spots on both. The end of her nose felt funny too. Once she'd realized she was becoming hypothermic, she'd done some funky dancing and some shimmying against the dirt walls, trying to get her hood over her head to preserve some body heat. It might have actually been the difference between life and death.

"You've got a badly sprained left ankle, too." Cullen brushed her cheek with his free hand. "What happened?" His voice was quiet, but the anguish came through loud and clear.

Piper did her best to squeeze his hand. She opened her mouth to tell him what she remembered when the door swung in. Ben poked his head inside and smiled when he saw she was awake.

"Hi. It's good to see you awake. How're you doing?" He came in, followed by another man Piper didn't recognize.

"I'm okay. Stiff and tired."

"Well, I'm glad you're on the mend. You had us all pretty scared."

Her gaze traveled to Cullen, who nodded, his eyes conveying his relief that she was all right.

"You feel up to answering some questions?" Ben asked.

"Sure."

"Great. This is Agent Finley Porter from the ATF." He hooked a thumb toward the dark-haired man standing next to him. "He's the head of the task force investigating this case."

Piper nodded and tried to offer him a smile, but it came out as more of a grimace, she feared. She just didn't have the energy.

"I know you're tired, ma'am, so we'll make this as brief as we can." Agent Porter gave her a small smile, softening his serious countenance. "Tell us what happened."

She pressed her lips together, gathering her thoughts, then delved in. "I was leaving work when I heard Dr. Henry and Kylie Stoss arguing in one of the offices. He wanted her to remove items from the shipment coming in the next day. She didn't want to do it because of the increased scrutiny, but he told her they didn't have a choice. That they—the cartel—already had his wife, and if they didn't do it, they would kill her and then come after them. She argued, telling him she wasn't even working. He told her to make Rosalina do it. To threaten her son like they had before to keep her quiet." She took a steadying breath.

"Finally, she gave in. I tried to walk away when I heard them coming out, but they didn't buy my excuse that I was just walking past. Dr. Henry made me call Agent Quartermaine and make up a story to get him away from the pharmacy so we could leave unseen. He threatened to send the cartel after Mackenzie if I didn't do it." Moisture gathered in her eyes, and she looked at Cullen. "And you."

Cullen squeezed her hand. His jaw worked, but he stayed silent.

"Anyway, he took me to the mill and explained what happened to one of the men there. He tied me to a chair in the upstairs office until the boss could come figure out what to do with me. I was there a few hours when they brought Kylie in." Her voice caught on the last word, and the first of her tears spilled over.

"We found her body," Ben said. "It's what led us to you. They dumped her in the river, and she got hung up on the bridge over Irvine Road. We worked upstream from there."

Piper nodded, glad she'd been found. "She died in my arms." She sucked in a deep, shaky breath, trying to hold herself together. "I couldn't do anything to save her."

"Jesus," Cullen whispered. He rose from his seat to lean over and press a kiss to her temple. "I'm so sorry, honey."

She closed her eyes and brought her other hand up to clutch his arm. Horror and grief for what she'd experienced, along with a healthy dose of relief that she was alive and safe, threatened to overwhelm her. Piper battled the tears, not wanting to dissolve into a hysterical mess. If she started crying right now, she wouldn't stop for quite some time.

Sniffing hard, she blinked away the moisture in her eyes and lifted her head. Cullen kissed her forehead, then sat down, dashing at the wetness on his face.

"You're doing great, Piper." Ben patted her knee through the blanket. "What happened after that?"

"The boss showed up right after she died. He didn't come out and say it, but from what he did say, I think he was the one to beat her. I guess she wanted to go to the police, but Dr. Henry wouldn't let her. He turned her over to Herrera."

"Herrera?" Agent Porter frowned.

Piper nodded. "He told me his name was Gustavo Herrera."

Ben glanced at Porter. "Does that ring a bell?"

Porter's mouth flattened, and he shook his head.

"He's a nasty piece of work. I'm only alive because he wanted to 'break' me." Piper used her free hand to air quote. "Apparently, he likes things rough. And I didn't hold back. I broke the chair they tied me to, trying to get free to help Kylie. I used what was left of it and my legs to fight him off." She shook her head. "He was too quick for me, though. He got the upper hand and dragged me out of the office. We were going to go somewhere else, but one of his men stopped him before he could leave with me and told him the police knew about Dr. Henry. Herrera asked where he was, and the guy said he'd left to take care of some things. I think Herrera thought Dr. Henry was running, and it changed his plans. That's when he shoved me in the shed."

"Do you know what happened to Dr. Henry?" Porter asked.

She shook her head. "No. He never mentioned him again. Did he show up dead too?"

"No. We don't know where he is. Or his wife. What happened after he put you in the shed?" Porter crossed his arms and widened his stance, listening.

"They left me in there a couple of hours. It grew dark and cold. I could hear vehicles going in and out. They were using the mill to package drugs and were moving everything to a new location. Herrera came back as the last van left. I knew going with him would mean things I didn't want to think about, so I fought. Being five-eleven—and not a rail—has its advantages. Anyway, I managed to get away and ran into the forest. He shot at me, but missed." She paused and shook her head. "Falling into that hole was actually a good thing. He knew the police were closing in and getting me out would take too long."

"Why did he leave you alive?" Porter asked. "No offense, but you could ID him. Why didn't he shoot you?"

"He wanted me to suffer. I was stuck in the hole and out of shouting distance of the mill. The temperature was in the twenties." She shrugged. "He thought I'd die of exposure before anyone found me."

"He'd have been right if it weren't for Maverick." Cullen shifted in his seat, his features tight.

"Maverick?" She frowned.

"My department's K-9," Ben said. "He tracked you into the woods and found you."

"Oh. Well, tell his handler I'm grateful."

Ben nodded.

"What can you tell us about Herrera?" Porter steered the conversation back to the investigation.

"He was about my height, lean, mid-thirties, with dark hair and eyes. And he had an accent."

"You said he tried to put you in a car. What kind was it?"

"A silver Mercedes SUV. It looked a lot like Cullen's car, actually."

"Did you see the license plate?"

She shook her head.

"Okay. Can you think of anything else that would be pertinent?"

Piper pressed her lips together, going over the encounter. Her eyebrows lifted, and she nodded as she remembered something. "Just before he pulled me out of the shed, I heard him talking to his men. He said something about a man named Manuel. That Manuel wanted all the cargo on the road as soon as possible. They were speaking Spanish, and my Spanish is pretty rusty, so that's all I got from the conversation."

"That's still pretty good," Ben said. He glanced at Porter,

who had the corner of his mouth between his teeth. A deep frown wrinkled his forehead. "What?"

Porter briefly turned his gaze to Ben, then looked at Piper. "Manuel, you say?"

She nodded.

"Did you catch a last name?"

"No. Why? Do you know to whom he was referring?"

"Possibly." He sighed and uncrossed his arms, rubbing his right temple. "There's a Colombian cartel boss named Manuel Vargas-Ruiz. We—in coordination with the DEA—have been trying to dismantle his operation in the U.S., but it's like a damn hydra. We take out one cell and two more pop up elsewhere. I'll have to get with my counterpart at the DEA and see if they recognize Herrera's name."

Piper blew out a breath, her eyes closing on a long blink. "Dr. Henry mentioned the cartel they were working with was Colombian. This isn't over, is it?"

Porter shook his head. "No. We need to root out the distribution network in the area, or the main hub will set up shop somewhere else and plug right back into it." He exhaled a quick breath. "Okay. Is there anything else?"

She bit her lip, thinking again. "Just that Dr. Henry and Kylie didn't get into this out of greed. He said they were trying to help people who needed it. The cartel was bankrolling them because it got too expensive."

Porter pursed his lips, then nodded. "All right. I'll leave you to get some rest. I'm glad you're okay." He reached into his pocket and pulled out a business card. "If you think of anything else, contact my office. You can also call Sheriff Davidson." He motioned to Ben, then handed Cullen the card.

"I will. Thank you, Agent Porter." Piper didn't try to smile this time. Fatigue was quickly pulling her back under. Her limbs felt like they weighed a hundred pounds each. The pain in her hands and feet still pulsed with her heartbeat. She just wanted some painkillers and to go back to sleep.

He gave a short nod and took a step back. "Sheriff, I'll talk to you soon."

Ben nodded, then Agent Porter left.

"I should get going too." Ben motioned toward the door. "Do you need anything?"

"Pain meds," Piper muttered. She hurt so much now.

Cullen stood up. "Sorry, hon. I should have thought of that. Hang on."

Piper surprised herself and held onto his hand when he tried to walk away. He glanced down at her with surprise in his hazel eyes. "Stay," she murmured. "Use the call button."

Ben reached for the remote lying on top of the covers and pushed the appropriate button. When the nurse's voice came over the speaker, Cullen requested the meds.

"I'm going to head out." Ben patted her knee again. "Call if you need anything." He pointed a finger, indicating them both.

"We will," Cullen said. "Thanks, Ben."

"Yep. Get some rest, Piper." He touched his temple with two fingers, then left.

Piper closed her eyes and tried to relax into the mattress. Sleep pulled at her mind, but the pain in her extremities kept her awake. "How long is it supposed to hurt?" Pain colored her voice.

"The worst of it should fade soon enough. You're nearly warmed up. Hopefully, when you wake up again, your pain will be a lot lower."

"I hope so, because this sucks." Disgust dripped off her tone.

He chuckled. The mattress dipped, and she opened her eyes to see him leaning close. He raised a hand, brushing her hair back. Intense emotion shone in the depths of his hazel eyes.

"You scared me. When I jumped in that hole—" He broke off and closed his eyes. When they opened again, she could name the emotion shining in them, and gasped. All her pain faded as she basked in the emotions swirling in his hazel eyes.

"I thought you were dead. Then you moaned and all the emotions I'd been suppressing tried to break free. It wasn't until we were here and had you rewarming that I let them all out and realized I love you." He leaned closer and pressed his forehead to hers. "I need you, Piper. Like I need air to breathe."

She raised a hand and touched his face, feeling the soft tickle of his beard on her palm. "I love you too." She pressed a gentle kiss to his lips, then pulled back and smiled. "This needs to be my last life-changing realization from a hospital bed, though. I'm not sure I can take another round."

His low chuckle warmed her from the inside. "Are you going to let me wrap you in bubble wrap and bulletproof glass?"

Piper laughed. "No."

"Then I can't guarantee anything."

She hooked her arm around his neck and pulled his face back down. "Safety's overrated."

He silenced her giggle with another soft kiss.

FORTY-THREE

The doorbell pealed through the house, and Piper paused on her way up the stairs to take a shower. She pivoted, careful not to fall as she balanced on her crutches, and saw two shapes through the frosted side windows.

Cullen came from the living room, glancing up at her as he reached for the doorknob. "It's Ben. I saw him through the front window." Unlocking the door, he opened it. Ben and Agent Porter stood on the porch.

"Hi, Cullen. Piper." Ben gave a small wave. "May we come in?"

"Sure." Cullen stepped back to let them inside.

Piper took the crutches from under her arms and slid down to sit on the steps. It was easier to scoot on her butt than to hobble down on the damn sticks. She made it two steps before Cullen bound up the stairs and held out a hand.

"Thanks." Smiling, she took it and let him pull her to her feet, then help her down the rest of the way.

"Let's go into the living room." Cullen tipped his head down the hall.

The four of them filed into the room. Piper sat on the

couch, and Cullen sank down next to her. Ben and Agent Porter each took a chair.

"So, what can we do for you?" Cullen asked.

"We actually came with an update," Ben replied.

"Oh?" Cullen shared a glance with Piper.

She raised an eyebrow, then turned back to the men, curious what they had to say. And why they were sharing.

"So, we interviewed Rosalina Morales and learned some things. Namely, the reason Dr. Henry and Ms. Stoss were involved with the cartel," Agent Porter said.

"It had to do with sending medications to disadvantaged countries, didn't it?" Piper shifted to rest an arm on the couch.

Porter nodded. "Yes. From what Ms. Morales learned, Dr. Henry found a flaw in the pharmacy's software that allowed him to order extra quantities of medicine, then later alter invoices. We're not sure how Ms. Stoss became involved, but it was likely the same way Ms. Morales did, and she overheard or noticed something. She either had something Dr. Henry could hold over her, or she voluntarily joined him. We're still digging into her life."

"What about the cartel?" Cullen glanced at Piper, then back to Porter. "We know from what Henry told Piper he needed their backing, but is this over? Are they out of the picture?"

"I don't have the answer to that. Vargas-Ruiz is a nasty, nasty man, but the major players here—Peter Henry and Kylie Stoss—are dead. Most of his operation is safe. We nabbed one van-load of workers the day after they abandoned the mill. None of them are talking, of course. With Herrera and the rest of the operation in the wind, we're pretty certain they'll leave you, Ms. Morales, and Dr. Trufant alone now. Indications are it was Herrera who put the screws to you and Dr. Trufant."

"So, any threat will come from him, then?" Piper picked at the couch, then folded her hands together to stop the nervous twitching. She'd had enough of that man, and the thought of being back in his clutches made her skin crawl.

"Most likely. But he's probably a state away now, at least. I talked to my DEA colleague. They think Herrera's the regional cartel boss."

"They think?" Cullen raised an eyebrow.

Porter nodded. "They've only ever photographed a man they believe is the boss. He matches the description you gave." He reached into his jacket and removed his phone, unlocking the screen. After a couple of taps, he turned it around to show them a picture.

Piper's heart skipped a beat, then thudded in her chest.

"Is this Herrera?"

"Yes." She picked at her fingers, then folded them together. "I'll never forget that face." She just hoped one day it would no longer haunt her nightmares.

Porter turned off the screen and pocketed the phone. "Then, yes, he's who they think is the regional boss. He's usually in Atlanta, and we think that's where he's gone again. At least temporarily. Because of the scrutiny, he may head to a different city, or even try to flee to Colombia until things die down some. We've got agents on alert in Atlanta and the other major cities in the southeast as well as at all the major transportation hubs."

"So, you don't think he's coming back here?" Piper asked.

"Most likely, no. Every law enforcement officer in the area knows who he is. It would be difficult for him to spend any time around here without detection. I must caution you that we can't rule it out, though. For the time being, I'm leaving an agent posted on the house, and I would prefer if you don't leave unless it's absolutely necessary. You, too, Dr. Tate."

Cullen briefly held up his hands. "I'm not going anywhere until she's mobile." He nodded to Piper.

"Good. I'll do my best to keep you apprised of Herrera's

movements. We may not have eyes on him, but our informants tend to know when the big players are around. Hopefully, that's the case here."

Piper's mouth twisted. She hoped he was right. Herrera wasn't one to be dissuaded or to leave business unfinished. And she was most definitely unfinished business. He'd badly wanted her for his plaything. And she could ID him. The question now was whether those things were enough for him to decide it was worth the risk to come after her.

Ben reached out and patted her arm. "You have the very best looking after you, Piper. Your guard isn't going anywhere anytime soon." He sat back, then looked at Agent Porter, who nodded, then stood.

"We'll be in touch. Stay inside. Close those blinds." He pointed at the window. "And call us if something seems off. No matter how silly."

Piper nodded. She had no qualms about doing that. Not when she knew what Herrera was capable of—and now the sort of reach he had. She had no intention of ending up on a plane to Colombia, never to be seen again.

Cullen rose and showed the two men out. Piper flopped back and stared at the window, not seeing anything. Her mind swirled with the information Agent Porter just imparted. She'd tried not to think much about Herrera since she woke up in the hospital. And aside from her dreams, she'd been mostly successful. But now his evil smile wouldn't leave her mind.

"Agent Porter is right. We should have been keeping the blinds closed," Cullen said, returning. He walked to the bay of windows, and lowered the blinds. "Especially once it gets dark." He peered through the slats at the setting sun.

"Yeah." She only partially registered what he said, her mind still stuck on Herrera's face and the depravity of his personality.

"Hey, are you okay?"

Piper blinked and met Cullen's gaze. She smiled. "Yeah. Just a little unnerved, I guess. I was hoping this was all over—even though I knew better."

"You weren't the only one." He leaned down and kissed her forehead, then leaned over and unfastened the straps holding the walking boot in place around her foot.

Piper lifted her leg free and wiggled her toes. It was nice to be able to do that without pain shooting up her limb. She still couldn't put any weight on it, though.

"Come on." Cullen set the boot down, then held out his hands. "I'll help you upstairs, then we can have some of your delicious hot chocolate and play a game."

She took his hands, and he pulled her to her feet. "Okay. That sounds nice." Maybe the combination of the water, hot cocoa, and some fun would dispel the fear Agent Porter's words brought forth. It certainly couldn't hurt.

FORTY-FOUR

Fresh and clean—and less anxious thanks to the power of hot water—Piper scooted down the stairs on her butt, holding her crutches in one hand. Cullen needed to rewrap her feet before she put the boot back on. Blisters from her frostbite had developed on her fingers and toes several days ago. He drained them and wrapped everything, and they were healing, but it was a slow process. She was glad she'd escaped further damage. It would take another week or so before she'd have full use of her hands. And probably another one to two after that before she'd walk without the boot.

Her feet hit the main floor, and she stood, tucking the crutches under her arms. Their rubber tips thumped on the hardwood as she moved toward the living room, looking for Cullen. "Okay, I'm done and ready to be wrapped again."

He glanced up from the laptop perched on his lap. Smiling, he closed the lid and set it on the coffee table, then shifted to the corner. "Have a seat." He pointed at the cushion beside him.

She sank into the couch's softness, setting the crutches on the floor. Lifting her legs she placed her feet in his lap. If it didn't sting so much to have him handle them, she'd enjoy the massage. One day, she would.

"They look pretty good. The blisters are drying out nicely." He tipped her foot, tilting his head to study her feet. "And your ankle isn't as swollen. How did the shower feel today?"

"Not as bad." Her skin had sloughed off in a few small spots, and water made the areas sting.

"How about your hands?"

She held them out to him. Only a couple of her fingers had blisters. The rest just had some frost nip. "They feel pretty good."

"They look good." He brought her fingers up and kissed the backs of her hands. "How about your head? Did the water wash away some of your worry?"

Piper nodded. "Yeah. That and the time alone gave me a chance to think and put things in perspective. We can't let our guard down, but hopefully, he's fled the country and Porter will figure that out soon."

Cullen's head bobbed once. "My thoughts exactly." He kissed her hands again, then let them go. "Okay, let's get these feet wrapped. I already made the hot chocolate. It's keeping warm on the stove."

Piper smiled. "That sounds wonderful." He'd been so good to her in the four days she'd been home from the hospital. She'd been amazed when he announced he'd arranged the next two weeks off so he could care for her. And he'd done exactly that. She was going to be spoiled rotten by all the pampering, but she felt beyond loved.

Cullen picked up several bandages and opened them, wrapping the thin strips around her fingers to cover the blisters. Once those were done, he reached for the gauze and wrapped it around her toes, then carefully taped it into place. "Feel okay?"

She nodded.

"Good." He set the supplies down, then picked up her boot and slipped it over her foot, fastening the straps.

Piper lifted her feet off his lap and set them on the floor.

He stood. "I'm going to get the hot chocolate. What game do you want to play?"

"I want a checkers rematch." She was still determined to beat him. He'd stolen her crown, and she wanted it back.

A rakish smile crossed his face. "Should we wager again?"

She wagged a finger at him. "Uh-uh. I learned my lesson the last time. No more betting until I'm sure I stand a chance."

He laughed. "Spoilsport. Okay." He rounded the couch, heading for the door. "I'll be right back."

Grinning, she watched him leave, then sank into the cushions with a contented sigh. She wanted to pinch herself; their relationship—the knowledge that he loved her—still didn't feel real. Maybe because they were cocooned together in this house while she healed. They hadn't brought things out into the world yet, so it still felt a little like a fairytale.

The room plunged into darkness, and she sat up, her heart pounding. "Cullen?"

"Piper, stay put. I'll bring a flashlight when—" His words cut off at the same time she heard glass break. A moment later there, a soft thud reached her ears.

"Cullen?" She twisted in her seat, looking over the back of the couch to the doorway. Silence met her inquiry.

Standing, she struggled to hear over the rush of blood pounding through her head. "Cullen?"

He still didn't answer.

Alarm bells clanged in her brain, and a neon sign flashed, "Danger!" Piper hobbled over to the fireplace and picked up the poker. She didn't want to believe Herrera had decided she was worth the risk to his freedom, but there was little other explanation for what was happening. It was a touch ironic, though, that Ben and Agent Porter had just left. And she couldn't help but wonder where the outside guard was. Shouldn't he be pounding on the door, wondering why all the lights went out so suddenly?

As fast as her bandaged feet would allow, she crossed the room and pressed her back to the wall beside the door and raised the poker. Her eyes strained in the low light coming in around the blinds from the pole light over the driveway. Whatever knocked out their power wasn't natural. It wouldn't just be the house that was dark. Maybe that was why the agent wasn't banging down the door. Maybe he thought they'd gone to bed early.

Or maybe he was dead in his car.

Piper shuddered and pushed that thought away. It wouldn't help her.

The soft tread of rubber-soled shoes sounded right outside the room. She tightened her grip on the poker, twisting it in her hands and raising it a little higher.

Her breath caught in her throat as the tip of a gun came through the door. When a forearm followed and he didn't announce himself as an agent, Piper brought the poker down with all her strength. The man let out a yell, and the gun clattered to the floor, skittering out of sight. She swung again, this time smacking him in the chest. A string of angry Spanish curses filled the room. She recognized that voice.

Fury ignited her blood, replacing the fear. Letting out an enraged screech, she whacked Herrera with the poker again, making contact with his shoulder. When she lifted it and brought it down a fourth time, he raised a hand and caught it.

"*¡Bastante!*" He ripped the poker from her grasp and threw it behind him. It thudded into the hallway wall, then clattered to the floor.

Piper scurried back, out of his reach, and put the couch between them. He'd have to come over it or around it to get to her. From the corners of her eyes, she searched for another weapon. If she could make it to the bookcases, she could pelt him with Cullen's medical tomes.

"Still so feisty, *princesa*." The whites of his eyes shone in the dim light, giving him a maniacal look. "You will require extra attention to break. That is okay. I have many frustrations to take out, thanks to you."

"You're welcome." She edged toward the bookcase as he stalked closer. "How did you know I survived? You were long gone when they found me."

"The news media. Such a large federal presence doesn't go unnoticed in this area. Neither do two attempts on the same woman's life." He stepped to one corner of the couch.

Piper went to the other, which sent her closer to the bookshelves. When she got away from this maniac, she needed to call the sheriff and ask how he knew that. They never released her name to the press. She took another step back. "What did you do with Dr. Henry and his wife?" The police still hadn't found them.

"I learned from my mistake and made sure they were dead. They'll be bones before anyone finds them. His children are lucky there's so much pressure to find me, or they would join them."

Another shudder went through Piper. He was truly evil. Those children were completely innocent. "Yet you still want me alive?"

"You intrigue me, *princesa*. Despite your—violent nature, you have the heart of a warrior. I must possess it. Bend it to my will."

She rolled her eyes. Was he for real? "I'm so glad I inspire such emotion in you." Sarcasm dripped from her words, though they weren't entirely a lie. His obsession with her could be his downfall. She just needed to keep him talking until she could get away. Piper took yet another subtle step toward the books piled in front of the bookcase. They were almost within reach.

"How did you get in here?"

He scoffed. "Your federal agents are pathetic. The one in his car was easy to sneak up on. He won't be calling anyone for backup. Tell me—I'm curious—did the man I shot in the kitchen appreciate your tongue?"

Piper's blood turned to ice. Shot?

Herrera's low, diabolical laugh drifted across the space between them. "I see I've rendered you speechless. Suppressors aren't as quiet as the movies want you to believe, but when used outside, the sound of breaking glass covers them up quite well."

A fine tremor started in her belly and spread outward. Rage chased it hard, fueled by an immeasurable pain. With a yell worthy of the warrior he accused her of being, she turned and dove for the books, scooping the top one off the pile and chucking it at his head in the same motion. He ducked, caught by surprise, which gave her enough time to grab several more and toss them as she circled the couch.

But, thanks to her booted foot, she wasn't fast enough. He dove at her, tackling her to the floor. Piper struck out at him, but he corralled her hands in one of his and lashed them to the floor above her head. She spit in his face.

The hard smack took her unaware. Stars swam in her eyes, but she kept struggling. Sudden pressure on her neck stilled her movements. The stars got brighter as he cut off her oxygen supply.

"My plan was to take you with me. Save our first breaking-in session for your new home in Colombia, but I see it will be necessary to start here if I'm to get you out of the house."

The pressure eased from her throat. Piper coughed, her windpipe on fire. Tears streamed from her eyes as she tried to catch her breath.

Her reprieve didn't last long. A folded knife appeared next to her face. He touched the side and a four-inch blade popped out with a soft snick.

"Since my gun is hiding somewhere in the dark, this is my assurance you'll comply." He dipped his head, his voice changing to a low whisper. "But please don't. It's more fun for me when you squirm."

The knife tip pricked her cheek. Warmth rolled down her face, but she couldn't tell if it was blood or tears or both.

He pushed up, straddling her waist, but still holding her hands. Piper lay frozen beneath him. She didn't know what to do. Lying still would ensure he could assault her, but if she fought, how much worse would it be?

Bile rose in her throat as he skimmed his fingers over her breasts. She shut her eyes, steeling herself for more.

What are you doing? Are you just going to lie there and take it? Her inner voice cut through the fear and disgust running rampant in her brain.

No. Her eyes opened, defiance shining bright. She raised her knees, ready to tip him forward and roll—knife be damned—when movement behind him caught her attention. A figure weaved into view a moment before the iron fireplace poker cut through the darkness and smacked into the side of Herrera's head with a sickening thud. His eyes rolled up, and he toppled to the side. Piper watched him fall, then her gaze flew to the figure standing hunched just a few feet away.

"Cullen!" She pushed Herrera out of the way and scrambled to her feet, hurrying to his side.

He dropped the poker as she reached him, and it hit the floor with a loud clank. Piper ducked under his arm, supporting him as his knees gave way.

"Oh my God, I thought you were dead. He said he shot you. Where are you hit?"

"Side." He raised his left arm, wincing, to point at his left flank.

"Here." She led him to the couch. "Sit down. I'll call for help."

He grunted as he sank onto the cushions. "I think it's just a flesh wound. Hurts like the dickens, though. So does my head." He touched the back of his skull. "I hit it on the cabinets on the way down, and it knocked me out for a couple minutes. Are you okay?"

"Shaken, but physically, I'm fine. Do you have your phone? Mine's still upstairs."

"It's in my pocket." He lifted his left hip, then groaned. "You'll have to get it."

Piper stuffed her hand behind his hip, feeling the edge of the phone. She grabbed it and pulled it out. Once she called for help, she laid the phone down, then looked at Herrera. He still hadn't moved, but she didn't want to take any chances. "I need to tie him up. Are you okay for a minute?"

Cullen nodded. "I was swinging to kill. I don't suppose I did, though, did I?" His voice took on a growl. "I saw him on top of you—heard the things he said—and it was like some other person took over my brain."

She was glad. It ended in their favor. Piper leaned down and pressed a hard kiss to his forehead. Tears stung the back of her eyes, and she blinked them away. "Okay." She straightened. "I'm going to check on him." Turning, she spotted the roll of gauze on the coffee table. She grabbed it and went over to Herrera, stooping to pick up the fireplace poker before she approached him.

A few feet away, she reached out with it and nudged him. He didn't move, so she dug into his side a little harder to check if he was feigning unconsciousness. When he didn't twitch and his breathing didn't change, she kneeled next to him and touched his neck. A weak pulse fluttered under her fingers. "He's still alive," she said over her shoulder to Cullen.

"Shame."

As bad as it was, Piper agreed. The world wouldn't miss Gustavo Herrera.

She made quick work of wrapping the gauze around his hands, binding them the best she could. It would hold until the police arrived. Picking up the poker and Herrera's knife, she went back to Cullen and turned on the flashlight on his phone and sat down next to him.

"What are you doing?"

"I want to take a look at your wound. Can't have you bleeding out on me."

"I'm okay."

She hummed. "You also sustained a head wound. Forgive me if I don't trust your judgment at the moment."

He huffed, but didn't protest when she raised his shirt to look. A furrow in his side oozed freely, soaking the waistband of his pants.

"We need to stop the bleeding. I used all the gauze to tie up Herrera." She pushed off the couch. "Hang on a minute." Leaving the room, she limped into the hall bath as fast as her booted foot would allow and grabbed two hand towels from the drawer, then went back to the living room.

"That'll work." He moved to take them from her, but she batted his hands away.

"Just sit there and look pretty. I can do it."

He laughed, then moaned. "Oh, don't make me laugh. That hurt."

She grinned. "Now you know how I felt after you sewed me back together."

"I'll definitely approach gunshot victims with a new understanding." He grimaced, then hissed as she pressed the towels to his side.

Faint sirens cut through the silence. Piper breathed a sigh of relief. Cullen needed stitches, and she needed Herrera out of her sight. Her adrenaline ebbed, leaving her shaky as the reality of what happened set in.

Cullen's hand stroking the side of her head shook her from her thoughts. "I love you, Piper."

She turned her head and pressed a kiss to his palm. A lone tear slid free. "I love you too." Sniffing, she offered him a wobbly smile and said a prayer of thanks that they were safe.

Thank you for reading Smoky Mountain Doctor! I hope you enjoyed it. Please consider leaving a rating or review on Amazon and/or Goodreads. It would be greatly appreciated! If you'd like a FREE romantic suspense novella just for signing up and EXCLUSIVE looks twice a month at my latest work-in-progress, you can join my mailing list at ashleyaquinn.com. You can also stay up-to-date on my newest projects by joining my Facebook readers' group, Ashley's She Shed. See you next time!

Keep reading for a sneak peek at Book 5 in the Foggy Mountain Intrigue series, Smoky Mountain K-9.

Smoky Mountain K-9

FOGGY MOUNTAIN
BOOK 5

ONE

The thump of the electronic dance beat coming from the speakers reverberated in Mara Roth's chest. She couldn't believe she let herself get talked into coming to this thing. It was one thing to agree to host the Valentine's bachelor auction at the equestrian center, but it was quite another to be part of the audience. She hadn't planned to come, but her friend, Brooke McGinty, showed up on her doorstep a half hour before the auction started and told her to change clothes, and she wasn't taking no for an answer. Mara tried to protest, anyway, but Brooke threatened to call their other friend, Gemma Davidson, who was co-conspirator for the auction benefitting the Foggy Mountain Women's Crisis Center.

At that point, Mara knew resistance was futile, so she changed into a black party dress and let Brooke usher her into the passenger seat of her car.

This was fun, though. She'd expected to feel out of place —she wasn't in the market for a man. But a lot of the women here had come in small groups, with only one of them bidding. Once Mara noticed that, she relaxed and started to enjoy herself. Some of these guys were total hams and worked the stage for all they were worth. It was great to see so much money raised for such a good cause.

"Okay, ladies. Next up we have Carter Townsend. He's Ferris County's K-9 deputy." The emcee's voice rose over the music. She held out an arm, gesturing to the man emerging from behind the curtain.

Mara's eyes rounded, and a tingle went through her lady parts. A lopsided grin sat on the man's square-jawed face beneath a shock of sun-bleached dirty blonde hair. In black tactical pants, black department polo, and combat boots, he loomed large on the stage. Beside him trotted an all-black dog.

She swallowed, hoping none of the drool ran out. Damn.

"Carter is accompanied by his partner, Maverick," the emcee said. "For his date, Carter has planned an evening at the zoo for a behind-the-scenes tour of the elephant exhibit. The tour also includes a paint-and-sip event with Thelma the African elephant. The event also includes dinner."

"That sounds like a fun date." Brooke glanced at Mara and grinned.

"What?" Mara's eyes flitted to her friend, then back to the stage. "Oh, yes. You're right, it does."

"One thousand!" Brooke's hand shot up, and she waved her paddle.

"What are you doing?" Mara frowned. She didn't understand why Brooke would bid on anyone. Her friend was happily engaged. They were just here tonight to watch, have fun, and support Gemma.

"Buying you a date."

"What? No." She grabbed Brooke's arm and yanked it down when she would have raised her bid.

"Oh, yes." Brooke wrenched her arm away and raised it. "Fifteen hundred!"

"You cannot spend that kind of money on a date for me. Are you crazy?"

Brooke giggled and held her arm out to the side as Mara made another grab for it. "No. I saw the look on your face when he stepped out. I've never seen you look at a man like that. And, honey, it's past time for you to go on a date. It's been three years since Blake died."

Mara didn't need that reminder. She was well-aware how long she'd been a widow. "So? There's no timeline on grief."

Brooke raised her paddle. "Eighteen hundred!" She glanced at Mara. "I know, but you're not grieving anymore. Not the way you want people to think. You wouldn't have looked at Deputy Townsend like that if you weren't ready to put yourself out there again. You're just scared." She grinned. "I'm giving you a push."

"Brooke—"

"Twenty-one hundred!" Brooke waved her paddle, hopping on her toes.

"Oh my God." Mara groaned and covered her face. "Would you stop? Please?"

"Do I hear twenty-two?" The emcee's voice carried over the crowd. "Going once..."

"Sweet Jesus," Mara muttered. This wasn't happening.

"Going twice..."

"Someone please bid. Anyone." She peeked through her fingers as she prayed for divine intervention.

Brooke giggled and bounced on the balls of her feet.

"Sold! To number fifty-two for twenty-one hundred dollars." The emcee banged her gavel.

Mara groaned. "I can't believe you did that."

"Believe it, sister. You now have a date for Valentine's Day."

"I hate you so much right now."

The smile on Brooke's face told Mara she didn't care. "You'll thank me one day."

"For setting me up on a blind date with a man you bought at a charity auction?"

Brooke's head bobbed once. "Yep. You watch." She wagged her paddle at Mara. "This will be the start of a new chapter in your life."

"I like the chapter I'm in." It was safe. Nothing could trample on her heart and make it bleed again.

"It's overdone, and you need to start a new one."

The emcee's voice echoed over the crowd, drowning out anything Mara would have said. She flattened her lips together and stared at the stage. There was no arguing with Brooke when she got an idea in her head. It didn't matter what Mara said at this stage. Brooke would still think she was right.

Well, fine. She'd just have to prove her wrong. She'd go on the date with Deputy Townsend, then tell Brooke she tried, but was happy with the status quo. He was sexy, but Mara was happy with her life the way it was. She didn't need a man.

The rest of the auction flew by for Mara. She barely paid attention, lost in her thoughts. When the final bachelor sold and the gavel banged, Brooke grabbed Mara's arm.

"Come on. Let's go meet your date."

Groaning, Mara followed her friend through the surging crowd toward the registration table, where women were lining up to pay for their dates.

"Do you see him?" Brooke stood on her toes, trying to peer over the crowd.

Mara shook her head. "No. There are too many people." She wasn't much taller than Brooke.

"Ladies, let's form a thinner line." The emcee walked up, clapping her hands to get everyone's attention. "Our bachelors are going to come up alongside everyone, so you can meet."

The crowd shifted, snaking out into the arena to accommodate her request. Mara glanced toward the stage and saw the line of men coming out from behind. It wasn't hard to spot Deputy Townsend. Not only was he the most attractive one of the bunch, but he had his K-9 partner at his side. The dog was as beautiful as he was.

Brooke leaned to the side and waved her paddle, a wide smile on her face. "Deputy Townsend."

Mara tried to shrink into the people around her as he walked up, a polite smile on his face.

"Hello."

A shiver went through Mara at the sound of his deep voice, leaving gooseflesh on her arms. It was like butter, but had a bit of gravel to it.

"Hi," Brooke chirped. "I'm Brooke McGinty."

He held out a hand. "Carter Townsend. It's nice to meet you. Thank you for your generosity to the women's crisis center."

"Oh, you're welcome. I was happy to do it." Brooke smiled up at him as she shook his hand. She let go, then stepped back, waving Mara forward.

Mara stood there, arms crossed, and blinked at Brooke, still not happy.

"Deputy, this is my friend Mara Roth. She's your date."

Carter blinked, nonplussed. "Oh." He frowned. "You bid on me for your friend?"

"Yes. I'm happily engaged." Brooke raised her left hand and waggled her fingers, showing off her engagement ring. "But Mara needs to get back out into the dating pool. This seemed like a good opportunity. No pressure or expectations."

He tipped his head, studying Mara. His liquid silver gaze burned into her, turning the gooseflesh to a heated flush.

"Well, it's nice to meet you, Mara." He extended a hand. "I'm sure we'll have a pleasant time."

Oh, God. He wants me to touch him? The feelings he evoked just standing there were bad enough. With a long blink, she steeled herself and took his hand. It was a brief handshake, but it was enough to send a tingle up her arm that electrified her entire body.

"It's nice to meet you, deputy."

"Call me Carter, please."

She gave him a tight smile and nodded.

The line shuffled forward, and Mara glanced at the dog at his side. "Your dog's name is Maverick, right?"

He nodded.

"What breed is he?" He looked like a German Shepherd, but she wasn't a good judge of dog breeds. Give her horses, though, and she could name it with a quick glance.

"Belgian Malinois."

"He's pretty."

One side of his mouth lifted, and he glanced at the dog, who looked up. "Don't listen to her. You're handsome."

Brooke laughed. Mara felt her lips twitch. "My apologies, Maverick." She unfolded her arms and glanced at Carter. "May I pet him?"

"Sure. He's off duty."

Mara held a hand out to let the dog sniff her, then scratched the side of his face near his ear. His tongue lolled out, and he stared up at her like a puppy.

Carter's rich laugh rolled over her. "You hit the sweet spot. He likes you."

"I'm glad. I wouldn't want to be on his bad side."

"Unless you're on the wrong side of the law—and running away—I think you're safe."

Mara smiled and scratched Maverick's ear again. She straightened, removing her hand, and he stepped forward to nudge her, making her laugh. "I guess I really did hit the sweet spot." She ran her fingers through his soft fur again. A smile still on her face, she glanced at Carter. He watched her with a slight furrow between his eyes.

His expression quickly cleared, and he smiled again. "I guess I should probably get your phone number and address." He withdrew his phone from his pocket.

"Right." Mara told him her information. A moment later, her phone vibrated as he texted her his number.

"It was lovely to meet you both. Mara, I'll see you Monday evening. Wear something comfortable. We'll be doing some walking."

Mara's smile turned tight at the reminder of their date. She nodded. "See you then."

He lifted a hand as he backed away. "Have a good evening." Turning, he and Maverick loped toward the exit.

Mara wished she could escape as easily.

Brooke squealed and grabbed her arm. "He's even hotter close up. And that voice." She rolled her eyes and laid a hand over her heart. "If I weren't blissfully happy with Johnathan, I would have bid on him for myself."

"Speaking of, is he going to have a conniption when he finds out you spent over two grand on a date for me?" Mara crossed her arms and lifted an eyebrow.

"It's my money." Brooke waved a hand. "I can do with it as I please. And you know I have plenty to cover the cost."

It was true. Brooke was a wedding planner, but she didn't need to work. Her family owned a local luxury resort.

"Besides, you'd do the same for me if I needed the push to put myself back out there." She grinned. "Well, maybe not spend two thousand dollars, but you'd set me up." Brooke waved a finger in Mara's face. "Don't deny it. You know you would."

A smile toyed with Mara's lips. "Maybe." She'd want her friend to be happy. And Brooke was right. If she thought putting herself out there would make her happy, she'd set Brooke up in a heartbeat.

Some of the fight leached out of her. Brooke just wanted her to be the best version of herself. And truthfully, Mara was a bit stuck in the mud. She'd lost herself since she lost her husband. But she wasn't sure she was ready to come out of her protective shell. It just hurt too much when things went sour.

Two

Crisp, wintery air filled Mara's lungs as she stepped into the outdoor arena with her horse, Stinger. The black gelding pawed at the dirt, ready for their morning ride. Dust rose to sparkle in the sunshine. It was a beautiful day.

Mara closed the gate, then mounted Stinger, nudging him into a trot to warm him up. With the bite to the air, she wanted his muscles nice and warmed up before she put him through some runs. He had other ideas, though, and she had to rein him in several times when he tried to work his way into a slow canter. Stinger loved to run.

Once she was sure he was limber enough, she trotted to the gate and turned to face the arena. Three barrels sat arranged in the dirt. Stinger tossed his head and let out of soft whicker. Mara leaned forward and patted his neck. "Let's do this, Stinger." She dug her heels into his sides, and he took off for the first barrel. Mara leaned low as he tore around the barrel and raced across to the next one. Dirt flew as he rounded it, launching them up the straightaway to the third barrel. In moments, they were around it and flying back the way they came.

She sat up and pulled on the reins as they passed the fence post Mara used as a finish line. Stinger snorted and danced in the dirt, wanting to go again.

Clapping drew her attention. She glanced back to see Gemma step up on the gate rails, a wide smile on her face.

"Hey, what are you doing here?" Mara trotted over. Gemma was still on maternity leave.

"I came to say good morning to Jasper." She hooked a thumb toward the building and her horse in his stall. "I didn't see Stinger in his stall, and you weren't inside, so I looked out here. He sure does fly. I'll never get tired of watching the two of you."

Mara grinned and patted Stinger's neck. She might not compete anymore, but she still enjoyed the thrill of racing. "Are you allowed to ride yet?"

Gemma wrinkled her nose. "I could, but things are still a touch sore. It's only been four weeks."

"Well, I'll saddle Jasper sometime today and put him through his paces."

"He'd like that. He's probably getting a little squirrely with only the sedate walks during therapy sessions."

"I've been exercising him. But not as much as he's used to, I'm sure."

"I appreciate it. It sucks not being able to ride." She wagged a finger. "Soon, though." Gemma crossed her arms over the top rail, and her smile changed. "So. Are you looking forward to your date tonight?"

Mara groaned. "I was trying not to think about it."

Gemma chuckled. "Why? Carter's nice. And nice to look at."

"I know, but—" She broke off and sighed. "I haven't been on a date since Blake died." Her husband's death left a hole in her heart that still wasn't filled in. She didn't think it ever would be.

"You can't spend the rest of your life alone, Mara. You're still young. Would he want you to end up a spinster?"

Mara's lips pursed. That was a question she'd asked herself multiple times this weekend. Every time, the answer was no. Blake would want her to move on. He'd want her to remember him, but he wouldn't want her to stay stuck in the past.

But it was damn hard to take that first step.

She shook her head. "I know he wouldn't, but that doesn't make it any easier."

Gemma's smile turned sympathetic. "Carter's a good guy to break into the dating scene with. He's easy-going and a gentleman."

Mara chuckled. "I just hope he can handle a nervous, slightly awkward thirty-four-year-old widow who was shoved into the frying pan by her two best friends."

"What?" Gemma laid a hand over her heart and feigned a shocked look. "I didn't bid on him. Nor did I tell Brooke to do it."

"No." Mara laughed. "But I'm sure you encouraged her to make me come. You also helped organize the whole thing."

Gemma shrugged. "I'll cop to that. But my goal wasn't to get you a date. It was to get you to have some fun. You work, then go home and bury your nose in a book."

"Hey. I like my book boyfriends."

"I like mine, too, but my husband is a whole lot more satisfying."

Mara's mouth twisted. She did miss sex. Her relationship with Blake had been fun. He wasn't the most spontaneous partner, but she had no complaints about his ability to satisfy her. He knew how to work her into a frenzy and had never left her hanging. Her problem now was getting past the idea that her sexual partner wasn't Blake. She never thought there would be another man in her life. But fate was a cruel bitch and had ripped him away from her.

"Well, regardless, my book boyfriends will have to suffice. I will not be welcoming Carter into my bed tonight." No matter how good he looked.

Her thoughts drifted to the memory of his shoulders and chest outlined by his department polo at the auction, and the dimple that formed in his cheek when he smiled that sexy half-smile of his.

Tendrils of heat started in her belly, spreading outward to her limbs. Mara slammed the door closed on her thoughts. Thinking about him like that would only make her more nervous and tongue-tied tonight.

"Never say never, Mara." Gemma grinned and shook a finger. She hopped off the fence. "I'm headed back in to hang out with my horse. I'll see you later."

Mara swung Stinger away from the fence and waved. "See ya." Her horse danced, ready to run again. She let him, hoping the race chased away her nerves.

ABOUT THE AUTHOR

Ashley started writing in her teens and never stopped. Her first novel, Smoky Mountain Murder, came out in 2016, and she has since published two more series and has plans for more. When not writing, you can find her with her nose stuck in a book or watching some terrible disaster movie on SyFy. An avid baseball fan, she also enjoys crafting and cooking. She lives in Ohio with her husband, two kids, three cats, and one very wild shepherd mix.

Website: https://ashleyaquinn.com

goodreads.com/ashleyaquinn

amazon.com/Ashley-A-Quinn/e/B07HCT4QST

Also by Ashley A Quinn

Foggy Mountain Intrigue

Smoky Mountain Murder

Smoky Mountain Baby

Smoky Mountain Stalker

Smoky Mountain Doctor

Smoky Mountain K-9

The Broken Bow

A Beautiful End

Wildfire

In Plain Sight

Close Quarters

Scorched

Light of Dawn

Pine Ridge

Sweetness

Loner

Shark

Katydid

Homespun